I0664195

Beyond the Red Sea Experience

By Angela Bolden-Thompson

An *iWrite Books* imprint

Beyond the Red Sea Experience

Cover Illustration by Angela Bolden Thompson

Trade Paperback

Bolden Thompson, Angela.

Beyond the Red Sea Experience / Angela Bolden Thompson

ISBN-10: 0-6922-0714-7

ISBN-13: 978-0-6922-0714-7

For further information,

Email: iwritebookz@gmail.com

Printed and Distributed in the United States

Dedication

I dedicate this book to my beloved grandmothers, aunts, and uncles who have gone on before me. I love and miss you, deeply.

Acknowledgements

With deep gratitude, I would like to thank God, my husband, and my family. To my husband, thank you for your support, patience, and understanding during my creative efforts. Special thanks to my entire family, both near and far. Your support and kind words keep my fire burning. God bless you. Sincere thanks to my immediate family, Mom, Dad, Lesa, Delwin, Kiara, and DeAngelo. You mean the world to me. I love you. A heart felt thank you goes to the Jones family for the good company, food, and writing breaks. Kathleen Wallace Irby, thank you for sharing your poem. Shine on! To my church family and close circle of friends, you rock! To all my readers who waited so patiently, thank you. I hope this is worth your wait.

~Angela Bolden-Thompson

Sometimes, your soul cries. The pain devours your body and stings your mind. You look for relief in a warm touch or a tender kiss, but the band-aid of lust doesn't heal you. You look for a willing ear or shoulder to cry on and none can be found. You fall to your knees and weep. Your tears splatter to the floor. As you lift your eyes to heaven for answers, a light shines in the distance. The glow draws you near. You walk towards it and bathe in its rays. Its light causes you to turn and see the tear stains on the floor. You see the lost years in the water, but the light calls you back. You find comfort in its glow and you smile. You reach to wipe your eyes and the tears are gone; dried in the sun. You walk back to where you cried to find the tear stained floor is dry. You smile, look to the sky and say, thank you.

~Kathleen Wallace Irby

Chapter One

Evelyn placed the cordless handset on the charger. Her heart pounded and millions of questions raced through her mind. She picked up the handset again and dialed her best friend's number.

"Hello, this is Rowena Patterson speaking."

"Ro, I need you."

Rowena tried to suppress the panic rising inside her. *"Is that you, Eve? What's wrong, honey? Is everything okay?"*

"Please, Rowena. Can you just get here as soon as possible?"

A barrage of questions plagued her brain and leaving the office was the only way to get answers. *"Sit tight. I'm on my way,"* Rowena said, slamming down the phone. She cleared the desk, turned off the office light and brushed past Morgan, her assistant. "I'll be out for the rest of the day. Call me on my cell if you need me."

"Yes, Miss Patterson."

Rowena rushed to the elevator. "God, please let everything be all right," she whispered, mashing the elevator button. The desperation in Evelyn's voice haunted her on the elevator ride to the parking garage. Rowena fought not to assume the worst. She hurried over to her white Land Rover, praying that Ms. Ella and the twins were okay. Using the automatic remote to unlock the car doors, she quickly undid the buttons on her cocoa brown suit jacket and tossed everything into the passenger seat. She climbed inside and nibbled at her nail while waiting for the engine to idle down. After a few seconds, she slammed the vehicle into drive and dashed out of the parking garage. Skillfully merging into traffic, she cruised onto the wet street towards Oak Lawn, IL where Evelyn resided.

*****

Dressed in her nightclothes, Evelyn sat on the corner of the bed, uncertain why something so devastating emerged rapidly. Her plan was to spend the better half of her morning soaking in a hot bubble bath with a cup of gourmet coffee, before starting a late workday. With those plans thwarted, everything grew disastrous. Tears formed as she began to hyperventilate. She perched her feet on the edge of the mattress and rested her forehead atop her knees. Drawing in deep, slow breaths, inhaling and exhaling, her heart rhythm slowed and ushered her mind back to their wedding day — a most beautiful and perfect day.

Only close friends and family attended. Her mother Ella Mae and the twins flew in from South Carolina. Ella Mae knew Evelyn's fixation with fairytales was only a set up for a let down. "Life is far from a fairytale," Ella Mae warned. "A man who pays the bills is plenty romantic." Those words fell on deaf ears. Evelyn was determined to have the entire package and didn't stop until she found it in Grady Simms. As she prepared to marry the man of her dreams, the air of magic permeated the room. In the vestibule, she seemed calm and angelic behind her lily-white veil, trying desperately not to ruin her flawless makeup with tears. The sound of music gave Nyeela & Nyasia their cue to start the stretch down the aisle. Grady, who had never been more handsome, waited anxiously for his bride at the altar. Evelyn never fathomed her father wouldn't be present to give her away, but having Ella Mae do the honors proved bittersweet.

Preparing for that day brought Evelyn a mass of challenges and urges to ease her nerves with a drink, but she refused. Nothing, not even alcohol, would rob her of the opportunity to be present for every moment of her dream, the dream that had now turned into a terrible nightmare. Chugging a drink now would be the perfect anesthetic.

Evelyn stood to her feet and slowly dragged herself from the bedroom, down the long, narrow hallway to the vast airiness of the kitchen. With her eyes closed, she leaned into the overshadowing grief and the warm tears began to trickle. She propped herself up against the wall to keep from collapsing to the floor. Her throat burned with agony. She staggered over to the fridge and reached inside for a bottle of water. The cool bottle against her face offered temporary relief and eased her mind into a trance.

*****

The streets were slick and chaotic. Rowena weaved in and out of lanes, yelling at the top of her lungs, "Move, idiot! Can't you see I'm in a hurry? Geez! Where do these people get their freaking licenses? Hold on Eve. I'm coming, just hold on." Fully focused on finding out what had Evelyn in such a panic, she effectively navigated her way through lines of cars, completely dismissing the dangers of speeding in such conditions.

Safely exiting the freeway, Rowena drew in a sigh of relief. After traveling five miles west on 95th Street, she made a sharp right, another sharp left, and sped up the street into a cul-de-sac slowing just enough to roll over a speed bump. Then she ripped her vehicle around the narrow curb and pulled into Evelyn's driveway. "Whew, I made it," she muttered, her mouth feeling like a sandbox. "Thank you, Lord, for watching over fools and babies," she said, throwing the gear into park and turning off the ignition. With a sense of urgency, she exited the vehicle hovering under her oversized handbag, and scurried up the walkway. Like the FBI, she approached the front door and banged, repeatedly. The commotion alarmed Evelyn. She placed the bottle of water on the counter and straggled to the front door, where she paused and drew in a deep breath.

Rowena held no reservations when the door opened in front of her. "What the hell is going on, Evelyn? Is everything alright?"

Clad in her unflinching pain, Evelyn scarcely managed her silence. As she walked away, it became apparent that she wasn't immediately interested in satisfying Rowena's curiosity. The grief in the house was palpable.

Rowena watched Evelyn move slowly toward the corner to flip on the grey torchère lamp. "Talk to me, Eve," she said, closing the door. "Tell me, what's going on? Where is Grady?"

Evelyn prefaced the verbalization of her pain by softly saying, "I hope you don't mind that it's dim in here."

Rowena slipped off her suit jacket. "Let me open up the blinds," she said, trying to swallow the thickness forming in her throat.

Evelyn walked past the smoked glass coffee table and plopped down in the center of the leaf green leather sofa. "No. I prefer the light from the lamp."

"Okay, Eve," Rowena said. "Out with it."

"He hates me," Evelyn announced, in a raspy voice.

"Who hates you?"

"Grady. He hates me," she said, pulling a piece of tissue from the pocket of her pajama pants.

Her response took Rowena by surprise. "Oh honey, that's not true," she said, reassuringly.

"Yes, Rowena. He wants to divorce me." Evelyn buried her face in the tissue.

"What? Why?"

Evelyn paused. "He said things aren't the same between us… that we don't share the same interests anymore."

Rowena and Evelyn shared six years of friendship since meeting at a writers' conference in New York City. The strength of their relationship rested solely on the fact that they were patient and understanding with one another and never hesitated to reach out for support in times of distress. However, the circumstance Evelyn faced was unfamiliar territory for both of them. Being her best friend offered Rowena impromptu encounters with various emotional aspects of Evelyn's personality, but never in that capacity.

No stranger to heartbreak, Rowena understood the magnitude of the situation. Seeing Evelyn so broken vexed her, but the task of finding out what happened remained at hand. She resolved to restrain her opinion until all the facts were gathered. "What did he mean?" Rowena asked.

Evelyn shrugged her shoulders. "I don't know. When I asked, he said he didn't want to discuss it over the phone."

"And this happened when?"

"This morning," Evelyn sniffled.

"Where is he now?"

"In Detroit on business."

"Ok, Eve, let me get this right. Grady told you he wanted a divorce … over the telephone?"

"Can you imagine the audacity?"

"Hell no! It doesn't make any sense. I mean you two have been the ideal couple since I've known you. I refuse to believe that this is anything more than a simple misunderstanding."

As far as business and education were concerned, Grady had an impressive resume. He obtained an MBA in communications and landed a position as a top exec for a large media firm earning him a six-figure salary. He came from a warm, close-knit family, whose company Rowena had had the pleasure of enjoying on occasions. His parents, Mason and Brenda, shared over forty years of marriage. His only sibling, Gail, was engaged to marry fiancé Michael and they were expecting their first born. During their seven-year marriage, Grady splurged on lavish vacations and romantic candlelit dinners for his wife. Even though she did everything she could to support him, Evelyn was successful in her own right. She had a degree and a job that sustained her independence. According to Rowena, most men could appreciate such efforts.

She slid close and lovingly embraced Evelyn. "I'm so sorry you're hurting right now, sweetie."

"This cannot be happening," she said, wiping her face.

"Can you tell me what happened between the two of you?"

"Ro, I wish I knew but I'm… I'm just not sure."

"I really want to help but I need something to work with here."

Evelyn scratched her brow. "He called me last night after checking in and said he was exhausted. I asked what time the meeting was tomorrow and he said, "8 a.m." I told him that I love him and to get some rest, then we said goodnight." She blew her nose into the tattered tissue.

Rowena got up to get more tissue. "Okay, so he wanted some peace and quiet. No big deal, right?"

"Yeah, but...."

"But what, honey?" Rowena handed Evelyn a tissue and took a seat. "What on earth happened in the span of several hours to make him call you bright and early asking for a divorce?"

Evelyn stood to her feet. "I'm still trying to figure it out."

"Did you two have a fight?"

"Absolutely not! I mean ... sure we had our differences, but certainly nothing to bring us to this point." Evelyn paced back and forth.

"What kind of differences? Give me an example, if you don't mind."

"Well, for one, he wanted kids and I wasn't ready yet."

"Okay, did that pose a problem for him?"

Evelyn rubbed her forehead. "I don't... I don't think so."

"Well ... what else?"

Evelyn threw up her hands. "I can't remember anything else, right now."

"Am I missing something? Because this isn't making any sense to me, Eve."

Evelyn drew in a deep sigh and sat down. "Um, okay. He and Gail always had a competition going. Grady found out about her pregnancy and promptly decided we should be next. He started pressuring me."

Rowena shrugged her shoulders. "Okay, but should that be grounds for divorce?"

Evelyn stood up again. "I don't know. I'm just trying to explain."

"I know. And I don't mean to press, but I'm a little confused."

"Hey, if it's any consolation to you, this isn't making much sense to me either, Ro," she confessed, rubbing her chin. "Every time Grady brought up the subject of children, I explained we didn't need to rush. But he insisted on getting the ball rolling and once he has his mind set, there's no use in trying to talk him out of it. Fortunately for me, he gave it a rest so I just assumed he understood," she said, plopping back down on the sofa. "I thought we were happy, Ro. God, what if he's cheating on me?" Evelyn shook her head and covered her face.

Rowena rubbed her back. "Listen, Eve. Don't start speculating. Maybe he just needs a little space right now. Perhaps a little counseling will get you guys through this."

Evelyn's cheeks were wet with tears. "No. I really think my marriage is over."

"How can you say that, Eve? Don't you love him?"

"I do. I do love him, but something isn't right. I think he may be hiding something from me."

"What makes you say that?"

"For a while, I kind of assumed he held it against me for refusing to give him a baby because...."

Rowena forged a frown and held up a firm hand. "Wait, wait, wait! Back up a minute," she said, demonstrating an air of confusion. "Did you say you *refused* to give him a baby? As in never?" She paused. "That's totally different from not being ready. When did you make such a radical decision? Why don't you want children?"

"Okay, Ro, I know I've never openly shared my position on motherhood, but please bear with me here. The night before Grady and I had this discussion, I found out that I was pregnant."

Rowena's mouth fell open.

Evelyn noticed her reaction as she explained. "His obnoxious behavior on the subject made me anxious," she said. "So I kept quiet about the pregnancy and had the abortion without him."

Rowena looked at her sideways. "Why am I just hearing about this, Eve? Couldn't you have shared this with me at the time?"

"My mind was already made up and I didn't want anyone judging me *or* trying to stop me."

"Wow! I don't believe it," Rowena said, shaking her head.

"Listen. I wasn't ready to sacrifice my freedom to be a stay-at-home mom. It's not who I am. Plus, the fear of raising the baby alone definitely shaped my decision."

Rowena folded her arms. "You still could've told me."

Evelyn placed her hand on Rowena's thigh. "You're right. I could have, but I didn't and I'm sorry." She tilted her head to catch Rowena's eyes. "Okay, what's with the annoyed look on your face?"

"Forgive me for feeling a little rejected, Eve, but you were completely unfair to assume that I would judge you *or* interfere. I mean, you don't know what I would've said! And when have I *ever* judged you?"

Evelyn sighed and turned to face her. "Yes, it was a mistake to shut you out. You're right. I'm sorry. You've never judged me and I love you for that. Now, can we move past this?"

Rowena rolled her eyes. "Fine." She leaned forward. "Tell me something. If Grady was so dead set on having children, why were you afraid of raising a child alone?"

"Because it happens. Most women don't dream of being alone when it comes to parenting, but it happens. Look at my mother. She never considered raising the twins by herself, but when my father died, what choice did she have?"

"Trust me. I understand. My mother struggled through the same thing after my dad died and while it's unfortunate, we have no control over death, Eve. We just have to take our chances and hope for the best."

"I'm not so sure I agree."

"Well, I certainly empathize with you, but I still think you were a little unfair to Grady."

"That sounds like judgment, Rowena!"

Rowena shook her head. "I'm not judging you, Eve. I'm just saying."

Evelyn scooted to the edge of the sofa. "For your information," she said, holding up a finger. "I never signed off on this parenthood thing to begin with and in case you've forgotten, this *is* *my* body!"

"Obviously, I'm in no position to tell you what you should or should not do with your body and I would never try. But you could have at least allowed me the opportunity to be there for you. I *am* your best friend, aren't I?"

"I *said* I was sorry. What more do you want from me?"

"Okay, Eve. Listen. I know you have more than enough to deal with right now and I'm not here to make you feel bad. But as far as parenthood goes, it has to be bigger than just one person. Since it takes two people to make a baby, I think both parties should have a say. Was the issue made clear in the beginning?"

"We never really discussed it in the beginning. Besides, I didn't know how he would've reacted and I certainly couldn't risk losing him at the onset of our relationship. Avoiding the subject gave me the time I needed to figure out what I wanted. His not knowing about the abortion was to protect his feelings. Why does it feel like you're taking his side?"

"I'm *not* taking his side. I'm just trying to be objective and keep it real with you. I mean… Come on, Eve. You can't control another person's reaction."

"I know, Rowena. But all that talk about having a family made me question his motives. It didn't feel as if he had *me* in mind," she said, fidgeting with a loose thread on her pajama sleeve. "But I wouldn't expect you to understand. You don't know him like I do."

"That's true. I *don't* know him like you do, but maybe you are trying to justify your actions a little bit."

"Why do I need to justify my actions? I'm the one who has to live with the decision, not you, and certainly not Grady!"

Rowena watched Evelyn tread a path on the gray carpet. "Fine," she said softly.

"You know, I can't shake this feeling that Grady hasn't been honest with me."

"What do you mean?"

"The past few months, I definitely sensed something going on with him."

"Because?"

"Because he seemed emotionally overdrawn. Every time I tried pushing him to talk, he shut me down. One day, I decided to reorganize the closet. Something I had been putting off for quite some time."

"Okay," Rowena said.

"And that's when I found them."

"Found what?"

Evelyn stared at her blankly. "A bunch of pornography stuffed in the back of his closet."

Rowena chuckled. "That's it?"

Evelyn nodded and chewed on her nail. "Mm Hm!"

"Come on, Eve. What man doesn't like a little porn here and there? And you never know, it may have done you both some good."

"I am not a *total* idiot, Rowena. Yes, those were my thoughts initially. It even excited me a little, but then I browsed through the titles…" Evelyn's face turned red. "…and it was gay porn."

An uncomfortable silence ensued. Rowena attempted to move the conversation forward. "Are you sure?" she asked.

"Yes, Rowena. I'm sure."

"What kind of titles did you find?"

"Titles like 'Stud Pups' and 'Cock Tales.' I needed to be sure, so I put one of them into the DVD player. After five minutes of watching, my heart dropped to the pit of my stomach. It made me nauseous. I ran to the bathroom and threw up. It took me hours to compose myself. I couldn't even bring myself to talk about it, until days later when I confronted him."

Rowena maintained a steady composure. "Maybe there's a logical reason, like a weird fetish that he hid from you." As soon as the words came out of her mouth, she didn't believe them anymore than Evelyn did. The awkwardness of the moment compelled her to say something to make it easy for them both, but there were no words. Entertaining the thought of Grady being gay seemed like such a betrayal on her behalf. Nevertheless, she pursued her interest. "How did he respond when you confronted him?" she asked.

"He told me that he and a couple of the guys at work were going to pull a prank on a co-worker, but they decided against it. So he stashed them in his closet and forgot they were there. Of course, it just goes to prove what an idiot I am for thinking of my husband in such a way. Who does that?" Evelyn desperately tried to appropriate her guilt. Unfortunately, Rowena's interest was in getting the rest of the story. "Anyways," Evelyn continued. "The uncertainty never left, and I made it my business never to bring up the subject again. Honestly, I'm relieved I didn't have his baby. Especially under these ambiguous circumstances."

Rowena paused to absorb what she had heard. "I can't imagine what went through your mind. I guess I understand your reservations, but you still don't know for certain he's gay."

"You're right. I don't know if my husband is gay, but I'm no fool either. Wouldn't you assume the same? Think about it. Grady isn't the most masculine guy you've ever met."

Honestly, Grady *wasn't* the most masculine guy, but it was much too soon to make a judgment call and Rowena had little interest in being his judge. She had another idea.

She grabbed Evelyn by the hand and led her into the kitchen. "Let me make you some herbal tea. It'll help you relax." Evelyn's kitchen favored a page right out of an interior design magazine. From the garish cranberry walls to the Italian marble floors, simply put, it was exquisite. Custom-made cabinets with beautiful glass doors lined the upper and lower kitchen walls. The stainless steel appliances appeared untouched. She retained expensive, formal dinnerware for almost any occasion, yet never hosted a single dinner party. Her silverware was spotless. You could carry a spoon in your purse as a compact mirror. The dining room table, poised for eight, added the final touch to a picture-perfect room.

"Ro, screw the tea. I need something much stronger. Perhaps a shot of Cognac would do the trick." She flounced down in front of the bay window at her mango-wood breakfast table.

"Fine. Let's see what you have in here."

Even though alcohol made her obnoxious, Rowena didn't have the heart to deny her friend an escape. Unfortunately, the last time they attended a cocktail party together, Evelyn made an impression that promised to haunt Rowena forever.

Social gatherings made Evelyn uneasy. She preferred staying at home and watching movies. Rowena insisted that they go out and stimulate their social skills. An hour after their arrival at said cocktail party, Rowena mixed in with the crowd and left Evelyn to her own devices. Evelyn knew exactly what to do. She headed straight to the bar and ordered herself two apple martinis. Rowena noticed a second drink in Evelyn's hand and assumed her friend made nice. When she encountered her in a heated debate with one of the party guests, she realized two meant too many for Evelyn. Unsure who to blame, she kindly apologized, guided Evelyn to their things and back to the car. She swore *never* to make the same mistake. However, in light of the circumstance, she needed to make an exception to the rule sooner than she preferred.

Rowena diligently searched the cabinets for a bottle of Cognac but found nothing. What a killjoy, she thought before spotting the wine rack above the sink. She smiled. "Sweetie, I didn't find any Cognac, but I *do* see some bottles of Chardonnay and Malbec. I thought you weren't into wine."

"Just consider it one more thing you can add to Grady's list of surprises. He became an overnight connoisseur," she said, dragging the scarf from her head.

"Wine will do just fine," Rowena said, with a grin. She extracted a 10–year-old bottle of Chardonnay from the collection, uncorked it and allowed it to breathe.

Evelyn propped her head against her hand. "At this point, I'll take whatever you give me."

Rowena pulled the stemware from the cabinet. "For someone who didn't drink, Grady sure has good taste."

"After years of refusing to take a single drink, he started complaining about being the only one at business socials who didn't indulge." She raked her fingers through her thick curly mane, as her mind drifted back to the first time she laid eyes on him. "I still remember the night we met so vividly," she said. *"It was my first Christmas party at the magazine and I kept a Martini in my hand. When I looked up, I spotted a beautiful, greyhound-thin man with coarse, russet brown hair. He majestically strode over towards me and instinctively I knew he was my Prince Charming."*

"Why aren't you wearing a nametag?" he asked. His copper skin smooth and flawless. The smell of Cool Water cologne escaped him as he casually approached.

"Excuse me?" I tried not to gawk at him.

"Nametag." He pointed to his own. *"You're not wearing one."*

"Maybe I don't want anyone to know my name."

"Ah, I see. And how's that working for you?" he smiled.

"Just fine until now, Grady Simms."

"No fair. You know my name and I don't know yours."

"I'm Evelyn. My friends call me Eve."

"It's a pleasure to meet you, Eve, if I may call you that." He took my hand in his.

"Oh, so I guess you want to be my friend now." I gave his hand a gentle squeeze.

"When you told me your name, I assumed you wanted to be my friend."

"Maybe you assume too much." I removed my hand. *"As a matter of fact, maybe Eve isn't even my real name. Maybe it's Wyndi."*

He laughed. *"And maybe this is my cue to exit while I still have a chance."*

I laughed. *"Why, Grady Simms? Am I too much for you to handle?"*

"Hey," he said, surrendering both hands. "I don't want any trouble. I saw a pretty girl and thought I'd come over and ask her name, but this is going sideways. I'm beginning to have regrets."

"Well, I don't want you to regret anything. Evelyn Banks is the name my parents gave me, but you have permission to call me Eve."

"Okay Wyndi ... I mean Eve," he said, nervously. "Again, it's a pleasure to meet you."

"Likewise, Mr. Simms."

"Please, call me Grady," he paused. "How did you come to be at this party?"

"I run an advice column for the magazine."

"Ah, I see. You wouldn't by any chance be 'Ask Eve' would you?"

"In the flesh."

"Wow! I've read your column once or twice, but my sister never misses an issue."

"Nice. It's wonderful to meet people who enjoy the column. So far, I've gotten a lot of positive feedback."

"I'm not surprised. From what I've read, you're very good."

"Thanks."

"It's nice to meet you in person, Eve."

"You may not think so, once I get this drink in me," I laughed.

"You're not going to bite me, are you?"

"I might." I laughed. "I'm kidding. Honestly, I'm much more comfortable with paper than I am with people, which is why I've been clutching this glass all night with no nametag."

"As a matter of fact, I noticed how much time you've spent with that glass and to be honest, I'm a little jealous."

"The jealous type, huh?"

"Not at all, I just figured I could be better company."

"Oh really? Are you here alone?"

"Actually, I'm here with a friend. See the short dude over there in the blue shirt, overloading his plate?"

I glanced across the room. "Yes."

"He's with me. We both work for Ketchum Incorporated."

"Oh?"

"Yeah, see I'm not much of a drinker myself, but he likes to hit all the Christmas parties for free food and alcohol."

"Oh. And are you the designated driver?"

"Unfortunately. So…" He took my hand again. "What's a pretty girl like you doing here all by yourself at Christmas time?"

"Damn! You make me sound pathetic."

"I'm sorry. I didn't mean to be insulting. I've been keeping my eye on you all night, waiting on your little companion there," he said, pointing at the glass. "To give you some space so I could make my move."

"So, you're making a … a move?"

"Oops! Did I say that?" He smiled and looked around.

"Yes."

"Okay, now I'm nervous." He wiped the sweat from his brow.

"I have to be honest with you. The whole drink/companion thing is a little corny, but the pretty girl comment is working for you. You might want to keep working it. Anyways, it's a little presumptuous to assume you can make a move on someone you just met. What kind of friend does that?"

"Okay then, I've changed my mind. I don't want to be your friend anymore."

"Wow! You don't play around, do you?"

"We don't have to be friends, pretty girl. Just marry me."

"How do you know I'm not seeing someone?"

"Are you?"

"No. But…."

"…Then I'm not leaving without you."

"You sure?" I smiled. "I can be very demanding at times, Mr. Simms."

"It's Grady, and I've got a pad and pencil somewhere in my pocket." He
searched his suit pocket.

I laughed. "I like a man who isn't afraid of a challenge."

"Challenges I can do. Letting you get away, I can't."

"How do I know you aren't some kind of serial killer or psychopath?"

"Okay, I confess." He leaned in and whispered to me. "I'm a part-time
thief and I did plan to steal from you tonight."

"Oh?" My eyes grew.

"Yeah, it was one thing that caught my eye."

"And what might that be?" I gave myself a quick once-over.

"Your dimples." He touched my face. "But you look like you might put up
a good fight for those."

I smiled and exhaled. "Well, I hate to tell you this, Grady Simms but these
belong to my Daddy, God rest his soul. However, you may keep the package
they came in."

"Where do I sign?" he asked.

"Girl, he kissed me gently on the forehead and I knew my
search for 'Mr. Right' had ended. He charmed me all the way to the
altar. Up until six months ago, we never kept alcohol in the house.

I suppose he just wanted to fit in," Evelyn shrugged. "He certainly learned how to indulge and as you can see, he's done his homework."

"Well, I must admit," Rowena said, filling their glasses to the rim. "A nice glass of wine *always* does my body good."

"Ro, you would have a glass of wine with your cereal if you could." Evelyn grabbed the glass and took a huge swallow.

"No, I wouldn't! Besides, you can't speak on the subject."

"Yes, I can. I only drink when my nerves are bad. You have a glass of wine every day."

"Haven't you heard? Wine has tremendous health benefits."

"Yeah, but only in moderation."

Rowena carefully made her way to the table. "Well, where the hell is a good moderator when you need one?"

Evelyn sighed. "I watched my husband slowly become a different person and I couldn't do shit about it."

"Eve, let me ask you something." Rowena swirled the wine around in her glass, before taking a sip. "If you felt things were changing between the two of you, why didn't you guys seek marital counseling?" she asked.

"I mentioned it a few times, but trying to get a man to go see a shrink is like trying to pull an elephant with a shoestring. He refused and that was my *one* bright idea."

Rowena raised a quick eyebrow. "Do you really think Grady is gay?"

"I'm not sure. After the porn incident, I didn't know what to think of my husband. I do know the suspicion never left." Evelyn chugged half the glass of wine.

Rowena poured a refill. "I hope this isn't too personal, but did you two enjoy sex?"

"Grady and I had great sex. He was in tune with my needs. There were times when we'd lay in bed for hours, cuddling before making love. Other times he would romance me without sex. Once, he washed my hair and massaged my scalp so intensely, I had an orgasm."

"Damn!"

"He was good at pleasing me with his hands and stimulating my senses. When the sex started to taper off, it never bothered me. Suddenly, we both were just too busy and intimacy went on the back burner, but his thoughtfulness never ceased. I wish I could say the same for his affection. His parents had to be present for him to show me any. Just another attempt to show off, I guess. He knew how proud they were of the life he chose for himself and he didn't want to give them any cause for concern. When we were alone, I would get a peck on the forehead at best. I never even stopped to consider if he was being unfaithful until now."

"Did you ask him why he wants a divorce?"

"Of course I did, Rowena! Haven't you been listening? I love my marriage and the last thing I want right now is to lose it."

"Never mind me. Do you hear yourself right now?"

"What?"

"You said you love your marriage."

Evelyn shrugged. "Am I missing something?"

"I don't know. You tell me."

"Are you saying I don't love my husband?"

"I'm not saying anything. I'm asking you."

"Have you gone mad, Rowena? What is wrong with you? Why are you suddenly questioning whether I love my husband?" Evelyn got up from the table and walked into the living room.

Rowena followed her with the bottle of wine. The alcohol did exactly as she expected. It made Evelyn a tyrant.

"Here we go," Rowena grumbled. "Ok, Ok, Okay! I'm sorry," she reconciled. "You're right. Forgive my ignorance. I know you love him and you have every right to want your marriage. You've invested seven years into this relationship and you deserve some answers. When is he coming home?"

"He's not." She eased onto the couch. "He's staying with a friend."

Rowena sat down next to her. "What friend?"

"I don't know. Some dude I've never met." Evelyn finished off her second glass of wine.

"How do you know?" Rowena reached over and poured a refill.

"Call it a hunch. A few nights before all of this jumped off, some dude kept calling here for him and when I asked to take a message, he hung up. Tell me that isn't strange," she solicited, growing more agitated and desperate for answers.

Rowena put her glass down, squared herself and grabbed Evelyn by the shoulders. "Listen to me. You are a strong woman. I know it doesn't seem like it now, but you are going to get through this, with or without Grady. I promise you. This whole situation is much too complicated to figure out by yourself. Grady is the one with all the answers and he's the one you need to talk to." She searched Evelyn's teary eyes for some glimmer of hope.

Evelyn was well-rounded and attractive at thirty-six. She had a blindingly bright smile and came from a long line of beautiful and intelligent women. After her move to Chicago, she had the drive and ambition to finance her way through college, find a job she loved, and snag a romance most girls only read about in books. At times, her changing personality proved challenging for Rowena, but their friendship made her proud.

Rowena's gaze pleaded with her. "Would you like me to call your mother?"

"Why? There is nothing she can do for me except worry and I don't want her worrying about me."

"Well, somebody has to look after you until you feel better. I guess it's going to be me."

"But..."

Rowena held up a firm hand. "Don't attempt to talk me out of it. I have a few vacation days left, so consider it a done deal."

"That must be some kind of mistake. How can you only have a few left, when you've never taken a vacation?"

"Eve, I travel all the time."

"The only time you see the friendly sky is for business, my dear. It's no wonder you don't have anything going on in your life," Evelyn said, batting her lashes and sipping some wine.

"Um, excuse me. It may not seem like it to you, but I have plenty of things going on in my life. For your information, I'm always meeting new people *and* I work out on occasion. So there! What more could a girl ask for?"

"Uh, a man."

It had been years since Rowena dated a man. Being emotionally dependent frightened her. After the death of her father, Rowena's mother went through a period of withdrawal, which incited a determination in her not to repeat the pattern. Over time, her career became a loyal companion. "Evelyn, having a man doesn't equal having a life," she countered.

"It does for some people, Rowena. I mean, don't get me wrong. I'm not trying to belittle your life in any way or imply that just because you don't have a man, you don't have anything going on."

"Try a little harder because that's exactly what it feels like."

"If it's any consolation to you, as of today, I don't have a man either." She paused. "All I'm saying is I would like to see you have some fun for a change. You know, do something other than burying your face in a computer. All work and no play? Come on."

"There is a bright side to all of this, you know."

"Which is?"

"We've got each other," Rowena said, displaying her pearly whites.

Evelyn rolled her eyes. "Why am I not excited?"

Her smile faded. "Evelynnn," she sang. "Your cynicism is showinnng!"

"No, seriously. If the only thing you and I have to look forward to is each other, we're headed down the rabbit hole."

"Will you lighten up a little?"

Evelyn shook her head and looked down at her wedding ring. "Girl, the sad part is I can't even imagine a life better than the one I had with Grady. Everything pales in comparison."

Rowena placed her hand under Evelyn's chin and lifted her head. "I've got news for you, 'Ms. Alice in Wonderland,' just because you don't know where you're headed, doesn't mean it won't be good."

"From your lips...."

Rowena lifted her glass.

Evelyn drew in a deep breath and clinked her glass against Rowena's.

"Sustained!" Rowena said, finishing the wine. She got up and grabbed her suit jacket. "I have to run home and pick up a few things. Can I bring you something?"

Evelyn grimaced. "Just my husband."

"Trust me. I wouldn't be very persuasive. Not tonight."

"I'm kidding, Ro."

"You're such a comedian."

Evelyn rolled her eyes. "Yeah, I'm a regular riot. Go on. I'll be fine," she waved.

Rowena opened the front door. "I'll be back in half an hour."

"Be careful. It's still wet out there and I know how you drive."

"I got this," Rowena winked.

"Ro!"

"Yeeesss?" she sang, looking back.

"I'm glad you're staying."

Rowena smiled. "Me too!" She closed the door. Outside, she took a deep breath and climbed into the SUV. On the ride back to Justice, where she lived, she mentally outlined the facts of their discussion. Even though she didn't want any of it to be true for Evelyn, she knew denial wouldn't make it go away.

Rowena felt everyone struggled to fit into society on some level. Being honest about one's sexuality, in settings where everything felt manipulated and forced, probably wasn't easy regardless of age, social status, or economic background. She wondered if either of those played as factors in Grady's dishonesty. At any rate, deception about such things could be a death sentence especially with AIDS on the rampage.

Rowena considered Grady and Evelyn lucky. No one expected their marriage to last as long as it did, especially with the divorce rate at an all time high. The whole *gay* theory made her a little skeptical. It lacked something concrete. A woman rarely questioned her spouse's sexuality unless there was a damn good reason and the pornographic video failed to incriminate him. Acting effeminate, hanging out with women at the mall, and forming platonic relationships with Evelyn's friends didn't convince her either, but it was definitely uncommon. Maybe those things made Grady special to Evelyn.

Rowena arrived home to find her neighbor peeping through his blinds as usual. Whether or not he knew she could see him was debatable, but Rowena made a point to wave. Rather than being grossly annoyed, she found it refreshing that someone in her building kept a watchful eye on things, or at least that's what she told herself. She collected the mail and thumbed through it as she walked down the hallway to her unit. The lighting above the door seemed dim, so she made a mental note to replace the bulb before she left.

As expected, the sound of the television welcomed her upon entering the apartment. Every day the automatic timer turned on the tube as a safety measure so no one, except her peeping neighbor, knew of her absence.

The next few days promised to be an emotional rollercoaster for both her and Evelyn, so she geared up. Besides the alcohol, she figured a movie would be a great distraction from the obvious. She didn't know if it would put a smile on Evelyn's face, but she had to be optimistic. During times of stress, music always eased her mind. Hopefully, it would do the same for Evelyn so she grabbed a few CDs. She thought of taking a Bible and some holy water, but Evelyn probably would've thrown her out. Rowena laughed at the thought, stuck to what she knew, and left the healing to the heavens. After wasting time gathering entertainment, she had to scramble to get clothes and toiletries. On the way out, she thought about the light bulb and went to the pantry to get a new one. Once she replaced the bulb, she remembered to check for messages.

Beep! "Rowena, it's me, Grady. Listen. I'm sure you've already heard by now, but I wanted you to hear it from me. I've asked Evelyn for a divorce. I don't want to go into details on the answering machine, but I would like it very much if you would check on her. This is a difficult time for us both and she probably shouldn't be alone right now. If you want, you can give me a call. I'll be back in town this evening. If you can't reach me, leave a message on my cell and I'll call you back. Take care!" *Beep!*

Rowena couldn't believe the audacity of his call. "Damn you, Grady Simms," she said, heading out the door back to Evelyn's house.

On the drive back, she continued the mental gymnastics. He could've fallen out of love with Evelyn, she thought. Or maybe he felt their marriage was empty, but according to Evelyn, there were no signs. After seven years together, she felt he owed Evelyn some kind of explanation, or at least the opportunity to fight for her marriage. Sure, people got divorced for one reason or another, but the way Grady handled things made Rowena's blood curdle. She shook her head. "I've got to keep a lid on my emotions and get into therapist mode. My girl needs me," she told herself.

Dressed in a purple, velour, sweat suit, Evelyn stood in the doorway watching, as Rowena pulled into her driveway.

"Going somewhere?" Rowena asked, removing the night bag from the truck.

"No. I just figured I'd do your eyes a favor and look decent while I fall apart."

"Oh no," she said, waving her finger. "There will be no falling apart. Not on my watch."

"We'll see about that. What took you so long?"

"I had to change a light bulb and check my messages," she answered, closing the trunk. "You okay?"

"I just don't want to be alone right now."

Rowena carried her small tote bag toward the house. "Nice ponytail."

Evelyn shrugged her shoulders. "What can I say? It's a ponytail."

"Well, you do look a lot better!" Rowena said, entering the house.

Evelyn closed the door. "I'll be damned if that's how I feel."

"How do you feel?" Rowena asked.

"I'll tell you when I find the words."

"You won't believe who called me."

"Who?" Evelyn inquired.

"Grady."

"What?"

Rowena tossed the bag on the floor. "Yep," she said, removing her suit jacket. "He had the nerve to leave a message on my machine, talking about he wants me to keep an eye on you. I don't know what the hell he's on right now." She shook her head.

Evelyn turned and walked into the kitchen. "He's worried because he knows he's guilty."

Rowena threw her jacket across the sofa. "Guilty of what?"

"Guilty of betraying me," she said, without looking back.

Rowena quickly trekked behind her. "Are you drunk?"

"Insufficiently," she mumbled.

Rowena took a seat on the high-backed stool at the breakfast bar. "Okay, let me get this straight," she said, blinking hard. "*Now*, he's cheating on you?"

Evelyn cut her eyes at Rowena. "Have you been paying attention?"

"Yes, Eve," she said, rolling her eyes around. "I *am* paying attention, but the last time we spoke you weren't sure. Now what the hell happened since I left?"

"I remembered this one incident," she said, opening the fridge.

Rowena folded her arms. "Go on."

"One of our interns, who met Grady once at a networking party we attended, told my assistant he saw Grady coming out of a known gay club, with some young stud. I'm not one who puts much stock in rumors, but something inside of me believed it. I mean, why would this young man lie? He doesn't know Grady from Adam," she said, placing a bottle of water in front of Rowena.

"Did you confront him?"

"Who?"

"Are *you* paying attention? Grady."

"No. I didn't want to face the truth. I didn't want to lose my husband." Evelyn grabbed the unopened bottle of water she left on the counter earlier.

"Damn, girl! This is a lot to take in. Why didn't you come to me sooner?"

"Do you know how embarrassing it is to tell anybody, let alone your best friend, you think your husband might be gay?"

"I really thought we could tell each other anything."

"We can," she said, trailing her finger across the rim of the bottle cap.

"But?"

"But," she paused, shaking her head. "I don't know."

"What?"

Her voice lowered to a pained whisper. "I feel like I'm the one to blame for all of this."

Rowena reached her hand toward Evelyn. "Don't you dare take the blame for this, Eve!"

"There must be something wrong with me."

"Listen. You are not responsible for Grady's freakish fantasies! Or whatever this is. There is nothing wrong with you. It is not your fault he's having trouble with his identity. And if he *has* betrayed you, *he's* the moron, not you. This whole situation is nuts!"

Evelyn drew in a deep sigh. "Yeah, but that doesn't lessen the pain."

"Okay, but assigning blame where it doesn't belong won't either. I refuse to let you do that."

Evelyn bowed her head and clutched the bottle of water. "Damn it! I feel like such a failure."

"Honey, you can't see past what you want right now, that's all."

She looked up at Rowena. "You seem to have all the answers."

Rowena stood up from the counter. "I *do not* have all the answers, Eve. I if I had all the answers, then I could explain to you why Grady would file for divorce knowing he has a gorgeous, intelligent woman at home, who has done nothing but love and support his ass for seven years. If I had the answers, I could help you understand why he would rather be with a man, *if* that were the case. But I don't. What I *do* know is that this has nothing to do with you. Or *who* you are as a woman. And as soon as you get past the pain, you'll see that."

"Okay. I'm sorry. I didn't mean to attack you. I know you are only trying to help."

Rowena scanned the room for the wine bottle. Despite her best effort, she had a hard time working through Evelyn's cynicism. Every sip of wine helped to ease her frustrations. She located the bottle and happily poured herself another drink. "You have every right to be upset. Why don't you make it easier on yourself and just ask Grady if he's gay?" She swallowed hard and took a seat. "There," she exhaled. "I said it, dammit!"

"I did ask."

Rowena's eyes grew. "You did?"

"Mm hm."

"And what did he say?"

"He hung up on me and I felt like an idiot!"

"Have you ever thought that maybe he wants you to feel like an idiot?"

"No. But if that's what he wants, he has succeeded."

"Being confused or unsure doesn't make you an idiot, Evelyn. If he had nothing to hide, then he would simply tell you the truth. Clearly, he's avoiding the issue."

"Something he's become very good at lately. It's so damn frustrating when you need answers and the only person who has them, refuses to give you any."

"That's for damn sure!"

"The only thing I'm certain of this very moment, is the fact that my marriage is over and there's not a damn thing I can do about it."

"Sure there is," Rowena said, taking a sip of wine.

"And what's that?"

"You can contest the divorce."

"Yeah, and it'll cost me thousands of dollars in court fees, without the promise of anything in return." Evelyn cracked open the bottle of water.

"No. It's going to cost *him* thousands. You get to walk away with the prize of knowing you fought for your marriage."

Chapter Two

The chime of the doorbell surprised Evelyn and Rowena.

"Eve, are you expecting someone?"

"No one that doesn't have a key."

Rowena opened the door. Evelyn's pregnant sister-in-law, Gail stood before her with one hand on her belly.

"Gail! How are you?"

"Not so good," she said, entering the house. "I just got off the phone with Grady and I came as soon as I heard. Is Evelyn okay?"

"No, but ask me again in about an hour," Evelyn yelled from the kitchen.

Gail waddled her 180-pound, five-foot, four-inch frame through the living room into the kitchen. Her round, brown, face was full of concern and perspiration as strands of hair stuck to her forehead. "Eve, I'm so sorry. I swear I didn't see this one coming."

"Neither did I, Gail."

"You guys seemed so good together."

"All couples go through trials, but I never thought for one second that we were beyond repair."

"How is that? Grady told me that you both agreed the marriage was going in a different direction."

Evelyn's eyes glazed over. "What?"

"Yeah. He told me you guys were completely unhappy."

Her voice transitioned from hurt to anger. "Oh, he did, did he? Well, he must've been the only one there for that conversation."

Rowena couldn't believe her ears. Once more, Grady's audaciousness made her sick with contempt. If he could lie to his family, then he certainly wouldn't have any reservations when it came to lying about his sexuality.

"Damn it!" Evelyn continued. "He is such a liar! He never even asked what I wanted. He called to say he had already filed the motion and I would hear from his lawyer. He didn't even have the balls to tell me to my face." She put down the half-empty bottle of water and refilled her wine glass.

Gail walked over and placed her hand on Evelyn's shoulder. "I'm so sorry, Eve. I had no idea."

Evelyn patted her on the hand. "It's not your fault, Gail," she said, walking over to sit down at the table.

"I can only imagine how this must make you feel."

"She's dealing with it," Rowena said, offering to take Gail's jacket. "And we're going to get through this, one way or another."

Gail handed Rowena the jacket and tried to get comfortable on the slender barstool. "I'm glad you're here, Rowena. She shouldn't be alone right now. I've been at the doctor's office all afternoon with these damn Braxton Hicks contractions. They've been going ever since last night. The doctor says I'm about 6 centimeters dilated and the baby could come at any time."

"Shouldn't you be at home resting or something?"

"I wish, Rowena. Between the doctor visits and the trips to the bathroom, there is no time to rest. Speaking of bathroom, I need to use yours. I'll be right back."

Gail wobbled to the bathroom and Rowena promptly relieved Evelyn of her glass. She could tell that Gail's feedback had her reeling. Both of them were at their limit on alcohol intake and

Rowena feared she wouldn't be able to protect Gail from the onslaught that was sure to come. Rather than leave things to chance, she improvised. "Um … you know what, Eve? We haven't eaten anything all day."

"Who can eat at a time like this, Rowena?" Evelyn slurred.

"Yeah, but we really need to put some food in our stomachs. You know. To absorb all the alcohol we've had."

"Help yourself. I'm fine."

"No, we both should eat. Let me see what's in the fridge."

Evelyn let out a hiss. "Not a damn thing!"

"Hmm … I'm afraid you're right. Wait a minute, I see some fettuccini," she said, opening the plastic container. "And it still smells fresh. Let's have some real quick." She warmed up the leftover pasta in the microwave.

Gail returned from the bathroom. "Whew! Much better. What are you making over there, girl?" she asked, trying to get back up on the narrow barstool.

"I'm heating up some leftover fettuccini I found in the fridge. Would you like some?"

"Oh, no. Thanks. I had a delicious tuna sub with lots of pickles and giardinera peppers."

"Ewe! That can't be good for the baby," Rowena said, standing in front of the microwave.

"Actually, tuna is great for the baby."

"Any idea what you're having?"

"A girl," she smiled, rubbing her belly.

"Congratulations! Have you picked a name yet?"

"Mike wants me to name the baby Layla, but Grady thinks I should name her Lilly, after our grandmother."

"Nice!" Rowena said, taking the hot container from the microwave.

"How ironic," Evelyn commented.

Gail gazed over at Evelyn. "What's that?"

"Well, he has thoughts about what you should call your baby, but he hasn't a clue as to what to call *himself* these days. Ha!"

"Here we go," Rowena muttered, spooning the pasta into a porcelain, soup, bowl. "Just like clockwork."

Gail shot Evelyn a blank stare. "What does that mean?"

"What does that mean?" Evelyn repeated, invigorated by her alcohol-induced courage. "It means your brother has a little fairy dust in his blood."

"Fairy dust? What on earth is this woman talking about, Rowena?" Gail asked, observing the half-empty wine glasses.

Rowena forced a hard laugh. "Girl, don't pay her any mind," she said, shaking her head. "We had a little joy juice to help get over this hurdle, but don't worry. Evelyn won't get any more."

"Apparently, she doesn't *need* any more."

"Excuse the both of you. I am not drunk. I know exactly what I'm saying. In fact, I'll say it again. Gail, your brother is gay," Evelyn said, getting up from the table and staggering toward the living room.

"Wait a minute!" Gail said, following Evelyn with her eyes. "Don't you think you're being a little insulting? I mean, just because my brother wants to divorce you, doesn't give you the right to tarnish his reputation. Try not to be so bitter. It's not a good look."

"Bitter?" Evelyn turned back and stood in the doorway of the kitchen. "Who the hell are you calling bitter? Walk a mile in my shoes before you try and judge me, Gail."

"Sorry, if that offended you," Gail said, shrugging her shoulders. "But how do you think I feel hearing you call my brother …your husband, gay?"

"It's okay if you can't handle it, Gail. But you need to trust me on this one. Your brother is gay."

Gail held up her hand. "Evelyn, please!"

"I know blood is thicker than water, but it's true. So deal with it." Evelyn continued into the living room and made herself comfortable on the floor.

"Well, I don't believe it," Gail said, shaking her head and turning to Rowena. "If Grady is gay, why isn't *she* the one asking for the divorce?"

"Good question," Evelyn yelled into the kitchen. "I don't know. Maybe denial. Hell, maybe even fear, but whatever the reason, it doesn't justify his actions. And you think I'm bitter. Ha! Girl, this is me being nice."

Gail looked at Rowena for an answer. Rowena shrugged her shoulders and placed the bowls of pasta on the table.

"You know what?" Gail said, climbing down from the stool. "I think I'm going to leave before one of us says something we can't take back. This is the craziest shit I've heard all day."

"Gail, take it easy," Rowena said, following her into the living room.

"No. How can she fix her mouth to say something like that about my brother? Her own husband? The man she says she loves."

"Because he *is* my husband, Gail," Evelyn chimed in. "And *I* should know. If you all weren't so busy putting his ass on a pedestal, then you could see it too."

Rowena put her hands on her hips. "Okay, Eve. That's enough."

"It's quite alright, Rowena. I'm out of here!" Gail waddled over to the door and let out a shriek. She grabbed her stomach and slumped forward. Seconds later, a trickle of water streamed down her leg onto the floor. "Oh, God! I think I'm in labor."

Evelyn and Rowena were in no condition to drive, but Rowena sobered up enough to grab some clean towels from the bathroom. She helped Gail over to the couch and placed a few towels down to make her comfortable. She positioned more towels between her legs to soak up the fluid.

"Where is your cell phone, Gail?" she asked.

"In my purse," Gail said, panting heavily. "He's number two on speed dial."

Rowena rumbled through the purse until she found Gail's cell phone. She hit number two on speed dial and Mike answered. She promptly explained the situation and Mike promised to get there as soon as possible.

Gail's pain intensified. She relaxed her body as much as possible and practiced her breathing techniques. "I can't believe this is happening now," she said between breaths. "I just left the doctor's office."

"Do we need to call him?" Rowena asked.

"No. Call Mike. He'll know what to do when he gets here."

"I did. He's on his way. What can I do to help?"

"Nothing. Both of you have done enough."

"Gail, please. Neither of us can presume to know what went on in their marriage. Evelyn is just having a tough time right now. Try not to take it personally."

"Ro, you don't have to make excuses for me. I don't give a damn what Gail thinks. She has her man. I don't."

Gail ignored Evelyn's comment and focused on her breathing.

Rowena began to pace the floor. "Okay, I think we're a little stressed right now. Let's try to calm down and think about this baby. Gail, how are you doing, honey?"

Gail perspired heavily. "Not so good. It hurts. It really hurts. I need to push."

She stopped in her tracks. "Don't you dare! Please. Mike will be here very soon. Just hang in there. Can I get you some water?"

"Pillows ... I need pillows."

Rowena rushed into Evelyn's bedroom and grabbed every pillow in sight. She managed to gather four small ones and fumbled back into the living room, dropping one on the floor.

Evelyn remained seated and in deep thought.

Rowena placed the pillows behind Gail's back. "Eve," she called. "Evelyn!"

"What?" Evelyn answered.

"Would you grab that pillow and come help me? We need to make her as comfortable as possible."

Evelyn staggered over and picked up the pillow. She clumsily tossed it to Rowena.

With all the commotion going on around her, Rowena forgot where she put the cell phone. After she located it, she calmed herself enough to dial Mike again. The call went straight to his voicemail. "Mike, where are youuuu?" she sang into the phone. "Gail is getting ready to have this baby right now and if we don't hear from you in the next five minutes, we are calling an ambulance." She began to perspire. "Gail, why isn't he answering the phone?"

"I'm really not sure," she panted. "But I can't wait any longer. I need to push now!"

"Gail, you have to wait," Rowena pleaded. "Just a few more minutes ... breathe ... breathe ... that's it. Inhale, exhale, inhale, exhale ... good job! Concentrate on your breathing."

The thought of traveling to the hospital in an ambulance made Gail anxious. The breathing exercise helped to keep her distracted.

Rowena could barely contain herself. The towels were soaked with amniotic fluid and Gail's urge to push had taken its toll. She scanned the room for Evelyn, who lay balled up against the corner of the sofa, sobbing. Rowena couldn't decipher which made her cry, the divorce, the baby or both. She didn't have time to figure out which, there was a baby coming and she had to focus on keeping it at bay as long as possible.

"Okay, Gail. I want you to keep breathing," she coached. "I don't know where Mike is, but I think we should call an ambulance." She barely got the words out of her mouth, when the doorbell rang. "What on earth took you so long?" she demanded, opening the door. "I tried to reach you on your cell phone, but your voicemail picked up."

"My battery died," Mike said plainly.

"We need to do something quick! It looks like this baby is coming and my guess is we don't have a lot of time."

"Okay ... Um ... Her doctor is at Christ Hospital, not far from here," Mike said. "Can you help me get her into the car?"

"Sure."

Michael and Rowena lifted Gail from the couch and carried her outside. Once she was safe in the car, Mike sped off toward the hospital.

Rowena rushed back inside to check on Evelyn, but she wasn't on the floor. "Eve!" Rowena called out.

"I'm in the bathroom," Evelyn answered, kneeling over the toilet.

Rowena handed her a paper towel. "Are you okay?"

"I will be in a few minutes," she said, wiping her mouth.

Rowena rubbed her back until she finished heaving.

After catching her breath, Evelyn inquired about Gail.

"She's fine," Rowena said. "They're on their way to the hospital. I told Mike we'd be right behind him. You up to going?"

"I have a slight headache, but I think so."

"Some aspirin should help."

"Fine. You get the aspirin and I'll wash up."

A half hour later, Gail gave birth to a healthy, beautiful, 6 lbs 11 oz, baby girl. Evelyn and Rowena sobered up enough to join them at the hospital.

*****

When Evelyn and Rowena arrived at the hospital, the attendant directed them to Gail's room.

Once they were outside her room, Rowena turned to Evelyn. "Are you good?" she asked.

"Much better," Evelyn said, smiling.

"Good," Rowena said, remaining in the hall.

Evelyn bravely entered Gail's room. To her surprise, Grady was present, standing alongside his parents. Mike was sitting next to Gail, holding their newborn. Tension followed Evelyn into the room. She offered Gail an immediately apology for her behavior. Gail graciously accepted. Evelyn acknowledged Mason and Brenda. They reciprocated with warm hugs.

Rowena stuck her head inside the room and offered a cheerful wave and hello to everyone. She caught Evelyn's eyes and silently mouthed to her, "Behave."

Evelyn winked and turned her attention to Grady. Before she could utter two words, he excused himself from the room. She followed.

"Grady, wait!"

"Eve, I don't want to do this right now," he said, brushing past Rowena. "I just got back and I'm really tired."

"Oh bull! You make time for everything else," she said, running to catch up. "When are you going to get the balls to tell me the truth?"

Grady stopped abruptly and turned to face her. "Tell you the truth about what?"

"You know exactly what I'm talking about. The truth about our marriage, the truth about you."

He continued walking. "I don't want to play this game with you, Evelyn."

"So this is a game to you?"

He slowed down, allowing her to catch up. "Look," he said, "I told you I don't want to do this right now. Please, leave it alone."

"No, Grady. I won't leave it alone. You owe me some answers and I want them."

"I gave you everything you wanted for seven years. It's time to do what I want."

"I thought you wanted me."

"Not anymore," he said, picking up the pace.

Evelyn stopped. Her eyes slowly began to water as the venom of his words seeped through her veins. She forced back the tears and continued in pursuit of him. "Grady, wait! Is it something I did?"

"No, Evelyn. It's me. All me."

"What do you mean?"

He slowly stopped. "You just can't let it go, can you?"

She searched his auburn eyes for some indication of their love but they were hard and cold. "No. I want answers, Grady. I want you to tell me our marriage isn't over. That what we had isn't a lie."

He shook his head. "I'm sorry. I never should have married you in the first place."

"Why, Grady?"

"It doesn't matter now," he said, walking away. "It's over. Accept it and move on."

"But what if I can't?" She kept at him. "Is there someone else?"

"Don't be silly."

"Who's being silly?"

He stopped and drew a long face. "We tried, Eve, and it didn't work."

"No, Grady. *I* tried, you didn't. I suggested counseling months ago and you refused. I tried communicating with you repeatedly, but you kept shutting me out. *Is* there someone else?" she asked, waiting for an answer.

Grady remained silent.

"Since you won't answer *that* question, answer this one. Are you gay?"

Grady glared at her for a moment and forced a fake laugh. "I won't even dignify that with a response." He walked away.

She followed. "It's true, isn't it? All it takes is a simple answer to make it go away, Grady. Come on, make it go away!"

He ignored her.

"Do you have something to hide?" she asked.

"Hell no!"

"Then why won't you answer?"

He turned to face her. "Why should I?"

"Because I need the truth. You say you have nothing to hide, prove it. Right here, right now. Put an end to all my suspicions, the mysterious phone calls in the middle of the night, hanging around with strange men, and patronizing gay clubs."

He laughed. "What are you talking about?"

"Someone saw you coming out of a gay club with one of your little men friends. Care to explain?" she asked, folding her arms.

"Why don't you get the person who told you that to explain?"

The possibility of the truth sent goose bumps down her face. "It's true, isn't it?"

"Believe whatever you want, Evelyn. I guess it shouldn't surprise me that you would believe a rumor, but it does. I expected more from you."

"Grady, I've tried to have this conversation with you a long time ago and you refused."

"Apparently, you've got the inside scoop. What more do you need from me?"

Evelyn grabbed his arm. "Why don't you just cut the crap, Grady? Be a man for once in your life and tell the truth. Are you gay?"

Grady looked at her and his eyes welled. He took her hand, the same way he did the night they met. He ran his finger over her wedding ring. "I wanted to give you the world," he said, looking into her eyes. "But the world is never enough when it doesn't include you." A single tear fell from his eye.

"I never asked you for the world, Grady. All I ever wanted was you," she expressed with all the love she could muster.

Grady shook his head. "Even if that were true, it doesn't change why we're here."

"Why are we here, baby?

"Because I can't keep agreeing to things I don't want."

"Do you hate me?"

"Evelyn, you can't believe…"

"Please, Grady. No more lies. Just tell me the truth."

"I'm sorry." He released her hand and walked away.

Without words, Evelyn continued behind him.

He stopped and turned to her. "You've got to let me go, Eve."

"Baby, why can't we just pretend that this is some terrible misunderstanding? Don't you want to come home with me?"

"No. And this isn't some terrible misunderstanding."

"What happened to 'till death do us part'? Why are you giving up on us, Grady?"

He continued walking. "Because I can't give you what you need anymore."

"All I need is the truth."

"And I need some time."

Evelyn continued to press him. "Are you sick?"

He turned and faced her again, this time with a frown. In that moment, he discovered the pain in her eyes. He reached out and pulled her close. She clung to him tightly and took comfort in his embrace. A voice called over the PA, "Dr. McDowell to the nurse's station, please."

Anger hit Evelyn like a hundred pound weight. She shoved Grady away from her. "Bastard! Don't patronize me. You owe me answers and I want them now."

"I have to go," he said, with a broken voice.

Evelyn didn't stop him. She wanted to collapse, but forced her legs to support her. She banged her fist against the wall and bowed into her grief. "I must've been a fool to think he ever loved me," she shouted, covering her face.

Rowena caught up to her in the hallway. "Eve, are you okay?

Evelyn wept. "Please, get me out of here."

Rowena escorted her back to the car and they drove home in silence.

*****

Rowena pulled into Evelyn's driveway. "Honey, is there anything I can get for you?" she asked.

"No, I just need to lie down for a while," Evelyn said wearily.

Rowena grabbed her purse and followed Evelyn inside. "Alright, I'll straighten up and then I'm going to lie down too," she said.

"Thanks for staying with me, Ro. I really do appreciate you."

"No problem, girl. I'm here for you." Rowena grabbed the soiled towels and empty wine bottles from the floor. "What a big mess," she muttered, buckling down on the leather sofa.

Evelyn kicked off her shoes and crawled into a fetal position in the center of her bed. "This can't be my life," she wept. "Please, God, make this go away. I'll cry a river, if You will drown my sorrow. I'll go to sleep, if You let me wake up next to my husband. If You do this for me, God, I won't ask for anything else. I promise."

Chapter Three

Darkness gave way to light and shards of sunlight filtered through the living room, casting a spotlight on Rowena. Awakened by the brightness seeping through her eyelids, she yawned, rubbed her eyes, and sat straight up on the sofa. Still dressed in her skirt and blouse from the day before, Rowena realized she hadn't cleaned a single thing. After stretching the stiffness out of her back, in one quick motion, she gathered the soiled towels and tossed them into the washer. She carefully placed the empty wine bottles into the trash, and tiptoed down the hall to check on Evelyn.

Fully dressed, Evelyn slept on top of the covers snuggled up with one of Grady's sweaters. Rowena grabbed a fleece throw off the sitting chair in the corner, and spread it softly across her peaceful form. She trekked lightly back to the guest room to make a few calls before starting the day. The first call went to Morgan, her assistant, explaining her absence. The next call went to Evelyn's supervisor. Rowena simply explained that Evelyn had a family emergency and she would be out for a few days.

With plenty of time on her hands, Rowena decided to shower and change clothes. She opted for her pale-pink, sweat suit and headed to the kitchen to make breakfast. The phone rang.

"Hello?"

"Rowena, is that you?"

"Ms. Ella? Yes, it's Rowena," she smiled. "How are you?"

"I'm well. How 'bout ya'self?"

"Oh, I'm not too bad."

Unaware of the circumstance, Ella Mae wondered why Rowena visited so early in the morning and why she answered the phone.

"Y'all havin a sleep ova or somethin?"

"Um, well… It's more like a girl's night out, since we haven't been spending much time together. I think it's safe to say we over did it a bit," she said, with a nervous chuckle.

"Oh, I see. Where is Grady?"

"He's out of town on business," she said, clearing her throat.

"How nice!" Her voice smiled. *"Where is that child of mine? I ain't spoke to her in months. I had a dream 'bout her last night."*

"Oh, uh...."

"Hello, Mother," Evelyn greeted from the other end of the line.

Rowena promptly hung up the receiver.

Ella Mae Banks had an innate ability to sense when things were amiss with her daughters. A few years back, Evelyn fractured her ankle and made Grady promise not to worry Ella Mae, but there was no need. A day or two later, Ella Mae showed up unexpected citing something about being lonely, while the twins were away on a college tour. But Evelyn didn't buy it. She accused Grady of breaking his promise not to tell.

Focused on breakfast again, Rowena took one look in Evelyn's refrigerator and remembered there wasn't anything in there to cook. She decided to get some take-out from her favorite pancake house half a mile away and do a little cardio in the process. She grabbed her wallet out of her purse and walked out onto the front porch. The serene ambiance of the neighborhood felt refreshing. The sky rendered a bright rich blue unlike the grayness that echoed their sentiment the day before, and the warmth of the sun ushered in a reassurance that things would somehow get better.

*****

Rowena began her walk to the restaurant. She hadn't anticipated a crowd, but sure enough, a small one gathered inside the foyer of the mid-size eatery. However, seeing such didn't thwart her ambition.

Mindful that Evelyn wasn't much of a breakfast person, when her turn came, she ordered strawberry waffles and a side of bacon for herself. Just in case Evelyn had a change of heart, she ordered sliced cantaloupe with a warm croissant and two large cappuccinos.

After placing the order, she stepped out of the way and watched the staff efficiently work the packed facility. Suddenly, the feeling that someone was staring overshadowed her like a cloud across the sunlit sky. The awareness grew more intense as she stood there patiently waiting. She threw a quick glance around the waiting area to validate the awkward suspicion, when she spotted a man in the corner wearing dark sunglasses and a baseball cap pulled low, gazing in her direction. The idea that he wasn't bashful about staring gave her the creeps. She turned her back and anxiously checked her watch. Fighting the nagging urge to look back, she shifted her weight from one leg to the other and discreetly gave herself a once-over to make sure her sweat suit didn't reveal anything private. Maybe there is something in my hair or on my face, she thought as time slowly passed. Grossly annoyed, she checked her watch a second time and considered confronting him, but she didn't have the courage. An unexpected tap on the shoulder jolted her. Her heart skipped three beats. She hesitated before slowly turning around. A short woman with a hair net on passed her the food she ordered. Rowena took the package and practically ran back to Evelyn's house.

*****

Evelyn sat quietly in the living room with her head in her hand replaying the conversation she had with Grady. She couldn't fathom why he insisted on being untruthful. If he were sick, she would've nursed him back to health, no questions asked. The fact that he didn't trust her with whatever troubled him made her angry. Not only was the marriage turning into a sham, but also trust and communication seemed obsolete. She couldn't help but wonder if the situation was somehow avertable or were they simply destined to fail? The only thing she did feel certain of was the myriad of emotions swirling through her exhausted body.

Rowena entered slightly out of breath. "Good morning!"

Evelyn slid her feet into the slippers lying in front of the couch. "It's morning, but I'm not sure it's good yet. What's in the bag?"

Rowena headed straight to the kitchen. "Breakfast for me and a cappuccino for you, unless you're hungry."

"You know I don't do breakfast, but something sure smells good."

"Have some. Maybe a little food will help." Rowena unloaded the food onto the counter. "I got some sliced cantaloupe and a warm croissant, in case you changed your mind."

"Maybe," Evelyn said, pulling a couple plates from the cabinet.

"You look a little rested," Rowena acknowledged.

Evelyn gathered the silverware and placed them on the breakfast table. "I dozed off here and there."

"How is Ms. Ella? Hearing her voice made me smile."

"Mother is fine. Of course, she wanted to know how things were and I couldn't bring myself to lie. So I told her the truth."

Rowena sat near the window. "I bet that wasn't easy."

Evelyn sighed. "No. But it was the only way to get her out of my hair," she said, placing the dinnerware on the table.

"How did she take it?"

"The same way she does everything — by treating me like I'm a piece of broken glass or something. And the worst part is she wants to fly here for a few weeks."

"What's wrong with that?" Rowena asked, placing a forkful of waffles in her mouth.

"She has the twins to worry about. I can take care of myself."

"For crying out loud, Eve, the twins are grown and in college now. It's not like they can't live without your mother for a few weeks."

"I wouldn't expect you to understand, Rowena. You're always one-sided when it comes to my Mother. Everything she does is okay by you and I know it's only because you miss your own so much."

"I do," Rowena said softly.

Evelyn tossed a piece of melon in her mouth. "What can she do for me in two weeks that she can't do over the telephone? I'm heartbroken, not handicapped. If I want my mother to dote over me, I know how to get on a plane and fly to her."

After a brief silence, Rowena's eyes grew big.

"What?" Evelyn asked.

She put down her fork. "Why not?"

Evelyn tore the lid off of her cappuccino. "Why not what?"

"Why not go home? It would do you some good to get away and regroup."

"There's a bright idea!"

"Don't be sarcastic. You know it's the truth. Besides, Thanksgiving is coming up. Don't you think you should be with your loved ones?"

"I *think* you should let me drink my coffee in peace and think about it later."

"Fine." Rowena picked up her fork. "I'll back off, but you know you'd rather have your mother's homemade pecan pie right now," she said, pushing portions of waffle around on the plate.

Evelyn smiled. "No. *You* would rather have her pecan pie right now. I would rather have my husband back."

*****

The sun left a shadow across the red sky as Evelyn lie in bed, on her right side, staring at the wall. Rowena walked in and took a seat on the corner of the bed.

"Hey, I brought some movies. Would you like to watch one?" Rowena asked.

"No. Thanks."

"You sure? I brought something funny."

"I don't feel like laughing right now," Evelyn stated.

"What *do* you feel like?"

"I feel like someone let go of my favorite balloon."

Rowena rubbed her leg. "Aw, sweetie. It's perfectly natural to feel the way you do."

"Like my life is over?"

"Eve, trust me. Your life isn't over by a long shot. You've got plenty to look forward to."

"I don't want to look forward. I want what I had."

"But what if that's not an option?"

"What if it is, Ro? What if this is just some kind of phase Grady is going through?"

"Click your heels three times and wake up next to your man, huh?"

"Well, I have to tell myself something, because I certainly don't deserve this!"

"Of course, you don't deserve this, Eve. And it's not your fault. The bottom line is this could've happened to anyone."

"It didn't happen to anyone. It happened to *me*, Rowena."

"Evelyn, I'm sorry. I really am. But you have to consider another option for yourself and your future."

"I can't."

"Holding on to what you had doesn't make sense."

"Nothing makes sense, Rowena. I keep going back to the beginning, when we were in love. Trying to make it stay at the forefront of my mind, but it doesn't. Sadly, the love we shared only exists somewhere out there, completely beyond my reach. This house, this room, none of it feels like us, anymore." A tear rolled across the bridge of her nose.

"It may not ever be the same again, Eve. And some day you *will* be okay with that. Right now, you have to take it one day at a time."

"A day at a time? Hell, I'm barely making it from one moment to the next," she said, wiping her face.

Rowena went to the side of the bed and knelt in front of her. "Listen, Eve. I know this hurts like hell. But remember, you are not alone. I'm here with you every step of the way. Just hang in there, okay?"

Evelyn sat up, scooted to edge of the bed. "I can't expect you to baby-sit me, girl," she said, hugging Rowena.

"Don't be silly."

"I think I'll take your advice and go to Mother's."

Rowena rose and took a seat on the bed. "Really?"

Evelyn sniffled. "Yeah, I can't stay here. As much as I hate to admit it, I need my mother right now."

"Good. You should go and be with your family. I'm sure your mom would like nothing more."

"Listen. I need to apologize for the comment I made earlier."

"What comment?"

"That comment about you being soft on my mother because you miss yours. It was totally insensitive."

"Oh, please!" Rowena waved dismissively. "I know you didn't mean any harm. Besides, it's true. I do miss her. Some days, if I look in the mirror at myself hard enough, I can see her face looking back at me." Her eyes slowly welled. "I look down at my hands and I can remember the way her hands felt on my skin, so warm and loving." She swiped at her tears.

Evelyn embraced her. "Every time you think about her, she's right here with you. Mother used to tell me that whenever I'd miss my dad. It got me through some rough days."

"I just regret not having the chance to tell her how much she meant to me. As teenagers, we spend so much time being angry with them, that we never take into consideration how precious and valuable life is. What a mess!" She cleared her throat. "Oh well, enough about me. When are you leaving?"

"I'm not sure. I think I might be able to catch an early flight tomorrow morning. I'll check in a minute."

"You shouldn't have any problems. Thanksgiving isn't for another week or so."

"Would you like to come with me? It'll give you a chance to travel for something other than business."

"Sounds like fun, but I've got too much work to do. Besides, you need this more than I do. You haven't been with your family in years. The twins are going to go nuts when they see you."

"You're probably right. I really wish you would reconsider, though. I don't know if I can handle my family alone right now. Plus, I haven't told Mother my theory about Grady yet. She only knows about the divorce."

"So what! You can tell her when you're ready. *If* you decide it's something you want to do."

"No. I won't be keeping any secrets for Mr. Simms. He's doing a good job all by himself."

"I don't blame you. Tell you what, let me finish my work here and then I'll join you guys in South Carolina for Thanksgiving."

"You will?"

"I promise."

Evelyn smiled. "Thanks, girl! I owe you one," she said, lying back on the bed.

"No, you don't. Everything is going to be fine. The only problem is you haven't packed a thing and tomorrow will be here before you know it. Would you like some help?"

"No, I got it. Thanks anyway."

"Okay. I'll leave you alone." Rowena really wanted to stay and curl up next to her best friend. She figured Evelyn had to be exhausted from crying so much and could use the distraction. Instead, she respected her privacy and left the room.

The phone rang. Evelyn shifted her position on the bed and contemplated whether to answer or not. After a few rings, she reached over to pick up the handset. "Hello?"

"*Evelyn?*"

"Yes?"

"*It's Brenda, sweetie. Are you okay?*"

"I'm tired," she said dryly.

"*Would you like for me to call another time?*"

"Yes. I'm sorry and it's nothing personal, it's just…"

"*Say no more. I understand. Get some rest and Eve?*"

"Yes?"

"*I'm so sorry.*"

"Good night, Brenda." She returned the handset to the charger. Overwhelmed with the urge to scream, she buried her face in a pillow. The tears kept her company until she fell asleep.

*****

At 6:30 the next morning, Rowena woke up to the buzz of an old alarm clock Evelyn kept on the nightstand. A note rested next to it, detailing her flight plans. Apparently, she had to be at Midway Airport by 11:15 a.m. So instead of spending the day mending a broken heart, Rowena had just enough time to shower and dress, without rushing. After her shower, she packed the remainder of her things.

Evelyn walked in fully dressed, but not well rested. Despite her best effort to doll her face with makeup, her stress leaked through. "Hey," she greeted, "I see you got my note."

"Sure did and I'm almost done. How are you feeling?"

"Like I've been hit by a Mack truck."

"And you lived to tell about it? I'm impressed!"

"I don't know if I would call *this* living."

"I'm glad you combed your hair," Rowena said, with a smile.

Evelyn nudged her with an elbow. "Anyway, I'll be gone for several weeks so be sure to take everything. You know how you always leave stuff behind."

"Damn! You know me too well." Rowena shook her head. "I'm sure I've made plenty of hotel staff happy leaving my expensive shit behind."

"You know what I always say," Evelyn smirked. "If your head wasn't attached to your body you would leave it, too," she said, slapping Rowena on the shoulder.

Rowena zipped her bag. "Thank God, it's attached then. On that note, we better get going before you change your mind."

"Thanks again for staying with me, Ro. I don't think I could've made it through the first few days without you."

"Yeah, well I charge $42.50 an hour and I want my money now."

Evelyn walked away. "Bill me," she said.

After driving Evelyn to the airport, Rowena had lots of time and energy. She decided to go home and clean up. The clutter of the closet seemed inviting and it was a good place to start. She refolded a stack of clothes strewn across the floor and placed them neatly on the closet shelf. Loose shoes were everywhere. Rowena meticulously paired and lined them all on the shoe rack. There were old hat boxes, albums, and journals stored on the top shelf of the closet. She reached up to push them back and a sheet of notebook paper fell on her chest. She glanced at it for a moment, before realizing it was a poem written when she was in high school. She paused, took a seat on the floor of the closet, and re-read "The Red Sea Experience."

An Abyss lays between the caterpillar and her wings- the dreamer and her dream. We pitch a tent on the shore of the Red Sea, this dreamer, the dream and me. The pain of yesterday is fast on our heels, we need an escape, quick. Do we retreat or try to swim free. Misery is gaining on us as our soul awaits a glimpse of destiny. Its prize we crave with the setting of the sun, entrapped with the suspense of the conception and the conceived one. The consequences of pursuing the Promised Land produce worn feet from treading the burning sand. Our soul is weary and our mind

drenched with presentiment for the sovereignty awaiting our journey's end. The climate thickens, the temperature drops, our vision is obscured, shall we pass, go or stop? The waves are stirring, have we run out of luck? Violent, unforgiving winds shake everything up. Night draws upon us leaving the dreamer, her dream and me alone. Alas, the past sits atop the hill and we hear a voice whisper, "Only trust and be still." The Sea opens up and summons us forward. Without another thought, our feet leave the shore. "Though foresight is dismal -don't stop- keep going. Forget what is behind and be not weary in well doing. Embrace change, seize the moment, this is your shot. In due season, you will reap, if you faint not."

Rowena submitted to her tears.

Chapter Four

Minutes before arriving in South Carolina, Evelyn continued to analyze her marriage. She recalled a time when something between them seemed slightly off. One Wednesday evening, while trying to meet a deadline for the magazine, she ran out of sticky notes and went to Grady's office to find some. While shuffling through empty file folders in his desk drawer, she discovered a male calendar full of half-naked men. Her heart sank. She didn't understand why something like that would be in his possession, not to mention his desk drawer. Unable to eradicate her confusion, she put the calendar back where she found it and pretended that it didn't mean anything. Like the incident with the porn, she never bothered mentioning it to Grady for fear of sounding ridiculous. In retrospect, maybe if she had asked questions and demanded answers, she could've saved herself the heartache.

The sun beamed heavily in Charleston, South Carolina. Nyeela and Nyasia waited eagerly at passenger pick-up for their big sister. Evelyn was anxious and excited as well. She could hardly hold back the tears when she spotted them. Though they were identical in appearance, Nyeela was always thinner than Nyasia and that's how Evelyn managed to tell the two apart.

Nyasia rushed to greet her with an enormous hug. Sporting baggy jeans, a faded blue sweatshirt and a big smile, she looked flawless. Her golden face and cinnamon brown eyes enhanced the chestnut highlights in her hair. "It's so good to see you, sis," Nyasia said, grabbing Evelyn's luggage and placing them in the trunk.

Evelyn smiled. "You too, baby girl!"

Positioned in the driver seat of the Ford truck they shared, Nyeela, the spitting image of her sister, looked like an attorney in her navy blue slacks and gold turtleneck. Despite her passion for a good argument, she had no desire to toil in a courtroom. Her dreams of becoming an accountant were non-negotiable. "Hey there, Eve," she greeted from the driver's seat.

Evelyn slid into the passenger seat and planted a kiss on her cheek. "Hi, sweetie!" She smiled. "Look at the two of you. You're all grown up! How have you been?"

"Great!" Nyeela smiled.

Nyasia closed the trunk and climbed into the backseat. They pulled away from the airport and headed to the house. Evelyn turned and gave Nyasia a once-over. "I can't believe how good you look, Nyasia."

Nyasia leaned forward and hugged Evelyn around the seat. "Thanks, sis. I'm so happy to see you!"

"What have you been doing with yourself?" Evelyn asked.

"Keeping busy with mid-terms and working part-time as a model."

"Interesting. How is that working for you? Are you able to maintain your grades?"

"It's definitely a challenge, but I'm staying focused," she said, leaning back into the seat.

"Does it leave you time for a social life? Or a boyfriend?"

Preoccupied with her cell phone, Nyasia paused before answering. "Um, I'm seeing someone. I'll tell you about it later."

"I look forward to it. What about you, Miss Nyeela?"

Nyeela quickly glanced at her side view mirror before changing into the left hand lane. "I'm doing well," she answered. "I've got a few offers from some major accounting firms looking to secure my skills."

"Already? You haven't even graduated yet. You must be kicking ass!"

"I know, right? It's been crazy. Mama thinks I should stay with the company I work for now, but I haven't decided yet."

"Well, you do what's best for you. Mother is probably worried about you leaving home. How is she?"

"What can I say? Mom is Mom. She finally has a boyfriend now. You know she was on a hiatus after Dad died."

Evelyn raised an eyebrow. "A *boyfriend?*"

Nyasia looked up from her phone. "Yeah. He's a nice guy. They seem to enjoy each other's company."

"His name is Melvin," Nyeela said, turning on the right hand signal. "They've been dating for about two years now."

"Melvin? Melvin who?"

"Melvin Pennington."

"I don't think I know him. Does he have any children?"

"No. He spent a lot of time looking after his mother until she passed away last January."

Evelyn frowned. "Sorry to hear that."

"Yeah, Ma was there for him the whole time." Nyeela cleared her throat. "What about you, big sis? How are you?"

"I'm okay. I just got a lot on my mind."

"Is that why you look so tired?"

"How's my brother-in-law?" Nyasia interrupted.

"Your brother-in-law is an uncle now. Gail had a baby girl the other night," Evelyn answered.

"Aw, how sweet! I hope I get a chance to see her before she's off to college," Nyeela said, looking at Evelyn side-eyed.

"I guess you're going to have to visit Chicago more often then," she said, pulling her sunglasses from her purse. "You too, Nyasia," she said, without looking back.

"Point taken. Anything new going on with you?" Nyeela pursued.

"Nope, same shit, different day," Evelyn said dryly.

"Hey, do you guys remember the time we were walking down this block eating ice cream and Mr. Green's horse of a dog started chasing us?" Nyasia laughed.

"Are you kidding?" Evelyn smiled. "Who could forget? I thought I was going to die when that thing knocked me down. I still have the scar on my knee."

"Twin and I dropped that ice cream and got the heck out of there," Nyeela recalled. "When we walked in the house without you, Mama let us have it. She said when one of us was in trouble, we all were in trouble."

"We are our sister's keeper," Nyasia added.

"A bunch of nonsense," Nyeela mumbled. "Well, here we are, ladies," she announced, pulling alongside the curb.

Evelyn surveyed the scene as she unleashed her seat belt. "This place hasn't changed a bit," she smiled. "I see Mother still keeps her lawn nicely trimmed."

"You know Ma. She believes you can tell a lot about a family by the way they keep their grass," Nyasia said, opening the car door.

Evelyn shook her head. "Hm! You can tell a lot about a lot of things just by simply listening to Mother," she grumbled, climbing out of the truck.

Nyeela turned off the ignition. "Sis, you can go inside. Twin and I will grab your things."

Evelyn removed her sunglasses. "Okay. Thanks, babe!"

Waiting in the doorway of the two-story bungalow, stood a top-heavy, full-figured woman, with long, graying hair, pulled loosely back into a bun. Her prescription glasses dangled from a thin, silver chain draped around her neck.

Evelyn approached slowly. "Hello, Mother!"

Ella Mae put on her glasses. "Evelyn?"

"It's me, Mother."

"Child, come ova here and let me look at you!" She reached out and grabbed Evelyn by the shoulders. "You look like you ain't slept in days!" She pulled her close and planted a kiss on her cheek.

"Gee, Mother. You're too kind." Evelyn said, reciprocating the hug. "Can I take off my sweater before you start on me?"

"I'm sorry, baby. Come on in. Let me take ya sweater. Can I get ya anythang?"

"No, I'm good."

Ella Mae hung the sweater on a rusted coat hook mounted on the wall near the door. "How was ya flight?"

"Fine, I guess. I slept most of the way."

Ella Mae fanned her hand. "Child, I don't know how y'all sleep on those thangs. Way too much activity goin on for me," she sighed. "But I'm glad you here."

The twins followed with Evelyn's bags in tow. Ella Mae directed them upstairs as Evelyn stood in silence, taking in the warmth of her childhood home. Ella Mae's voice interrupted her sentiment.

"I fixed ya room up for ya, Eve. You can go up wheneva ya want."

"Thanks, Mother. I'll go up in a few. How are things with you?"

"Oh, you know me, child. I won't complain." She closed the front door and linked arms with Evelyn, guiding her into the kitchen. "I'm jus' grateful to be here wit my three babies. Thanksgivin gon' be here soon and I got tons of thangs to do. Have ya spoke to Grady yet?"

"No," she said, allowing herself to be guided. The intimacy she felt being close to her mother produced a cry in her throat. She forced it down. "This kitchen seems much smaller than I remember," she said, her voice cracking.

"Well, it ain't as big as the one you got, but it suits me jus' fine," Ella Mae said, releasing her arm.

"I can't believe this is the same yellow paint I hated growing up. Mother, it's time for a change."

Ella Mae pulled out a chair from the round breakfast table for Evelyn and continued over to the sink. "Child, ain't nobody thinkin 'bout the paint on these ole walls," she said, without looking back. "Now, why ain't you spoke to Grady?"

Evelyn took a seat at the table. "What is there to talk about? It's over between us."

"What eva happened to workin thangs out?"

"It's much more complicated than you could possibly know."

"Evelyn, ain't nothin *that* complicated. 'Specially, when two people been togetha as long as y'all have. It jus' don't make no kinda sense to me."

"Trust me, Mother. You don't know the half of it."

Ella Mae turned to face Evelyn, folded her arms, and leaned against the sink. "Well, you jus' go right on and tell me, cuz I got two ears and plenty of time. You been foolin 'round?"

"Now, why would you assume that I was cheating, Mother?"

"Who's cheating?" Nyasia asked, prancing into the kitchen.

"Child, ya big sista and Grady gettin a divorce."

"You cheated on him, Eve?"

"Who cheated?" Nyeela asked, strolling in on the conversation.

"Thanks a lot, Mother," Evelyn said, rolling her eyes into the air. "I wasn't ready to tell the twins yet."

"Evelyn, ain't no secrets in this house. Ya sistas love you and they got a right to know when you hurtin."

"Eve cheated on Grady and they're getting a divorce," Nyasia announced, grabbing the milk from the refrigerator.

Nyeela approached Evelyn and gently touched her on the back. "I thought you all were happy. What happened, sis?"

Evelyn rubbed the space between her eyebrows. "First of all, I did not cheat on my husband. Things just didn't work out," she sighed.

"Child, you want me to call him?" Ella Mae asked, looking over her glasses.

"I appreciate the offer, Mother, but no. Thank you," she said, fidgeting with the place mat. "Besides, it wouldn't do any good. I've already tried talking to him. He won't open up to me."

"Sis, after all these years, you mean to tell me things just didn't work out?"

"Years are only years if they haven't accrued in value, Nyeela," she said, placing her hands in her lap.

"See, I told ya. You shudda gave that man some babies."

"Mother, babies or no babies, Grady is no longer a part of my life, so can we please drop it?" she said, lowering her head.

"Why should she have a baby in order to keep a man? If she doesn't want children, it's her choice, Mama."

Evelyn emitted a desperate gaze at Nyeela and nodded.

"Child, that ain't the right kinda attitude to have in a marriage."

"Oh, Mama. Does everything have to revolve around men and what they want?" Nyeela asked, pulling her hair back into a loose ponytail. "I'm sick of everybody making it seem as if we have to cater to men and forget about what we want and need."

Ella Mae took off her glasses and turned on the tap. "That's the reason why you ain't got one now, young lady."

Nyeela folded her arms and leaned against the wall. "Honestly, you don't know what I have, Mama."

"I know that attitude ain't helpin ya none. Why you think Evelyn sittin there?"

Evelyn heaved a heavy sigh and slapped her forehead with her hand.

"Please, Mama," Nyeela frowned. "There is nothing wrong with knowing what I want and going after it. If I choose not to compromise my career to wait on a man hand and foot, that doesn't make me undeserving of love."

Evelyn cast Nyeela a concerned look. "No, it doesn't, baby girl. And every man doesn't want or need you to wait on him hand and foot."

"Good, because I'm not going to dumb myself down for some man who can't handle me or my success. Besides, I have plenty of time to think about settling down if I decide to."

Ella Mae turned off the water and spun around. "Says who? We on borrowed time and havin a job don't equal no success."

"Oh and love does?"

"Do you see what you miss out on, Eve?" Nyasia interrupted. "Ma and Twin are constantly debating over everything and it drives me crazy," she said, stepping around Ella Mae to empty her glass into the sink.

Ella Mae turned the tap back on and filled the teakettle. "*Both* of y'all drive me crazy, 'specially wit them hard heads."

"Mama, you were the one who said there's no such thing as a fairytale. If you believe in love so much why did you reject it for so long?" Nyeela asked, taking a seat across from Evelyn.

Ella Mae put the kettle on the stove. "I told ya big sista that cuz I didn't want her gettin hurt like she is now."

Evelyn threw up her hands. "Gee, thanks, Mother! I was wondering when the old proverbial 'I told you so,' would come up."

"Child, hush. I'm tryin to tell y'all somethin. None of y'all got a clue 'bout what it's like to lose your betta half, knowin he ain't neva comin back. I didn't feel complete witout ya father and yeah, it took me some time to move on, but I couldn't help that."

"We understand, but fifteen...." Nyasia paused and counted silently. "No, I think its a little more, right?"

"It's been eighteen years, to be exact," Evelyn confirmed.

Nyasia grabbed a handful of unshelled pecans. "Eighteen years is a long time to grieve, Ma."

Ella Mae pulled out a few tea bags and dropped them into two coffee mugs. "Nyasia, when was the las' time you been on a date?"

"I've had plenty of dates," she said, munching loudly. "I may not always bring them home."

"And why not?"

Nyasia shrugged her shoulders. "Maybe I'm not ready yet," she snapped.

"Somethin *mus'* be wrong wit him if ya scared to brang him home," Ella Mae said, looking over her glasses.

"I'm going to work," she said, walking over to claim her kiss from Evelyn. "Sis, I'll see you later."

Evelyn reciprocated. "See you later, Nyasia."

Ella Mae bent over and started pulling out pots and pans from the lower cabinet. "I'm gon' start dinna."

"You need some help?" Evelyn offered, scratching her brow.

"Naw. You jus' relax, child. Mama got this."

"Sis, are you going to be okay?" Nyeela asked.

"Yes, baby girl," she said, reaching across the table for her hand. "Mother is right though. You have to give yourself a chance to experience love at some point or life will pass you by." Evelyn paused. "I can't believe I said that."

Nyeela rose from the table and pushed her chair in. "I know and there *is* someone special. It's a long story and I don't have time to get into it right now. I have to get dressed. My friends and I are going out tonight."

"What about dinner?" Evelyn asked.

"I'll grab something while I'm out. Besides, I'm a vegetarian and Mama doesn't know what I like," she said, forcing a laugh. "I'll be home early, I promise."

Evelyn smiled. "Okay."

Nyeela leaned in and kissed Eve on the forehead. "I'm glad you're home."

"It's good to be home, baby girl. Go have your fun, I'm going to unpack."

Ella Mae filled the two coffee mugs with steaming water. "Honey, right?"

"Uh, I'll take a little lemon and sugar, thanks!" Evelyn smiled. Although she had no desire to eat or drink anything, she knew if she attempted to drink the tea, it would satisfy Ella Mae. However, making it through the night without falling apart was another story.

Ella Mae dumped two spoons of sugar and squeezed a slice of lemon into the mug. She stirred a few times and slowly passed the steamy mug to Evelyn. She rose from the table with the mug in her hand. "If you don't mind, Mother, I'm going to take my tea upstairs. I need to unpack while I still have the energy."

"Okay, baby. Take all the time ya need. Dinna gon' be ready in a lil bit."

Evelyn forced a smile and slowly trekked up the stairs. She looked askance at all the old faded photos of herself lined along the wall of the stairwell. They reminded her of all the insecurities she wrestled with back then. Developing earlier than most girls her age proved awkward. In her old bedroom, everything remained the way she remembered. Ella Mae kept everything from her middle-school ribbon awards to her white, rustic daybed. Her entire childhood seemed frozen in time. She smiled at the thought of sleepovers and long nights on the phone with her best friend Yolanda. They were inseparable until Yolanda's parents divorced and moved away.

Evelyn sat the hot mug on the corner of the worn cherry-wood dresser. She pulled open the top drawer, hoping not to find any old sweaters or underwear from her days as a teenager. To her satisfaction, only a single button and safety pin remained inside. She began the task of unloading her luggage when grief surged over her like a tidal wave. She fell across the bed in tears. Her cell phone rang. "Hello?"

"*Eve, how's it going?*"

"Okay, Ro," she said, with a brittle voice. "Just unpacking."

"*Are you sure? It sounds like you've been crying.*"

She cleared her throat. "I'm okay. Happy that you're on the phone."

"*Aw, sweetheart. Where is your mother?*"

"She's in the kitchen working up some of her magic."

"*Mmmm, I can only imagine. Anyway, how was your flight?*"

"Long, but I slept most of the way."

"*Good. You need the rest. How are the twins?*"

"Grown and doing their thing. I can't believe my baby sisters have turned into little women. I'm so proud of them. Seems like they've gotten along just fine without me. I guess I knew they would. After all, they have each other."

"That's the point, Evelyn. You need them, not the other way around. Put your pride aside and let your family help you through this."

"Rowena, it isn't that simple. They have their own lives to live. They don't have time for my drama."

"Wrong, Eve. That's what you want to think. Give them a chance. They probably want to be there for you and you probably won't open up and let them. You have to start trusting the people who care about you."

"I'll try."

"Good. Now, I have to get back to work. I'll talk to you soon."

"Bye." Evelyn wiped her face and lay there in silence before attempting to finish unpacking. She caught a whiff of Ella Mae's oven baked chicken and homemade corn muffins, when the doorbell rang.

Ella Mae yelled from the hallway. "Eve, get the door! I'm in the bathroom."

"Okay, Mother." Evelyn hurried down the stairs and opened the door. Standing in front of her was a fine-looking, elderly man, with a gentle face and a bouquet of pink carnations.

"Hi, can I help you?" she asked.

"Evelyn, I presume?"

"Yes."

He extended his hand. "I'm Melvin Pennington, a friend of Ella."

Evelyn mustered up a smile and shook his hand. "Hi!"

"Ella dun told me so much, I feel like I awready know ya," he laughed.

"Oh, I can imagine," she grimaced. "It's a pleasure to meet you, Melvin. Come in. Mother will be down in a minute."

"I brought ya flowers," he said, kindly handing her the bouquet.

"That's very sweet! Thank you. Won't you stay for dinner?"

"I guess I will. Thank ya."

Evelyn walked over to the burnt orange sofa covered with knitted throws. With an outstretched hand and a strained smile, she offered him a seat. "Mother hasn't said anything about you. I feel like I don't know you at all."

"That's awright," he said, waiting for Evelyn to take a seat. He took one right next to her. "Let's see, ain't much to tell. You can ask me anythang, really."

"Where did you two meet?" Evelyn asked.

"At church. 'Course I don't go near 'bout as much as Ella, but…"

"Are you from here?" she asked, placing the carnations on the coffee table.

"Born and raised. I'm the oldes' of four siblins. Two of 'em gone on to glory; one brotha and one sista."

"I'm sorry."

"It's awright. They didn't suffer or nothin."

"I see. Do you have any children?"

"Naw. But I got a few nieces and nephews."

"Ah, I see. Have you ever been married?"

"Neva got married," he smiled. "I came pretty close, though."

Evelyn considered herself quite trusting, but her circumstance compelled her to dig deeper. "Pardon me for being so inquisitive," she said, with uncertainty. "But Mother is all we have and I just want to make sure she's happy. How come you never married?"

"Oh, I don't mind sharin. The woman I was gon' marry found out her daughter had cancer, so she moved to Atlanta to be wit her. We stayed in touch at firs' but aftawhile, we kinda los' touch."

"I'm sorry."

"It's awright."

"Why didn't you go with her?"

"She didn't want me to. Broke my heart. Then my mama had a stroke and that took mos' of my time. God res her soul."

"Yes, sir. I'm sorry to hear that."

"I'm so happy and blessed to have Ella in my life."

"She is wonderful, isn't she?"

Ella Mae came down the stairs. "Evelyn, you in here botherin my friend?" she asked, putting on her glasses.

"Yes, Mother, I'm giving him the third degree," she teased, rising to her feet.

Melvin stood and greeted Ella Mae with a kiss on the cheek.

"Melvin, don't pay her no mind. She jus' upset 'bout her marriage."

"Mother!"

Ella Mae took a seat on the couch. "Don't be shamed, child. It's true. Melvin, my baby gettin a divorce."

"Thanks, Mother. Would you like me to leave the room now so you can give him all the details?"

"Don't be silly. Sit down and tell him ya'self."

Evelyn stood there shaking her head in disbelief.

Melvin took a seat next to Ella Mae. "It's quite awright," he said, clearing his throat. "We jus' met and it ain't none of my business. Somethin smells good. What you cookin in there Ella Mae?"

"You gotta wait 'til dinna to find out. You stayin ain't ya?"

"Yes, ma'am. Evelyn, ya mama tells me you live in Chicago."

"Actually, I live in Oak Lawn, which is a small suburb just outside of Chicago."

"Is it anythang like what they say?"

"What do people say?"

"They say it's real bad up there in the winta."

"Yes, our winters can be brutal, but it's one of the reasons I love Chicago. The winters are perfect for snuggling and cozying up with the one you love."

"You eva been there in the winta time, Ella?"

"Naw, Melvin. I don't hardly like the cold no how. Maybe we oughta plan a trip when it's warm up there."

Melvin nodded. "Yeah, okay."

"Well, I'm going to excuse myself now." Evelyn picked up the flowers from the table. "Melvin, it was lovely to have met you. Mother, call me when dinner is ready," she said, leaving the room.

Ella Mae caught the regretful look in Evelyn's eyes. "Okay, baby," she said, putting a finger to her chin.

Evelyn marched up the stairs, back to her room swearing under her breath. "What in the hell am I doing here? I knew this would be a mistake. I never should've let Rowena talk me into this. I don't believe her. That is exactly why I never tell her anything. I wouldn't be surprised one bit if my divorce ended up making local headlines by morning. *Shit!* She hasn't even heard the whole story yet. God help me!" Evelyn tossed the bouquet on the dresser and flopped across the bed on her stomach. Minutes later, a gentle knock came at the door. "Come in."

Ella Mae entered, slowly.

"Is it time for dinner already?" Evelyn asked, resting her head on folded arms.

"Naw, baby. I jus' came up here to talk to you."

"Where is Melvin?"

"I sent him to the store for some wine," she said, clasping her hands in front of her.

"When did *you* start drinking? You never drank when Daddy was alive."

"Child, that's history. Me and Melvin like to drink a lil wine wit our dinna."

"I guess some things do change, huh?"

"What?"

"Oh, never mind, Mother. How on earth could you embarrass me in front of a complete stranger?"

"What stranga? Child, Melvin ain't no stranga," she said, waving her hand.

"He is to me." Evelyn sat up and swung her feet around to the side of the bed.

"Well, in this house he ain't. And he certainly ain't no stranga to bad news," she said, taking a few steps closer to the bed. "Baby, everybody get they heart broke at leas' once in life. I keep tellin ya I know how it feel to lose a man. Maybe not the way you losin

Grady, but it's still a loss. You got a chance to get Grady back if ya want him. Mine ain't neva comin back," she said, casting a look of sorrow.

Evelyn lowered her head and let out a tremulous breath. It was the first time she realized the depth of her mother's struggle, during her absence.

Ella Mae lifted Evelyn's head and looked intently into her eyes. "I stop livin when ya daddy passed and I don't want the same thang to happen to you."

In that fleeting moment, Evelyn got a sense of her mother's pain, but couldn't stop thinking of her own. "How did you do it? I mean, for me, if I'm not Grady's wife, then I don't know who the hell I'm supposed to be. When I vowed to love him 'til death do us part, I meant every word. I never dreamed he would stop loving me."

"Evelyn, we all put our hearts on the line for love. Nobody can say how its gon' turn out. When folk get married, they want it to las' foreva but sometimes it jus' don't happen that way. You jus' gotta cherish the good times and thank the good Lawd ya had a chance to participate."

Evelyn ran her toe across the top of her tennis shoe. "I don't think I'll ever love again. It doesn't feel good to lose. All this pain feels like a slow, silent death."

Ella Mae pushed her glasses up on the bridge of her nose. "Baby, I'm sorry you havin a tough time. You was so serious 'bout findin romance, I didn't know how to help you. I thought if I told you 'bout the simple thangs to look for in a man, you would get the hint. But some thangs you gotta learn for ya'self. Trust me, that pain is only here to remind you that you still alive," she said, gently rubbing Evelyn's back.

"Did you ever think you would love again?"

"Child, I don't know what I thought," she said, placing her hand on her cheek. "I jus' knew I was hurtin.' Loneliness and heartache became my best friends. Next thang I know, eighteen years had dun passed me by."

"No offense, Mother, but I don't want that."

"If you hurry, you can still save ya marriage," she said, folding her arms. "All ya gotta do is call ya husband."

"Mother, there is something I need to tell you."

"No more excuses, Evelyn," she said, slapping her thigh impatiently. "Put ya pride to the side and call ya husband."

Evelyn looked up at Ella Mae. "You don't know the whole story."

"I know y'all can fix this mess if you jus' forgive each otha."

"Some things can't be fixed, Mother."

Ella Mae put her hand on her hip. "Like what, Evelyn? Ya stubbornness? Girl, don't you know love is stronga than pride?"

"Mother, Grady is gay."

Ella Mae gasped and covered her mouth.

"That's what I've been trying to tell you."

Ella Mae shook her head. "Aw, now that ain't nice, Eve. I know you a lil angry, but if you ain't got nothin nice to say 'bout ya husband, then don't say nothin at all."

"Mother, I really do believe Grady is gay." Evelyn lowered her head. "Well, he hasn't exactly confessed or anything, but I would never make up a lie like that."

"Gay, Eve? Tell me why."

"Well, there are things I can't explain and he won't either."

"What do you mean? What thangs?"

"It's sort of complicated. There were weird things like calendars of half-naked men, strange phone calls in the middle of the night and the list goes on. If I had to go on my instincts I would definitely say it's true."

Ella Mae sat on the side of the bed next to Evelyn. "Was he tryin to hide it from you?"

"Yes, Mother."

Ella Mae put her hand to her cheek. "Oh, my God!"

"And I just don't know what to do." Evelyn covered her face.

Ella Mae looked upon Evelyn with sympathetic eyes. "I'm so sorry, baby."

Evelyn wiped her tears. "I feel like I've been walking around with blindfolds on all this time. Now, I'm back where I started," she sniffled.

Ella Mae lovingly wrapped her arms around Evelyn. "I don't like seein you like this. I know exactly how you feel too. I didn't know how I was gon' make it witout ya daddy," she said, shaking her head and rocking back and forth. "It sho wasn't easy. 'Specially wit the twins bein so young. I had to start all ova again, but it taught me to be strong. You gotta be strong okay, baby?

Evelyn laid her head against Ella Mae's shoulder. "How?"

"By trustin God," Ella Mae said, with a gentle squeeze.

"Okay," she sniffled.

"He'll make it awright."

"Yes, Mother."

"Now, dry them tears and let's go get some dinna."

"You go ahead, Mother. I'll be down in a minute."

"You sho?"

"Yes."

"Okay." Ella Mae left.

Evelyn grabbed her cell phone and sent Grady a text message:

We need 2 talk. No anger this time. I promise.

He responded a few seconds later:

Fine. I will call u in a few hours.

Evelyn changed her shirt, washed her face, and joined Ella Mae and Melvin in the dining room for dinner. She forced herself to eat a few bites of chicken and half a corn muffin. After dinner, they opened a bottle of wine and relaxed in the living room.

"Y'all know what? I think I'mma get my hair fixed for the holiday."

"Sounds nice." Melvin smiled.

"It's so long and pretty. A nice roller-set would look good on you, Mother."

"Child, I don't know. I jus' want somethin diff'rent."

"Ella Mae, I love how make up ya mind to do somethin and jus' do it."

"Thank ya, Melvin. I try," she said, blushing.

Nyeela returned home and joined everyone in the living room. "What's going on?" she asked, dropping her keys on the coffee table.

"Nyeela, where you been? You dun already missed dinna."

"Mama, I told you earlier about my plans. Besides, I don't eat the stuff you cook."

"Listen at you," Ella Mae said, crossing her arms. "You dun had cow, chicken and pig growin up. None of em was *mad* or had the flu. All ya gotta do is bless the food before ya eat it and it'll be fine."

Nyeela rolled her eyes and waved a dismissive hand.

"Mother, I forgot to tell you I invited Rowena to spend Thanksgiving with us. I hope you don't mind."

"Eve, you know we considda Rowena part of this family. She welcome anytime. Somebody gotta help eat all the food. How is she?"

"Compared to *me*, she's doing great," Evelyn said, sipping some wine. "Just a workaholic is all. Every now and then, I catch her in a sad place and I think it's because she really misses her mother, otherwise she's the best girlfriend in the whole world."

Nyeela smiled. "You two have been friends for a long time. Does Rowena have a boyfriend?"

"Rowena is the *last* person thinking about a man right now. She's had some bad encounters."

"Child, ain't we all?" Ella Mae said, pouring herself a glass of wine.

"That job is her man, right now. Rowena has her life tailored so she doesn't even have the time to consider romance."

Ella Mae shook her head. "Did I miss somethin? I don't understand y'all workin women, now-a-days."

"Mama, I think some men find a woman's independence intimidating."

"You've got a point, Nyeela," Evelyn agreed. "Consequently, strong women are not approached as much. And when they are, the relationship is short-lived."

"Most are finding they don't even *need* a man these days."

Melvin scratched his brow. "Oh, I don't know 'bout that, Nyeela," he said. "No matta how much a woman try to convince herself she don't *need* no man, it's jus' anotha lie at the end of the day. I mean, come on now. It's certain thangs *only* a man can give and ain't no technology in the world gon' replace it. Independence is one thang and I respect it, but God put man and woman togetha for a purpose."

"I thought so, Melvin," Evelyn said, crossing her legs. "I really did. But honestly, after what I've been through, I don't know what to think anymore."

Nyeela straightened her posture on the sofa. "Melvin, I'd like to know exactly what it is you're trying to say."

"I'm sorry, Nyeela. Let me make myself clear. I ain't talkin 'bout supaficial thangs like affection or support. A dog can give affection and friends give support all the time. I'm talkin 'bout a deepa level of connection. For instance, nobody can nurture a man the way a woman can. Nothin can replace the security a woman feel when she in her man's arms."

"Why does it have to be so deep? I mean, what ever happened to mere companionship?"

Evelyn raised her hand. "Okay. Melvin, I have a question for you since you seem to be more enlightened than the rest of us," she said. "How can a man find comfort in another man?"

"Sis, people can't help who they find themselves attracted to," Nyeela offered.

Evelyn ignored her and poured a refill.

Melvin continued. "Well, I don't have all the answers, Evelyn. I can't speak for all men. I'm jus' talkin 'bout what I know to be true."

"I don't see what the big deal is," Nyeela said. "Everybody doesn't need nurturing or security. Some people are just looking for companionship and a little romance."

"Ya jus' don't get it, Nyeela," Ella Mae commented. "Jus' keep on livin and someday you will."

"Mama, I don't see why women have to compromise all the time. It's an outdated concept and if you all don't get with the times, you are going to miss out on so much."

"From where I sit they aren't missing out on much," Evelyn said, pursing her lips.

"You're just angry because Grady left you high and dry, which goes to prove my point about all those old skool theories."

"Don't go there, Nyeela. Seriously, you don't have the slightest clue." Evelyn tilted her glass and took a huge swallow.

"If a 'deeper connection' can cause a beautiful and intelligent woman like you, to look, feel and act like death rolled over, then I'm good without it."

"Nyeela Marie Banks, don't speak to ya sista that way," Ella Mae ordered, taking off her glasses.

"Girl, you don't know shit! You probably never experienced love, in your whole little baby life."

Melvin stood up. "Well, I betta get goin."

Evelyn held up her hand. "No, Melvin, you don't want to miss this. Twin, with all the silver rings, wants to school us old folk on the art of love," she said, slamming her glass down on the coffee table.

Melvin kissed Ella Mae on the cheek. "Dinna was good. Great meetin ya, Evelyn. Night, ladies!"

Melvin left. Nyasia returned.

Ella Mae stood up and put her hands on her hips. "See what y'all dun went and did."

Nyeela got up from her seat. "Oh, Mama," she said, throwing her hand. "Get a grip! He'll be back tomorrow. I'm going to bed." She brushed past Nyasia and went up the stairs.

Nyasia's smile slowly faded as she walked into the living room. "What did I miss?"

Evelyn stood up and stumbled past Nyasia. "Sorry, babe, you're going to have to tune in tomorrow to find out."

"What is she talking about, Ma? Are you and Nyeela at it again?"

Ella Mae didn't answer. She stormed up the stairs to her room and slammed the door.

Nyasia shook her head. "I'm *so* glad I wasn't here."

Evelyn returned to her room, kicked off her shoes and flopped down on the bed. She tried to dream about the good times she and

Grady shared. Her thoughts went back to a romantic weekend they spent together.

Grady had everything planned right down to Sunday evening. Friday night, Evelyn came in from work to a tub of hot bath water littered with red rose petals. Scented candles flickered all around and soft music played in the background. He orchestrated the perfect finish to a long week. Grady approached Evelyn from behind and wrapped his arms around her waist, drawing her close to him.

"All this for me?" she said, with a smile. "I must've been a good girl."

"You are my good girl," he said, kissing her on her neck.

She turned around to kiss him on the mouth, but he broke away and walked over to the tub to test the temperature of the water. Evelyn quickly undressed and climbed into the tub, hoping he would join her. Fully dressed, he sat on the edge of the tub and washed her back. Maybe he needs an invitation, she thought. So she nibbled on his fingers hoping he would take the hint. Obviously not in the mood, he smiled, slid down to the end of the tub, and washed her feet. Evelyn became annoyed.

"Is something wrong?" she asked.

"No, why?"

"Well, there's plenty of room in here. I thought maybe you'd like to join me."

"Honey, can't you just appreciate the gesture? I want this night to be all about you. So please, try to stay in the moment and relax."

"Fine," she sighed. "Mmmm, that feels nice! How was your day?" she asked, after a long pause.

"Why are you asking me about my day? Didn't I say this night is all about you?"

"Alright. Out of curiosity, what's the special occasion?" she pried.

"Damn! I guess I just can't be nice to you, huh?"

"Forgive me for being a little surprised. You haven't been spreading the love lately."

"Okay, so I haven't been the easiest person to get along with, I know. I've been under a lot of stress at work and I admit I've been taking it out on you. I'm trying hard to make amends by putting some romance in the air. So please don't ruin it."

"I'm sorry. I do feel the romance and I appreciate you doing this for me."

"This is just the beginning. I have the perfect weekend mapped out for us," he smiled.

"Do tell," she said, with a naughty grin.

"You'll have to wait and see," he teased.

"You always know how to make me smile."

"You're an easy crowd."

"I love you."

"I love you more, Eve."

Chapter Five

The next morning, guilt greeted Nyeela as she rolled over in bed. The insults she hurled at Evelyn the night before left a bitter taste in her mouth. She climbed out of bed and went down the hall to apologize. She started to knock, but hesitated when she heard Evelyn's cell phone ringing.

"Grady, what happened?" Evelyn asked. "I thought you were going to call me last night."

"I did, Eve. Check your voicemail. I called twice and you didn't answer."

Evelyn scratched her head. "I guess I didn't hear it ringing."

"Listen. What happened at the hospital was not how I intended things to turn out. I didn't mean for it to turn so messy."

"Grady, everything you've done, up to this point, has been messy."

"For what it's worth, it's not my intention to hurt you."

"You've failed, miserably."

"This hurts me just as much, Eve."

"I doubt that."

"Look, if you want to get past this, you need to be ready to hear the truth."

"I'm all ears."

"The truth is…Being married to you felt a little one-sided. After all of the expensive cars, lavish vacations, and fancy dining, I have nothing to show except a bunch of high credit card bills."

"What are you saying, Grady?"

"What did you sacrifice for this union?"

"Why did I have to sacrifice anything? I never asked you for those things."

"You didn't turn them away either, did you?"

"Hell, if I had known you were going to use it against me, I would have."

"The only thing I asked for was a family, Eve. But you refused to do it."

"Grady, I gave you a family. I gave you me, but I guess I wasn't enough. You always have to have more. Is that the real reason you filed for divorce?"

"The reason I filed for divorce is exactly what I said."

"Well, you haven't said much. All this foolishness about what you did for me, is as tired as you are. I have a good education and a career that pays me well, so don't get it twisted. I *thought* you did those things because you loved me, but I guess you were only looking for some kind of trade-off."

"No. I wasn't."

"Let me get this right. You bailed out of this marriage, because I refused to be a baby factory? I have to say, I'm a little disgusted and disappointed in you, Grady."

"That makes two of us, Eve."

"I never told you I wanted kids."

"You never said you didn't."

"I don't recall you asking. You were too busy assuming, while you were planning those lavish vacations."

"Marriage is about compromise."

"Marriage is about a whole lot of things, but whatever!"

"My needs weren't fulfilled, Eve."

"Okay. So now, I didn't fulfill your needs. You were the one who refused to get counseling, Grady. If you really wanted to fix our marriage, you would've jumped at the opportunity."

"Why pay some stranger to tell me what I already knew?"

"Well if you knew, why couldn't you tell me?"

"Because I knew it wouldn't change anything."

"And you know *every* damn thing, right? This is exhausting. Let's get some damn closure, so we can end this."

"Eve, I know you don't believe this, but I love you and I never meant to hurt you."

"Please, Grady. Spare me the "I'm so sorry" speech."

"What do you want from me?"

"I want you to be a man for once...."

"I am a man—one hundred percent. I think I've proven that over the years."

"Don't flatter yourself, Grady."

"You can be so damned mean."

"You certainly aren't in any position to judge me."

"Hey, you wanted a knight in shining armor and you got it. You didn't seem to care much about anything else."

"Are you saying I didn't care about you?"

"Sometimes, it felt that way. It seemed like all you cared about were the people who needed your advice."

"That is not true, Grady. And you know it! I had a job to do and it was important for me to do it well. I gave you all of me, even when I didn't feel like it."

"That's a matter of opinion."

"I never asked you to choose me over your job."

"You never had to."

"Are you saying it's my fault that our marriage failed?"

"I'm saying it never really had a chance."

"Why?"

"I think you already know."

"Damn it, Grady. Stop assuming what I already know and tell me."

"This isn't easy for me to say to you."

"You seem to be doing just fine."

"Eve, I'm attracted to men."

"What?"

"You heard me."

"Did you say…?"

"Yes, Eve. I'm gay."

"You're ...." Evelyn couldn't say the words. The phone slid halfway down her face and her stomach fell into a knot. For a moment, her heart stopped and everything seemed a big blur. She didn't even feel the tears surface, but they came in full force. She wanted to throw the phone across the room, but nothing on her body functioned except her tear ducts. After a long numbing silence, she found her hands and positioned the phone back to her ear.

"Hello? Are you still there?"

She forced her voice to give sound to her words. "I specifically asked you," she said, in a pained whisper. "How could you?"

"Eve, I couldn't even say the words out loud, let alone say them to you."

"Oh, God! This can't be."

"It's who I am."

"But we ... Oh, I'm going to be sick."

"Eve, you said you wanted the truth so here it is. I knew you couldn't handle it."

"How the hell do you expect me to react, Grady? Do you expect me to be happy to hear this shit?"

"Hell, I wasn't happy to say it but ..."

"You've been lying to me all these years."

"I've been lying to myself."

"How hard is it to be a real man and tell me the truth?"

"I wish you would stop insulting my manhood. You have no idea how difficult this is for me and for your information, being gay doesn't mean I'm not a man. I'm just not the kind you want."

"Grady, you have the biggest ego I've ever seen. You want so badly to make this all about you, but you are the one who deceived me."

"And I'll regret it for the rest of my life."

"Your regret doesn't bring me any comfort right now."

"I wanted to tell you, but…"

"Grady, we had sex. How could you be gay and have sex with a woman?"

"Because I wanted to. I wasn't lying when I said I love you."

"I don't believe it."

"Well, I guess it doesn't matter what I say then, does it?"

"No, because everything that comes out of your mouth is a big fat lie. All these years, I thought I knew who and what you were. Now, I don't know shit!"

Grady drew in a deep sigh. *"Evelyn, I'm really trying to offer you something here. The love and the sex were real and nothing is going to change that."*

"Wrong! This changes everything. Did you cheat on me?"

"No, Eve. I didn't."

"Come on, Grady. You can't expect me to believe that."

"I swear to you, I did not cheat."

"So how do you know?"

"Know what?"

"That you're…"

"Gay? Because I've struggled with it for years. It came to the point where I just couldn't live a lie one more second."

"Exactly how long have you known you were attracted to men?"

He paused. *"I don't know. Early I guess."*

"You guess? Are you sure you aren't bisexual?"

"I've gone over this in my head a thousand times. Trust me, I'm not a bisexual."

"How do you know?"

"Other than you, I'm simply not attracted to women. My attraction is for men and it won't go away."

"Maybe you're confused."

"This isn't some cooked up scheme to hurt you, Eve."

"That depends on who you ask. To marry me, knowing you're gay is pretty damned deliberate, Grady."

"Was it okay for you to marry Prince Charming? Get the world on a silver platter and refuse to give me children?"

"Prince Charming lived in a closet. You spent the last seven years watching me turn our house into a home. I gave my body and soul to you without a clue that you were thinking about men. And you have the nerve to point the finger at me!"

"I guess we both ended up with the short end, huh?"

"You smug bastard!"

"Okay, that was mean. I'm sorry. I don't want to argue."

"Too late!"

"Eve, if I could take it all back and do things differently, I would."

"So would I."

"I don't have any regrets about what we shared."

"Surely, you *must* regret wasting all these years on a woman who wouldn't give you children. Isn't that the real reason you married me?"

"No."

"So why marry me, when you could've had a man?"

"That's not fair, Eve."

"Fair? Don't talk to me about what's fair!"

"Look, this is not some disease to be cured. I can't change who I am. I'm sorry for misleading you, but I'm sorrier for misleading myself. The truth is out in the open now."

The awkwardness that came with his words, prompted Evelyn to switch positions on the bed. She folded her lips and closed her eyes. "So what now?" she asked.

"I don't know. You tell me?"

"Grady, were you using me to bear your children? Do you have any idea what this would have done to them? Damn! I'm so angry with you right now."

"Eve, I swear on my life, I never used you to bear children. I honestly just wanted us to have a family. My love for our children would never have suffered in any way."

"So you were prepared to continue living a lie."

"I believe I would have done anything to keep my family together."

The abortion crept to the forefront of her mind. Guilt surged through her like a bolt of electricity. "I suppose none of it really matters now," she said, shrugging it away. "What's important now is what happens from this point."

"To make things go as smoothly as possible, I'm willing to give up the house and everything in it. I just want my clothes and all my fitness equipment."

"Fine."

"This may sound redundant, but I need to ask. Will you be seeking alimony?"

"Contrary to your opinion, I don't need your money. However, considering all the pain and humiliation you've caused me, I think it's only fair that you compensate me."

"Eve, all the money in the world won't fix a broken heart."

"Oh, I know. But it will surely help the healing process. I don't want to get into this over the phone. You can discuss it with my lawyer. And just so you know, I plan to sell the house. It makes no sense to hold on to all the lies."

"Do what you want with it. I don't care."

"How can you act so nonchalant? Am I that dispensable to you? You know what … never mind."

"I didn't mean it the way it sounded, Eve."

"Should I be expecting the papers any day now?"

"I suspect some time after the holidays."

"Okay then, I'll talk to you later."

"Okay."

"Goodbye."

Still eavesdropping outside the door, Nyeela ducked into the linen closet when she heard Evelyn get off the phone. Feeling nauseous, Evelyn opened the door and rushed down the hall to the bathroom.

Nyeela poked her head out of the closet before tiptoeing down the hallway. She gently knocked at the bathroom door. "You okay in there, sis?"

"Uh, yeah. My stomach is a little queasy this morning," she said, in between breaths.

"Is it something you ate?"

"No. I think I had too much to drink last night. Is there anything in here for an upset stomach?"

"I think we have some Mylanta®. Can I come in and get it for you?"

"Please."

Nyeela entered the bathroom and pulled the Mylanta® from the medicine cabinet. "Here. This should help," she said, uncapping it and pouring a dose.

"Thanks."

"Hey, I really want to apologize about last night. I didn't mean to be insulting."

Evelyn swallowed the milky antacid. "It's okay."

"I get so worked up when Mama and Melvin start to preach that old skool stuff. What worked for them all those years ago doesn't mean it's going to work for everybody."

"Baby girl, there's so much you don't understand right now."

"I swear if I hear those words one more time, I'm going to scream."

"Maybe you should try listening to Mother. You might be surprised at the results."

"I wish somebody would listen to me and give me some credit. I understand a whole lot more than everybody thinks and in case you haven't noticed, I'm not a little girl anymore."

"I see. I know you're a smart girl, Nyeela, but you still have a lot to learn about life."

"Anyways, I hope you feel better."

"What in the world is that awful smell?"

"Smells like breakfast, but Mama isn't here. She left early this morning."

"Must be your other half in the kitchen then."

"I guess," Nyeela said, heading down the stairs.

Evelyn followed.

In the kitchen, Nyasia scrambled eggs, fried bacon, and heated toast for everyone. Nyeela crept up behind her like a cat and poked her in the side. Nyasia grabbed her chest. "Girl, you scared me," she said, closing her eyes and taking a deep breath.

"Dang! You haven't cooked like this in a long time. What's the occasion?"

Nyasia smiled wide. "I'm just glad to have our family together again."

"I hate to burst your bubble, but you already know I don't eat meat or eggs," Nyeela said, with raised eyebrows. She walked over to the cabinet and grabbed an empty glass.

"Dang! I forgot. What about you, Eve?"

Evelyn shook her head. "Sorry, baby girl. I'm not a breakfast person," she said, with a finger under her nose. "Besides, I don't feel so great this morning."

"Maybe you should lie down on the couch," Nyeela said, pouring a half glass of orange juice.

"I would much rather lay in my bed," Evelyn said, turning back toward the stairwell. "No offense. But I can't take the smell of food, right now."

Nyasia folded her arms. "I cannot believe after all the effort I put into making this breakfast, no one is going to eat anything."

Ella Mae returned home and calmly strode into the kitchen. "Surpriiiise," she sang.

Nyeela put her hand over her mouth. "Oh my goodness," she muttered.

Evelyn's eyes grew as she turned back and looked over her shoulder. Standing in the doorway of the kitchen was her sixty-one-year-old mother, looking ten years younger.

Nyeela approached her slowly and touched her hair. "Mama, you cut your hair!"

"Yep!" Ella Mae said, taking off her glasses. "Go on and touch it!"

Nyasia turned off the stove and walked over to Ella Mae with an approving smile. She gently ran her fingers through her mother's new do. "You look like a brand new person."

"Yeah, Mama," Nyeela agreed. "You look so young."

"Well I don't know if I look younga, but I sho feel lighta. I dun had that hair on my neck for sixty-one years and now it's gone. What a relief!"

"Mother! How could you?" Evelyn blasted from the stairwell. "You always preached to us that a woman's hair is her glory. Because of you, I've never cut mine."

Ella Mae fanned a dismissive hand. "Child, my glory years are long gone. I needed a change. Somethin to show how I feel on the inside." She smiled.

"What does cutting off all of your hair say, Mother?"

"Sis, maybe you should take a lesson from Mama and do something with your hair," Nyeela teased.

"I don't think so. Besides, it looks a little boyish to me," Evelyn said, leaning against the oak banister.

Nyeela shot Evelyn a disapproving look. "You are totally out of pocket. How could you say something like that to Mama?"

"Child, I ain't hardly thinkin 'bout Evelyn," Ella Mae said, trying to catch Nyeela's eyes. "She can say whateva she wants. That hair is gone and it ain't comin back," she said, grabbing Nyeela's face and turning it toward her. "Pay no mind to Eve. She jus' emotional right now and it's okay."

Evelyn took a few steps down the stairs. "But, Mother ...."

"I don't wanna hear anotha word, Evelyn Renee," Ella Mae said, showing a firm hand. "I'm done talkin 'bout it and if you eva take that tone wit me again, you best pack ya bags and gone back to ya own house where you pay the cos' to be the boss."

Evelyn turned and stomped up the stairs. The twins looked at each other and shrugged their shoulders.

Ella Mae walked into the kitchen. "Mmmm, what smells so good?" she asked, examining the contents on top of the stove.

"I made breakfast especially for you this morning, Ma," Nyasia grinned.

"Aw, you always know how to make Mama smile."

"Ass kisser!" Nyeela whispered, brushing past her sister.

"Hater!"

"You still can't cook."

"Shut up, Nyeela! Maybe if you ate some meat, you might not be such a ...."

Ella Mae slammed the lid down on one of the frying pans. "Y'all knock it off! Nyeela, leave ya sista alone."

"At least, I eat healthy. If *she* keeps eating the way she does, her hips are going to start looking like saddlebags. What kind of modeling agency is she going to work for then?"

"Excuse you. But I don't have to worry about saddlebags, because I get my workout on *everyday*. So don't hate – appreciate!"

Nyeela rolled her eyes and twisted her hand. "Whatever! I'm going to get dressed. Mama, no matter what Evelyn thinks, your hair looks great!"

"Thank ya, baby."

Nyasia grabbed a piece of bacon from the stove and took a small bite. "What's her problem, Ma? I know she's going through it right now, but why is she so hateful?"

"Cut ya big sista some slack, Nyasia. She can't help it. Don't none of us really know how she feel."

Nyasia shrugged her shoulders. "I guess."

"Ain't you late for class this mornin?"

"Not quite. I'm leaving in a few minutes. I was just trying to show some love for my family this morning."

"You did good, baby. Now get outta here!"

Nyasia grabbed another piece of bacon and a slice of toast. "You got the dishes?"

"Don't I always?"

"Love you, Ma."

"Love you too." Ella Mae nibbled on a little breakfast, finished the dishes and started the laundry.

Evelyn sat in front of the dresser mirror hating the image staring back at her. Her cell phone rang. She grabbed it off the corner of the dresser and pushed the talk button, waiting to hear a voice.

"Hi."

"Rowena?"

"How are you today?"

"I don't know," she said, rubbing her temples.

"Why?"

"This isn't working."

"Eve, what's going on?"

"I can't get a handle on things. This morning, I snapped at my mother for cutting her hair. Last night, I practically bit her friend's head off for giving his opinion. And let's not mention the fact that I almost called my sister a lesbian. The one person, whom I'm infuriated with, receives a free pass from me this morning."

"Who? Grady?"

"Yes," she said, leaning forward and covering her forehead with her hand.

"So, you've spoken to him?"

"I spoke to him briefly this morning and he didn't even come close to making me feel any better."

"Well did you think that one conversation with him would?"

"I guess I did," she said, looking at herself in the mirror with disapproval. "Ro, I still have so many questions to ask and so many things to say, but every time I try, I can't seem to find the words. The killer part is I still love him. Isn't that nuts?"

"Of course not, Eve. He's your husband. You've only spent the last seven years of your life with him."

"Why do I feel so stupid?"

"Honey …."

"Is it even possible to love and hate someone at the same time?"

"Honey, you're going to go through a gamut of emotions before it's all said and done."

"Right now, I'm furious with him. I don't think I'll ever be able to trust men again."

"It's all too fresh. The pain is still raw. Give yourself some time."

"You know what really gets me?"

"What?"

"How long it took for him to admit he's gay."

"He finally admitted it?"

"Yeah, he did. I even asked if he was sure."

"Wow! What did he say?"

"He swore up and down it wasn't an act. I asked him how he knew."

"My goodness, you weren't beating around the bush, were you?"

"Hell, I needed answers and he was offering."

"Well, what did he say?"

"He told me he's always been attracted to men."

"I guess it isn't a phase after all, huh?"

"If only…"

"Listen, Eve. Grady has told you, with certainty, that he's gay. What more do you need?"

"I need to know if he cheated on me."

"Okay."

"I mean, I need to make sure he didn't sleep with other men while we were sleeping together because I swear, if I find out he did I'll … I'll kill him, Ro."

"Honey, there is no way to be absolutely sure. At this point, you can't trust anything that comes out of Grady's mouth. You need to go and get tested for HIV."

Evelyn began to heave. "I'm going to be sick."

"Calm down, Eve."

She took long, slow, breaths to calm her regurgitating instincts.

"Evelyn, are you there?"

"I'm here," she whispered.

"Honey, don't cry. I know it all feels crazy, but you can't beat yourself over the head with this shit. Promise me you will get some rest. Take in some love and support from your family. You need it right now. You can worry about the other stuff when you get home. Okay? Promise me."

Evelyn paused to gather her words. "Hell, I don't even love myself right now."

"*Evelyn…*"

"They probably hate me too because I certainly haven't made it easy. And it doesn't matter what I do, I can't seem to focus on anything other than this craziness, Ro."

"*I know it's hard.*"

"Do you know that bastard actually had the nerve to tell me he still loves me?"

"*Maybe he does.*"

"I swear it took everything in me to keep from breaking down. I wanted and needed to hear him say it, even if it was a lie."

"*Hm.*"

"Part of me thinks he was just using me to give him children. I must have been blind as hell to fall in love with a gay man. It's official. I'm a nut case."

"*Okay, Eve. Slow down.*"

"I couldn't even think of one damn thing to say that would make me feel vindicated. I even considered telling him about the abortion just to hurt him, but I couldn't do it."

"Because you are not the monster you keep making yourself out to be. He is."

"Try telling my family that."

"I don't need to. They already know it. You just promise me you'll take it easy and be gentle with yourself, Eve."

"You make it sound so easy."

"Just keep yourself busy and you'll get through this."

"I'll try."

"Give your family permission to fill up the space."

"After what I pulled this morning, I don't think they want to," she paused. "Anyway, I appreciate you and can't wait until you get here."

"Me too. I'll see you soon. Love you."

Evelyn crawled into bed half-dressed and pulled the covers over her head. Hours later, Ella Mae crawled into bed with her. Evelyn woke up to her mother lying there. She yawned deeply. "What time is it, Mother?"

"It's five o'clock."

Evelyn sat up in the bed. "Why didn't you wake me?"

"For what, child? The girls ain't here and I jus' finished cleanin."

"I didn't realize I was so tired."

"Well, ya only had a small catastrophe. A nap shudda did you justice."

"Very funny, Mother. How could you find humor in the midst of all this craziness? Especially after all the nasty things I've said to you."

"Baby, its gon' take more than a smart mouth to get my goat."

"I'm sorry for being so mean. My emotions are all over the place."

"Mama undastands," she said, turning over on her back.

"Do you think I'm a fool for falling in love with a gay man?"

"Child, you can't tell ya heart who to love. Grady is the one who should get the blame, not the otha way 'round. The bes' thang you can do for ya'self is forgive him and move on."

"But what if I can't forgive?"

"You can always forgive, Eve. The question is do you really want to? We all make mistakes. That's what make us human."

"I don't know. I really want to hate him, Mother. Especially, when I think about how much it hurts."

"Baby, hatin him ain't gon' do you no good. He fell short, I know. But you can't depend on one person to be ya ev'rythang. It ain't possible. That's why the good Lawd give us friends and family. What you can't get from one, you get from anotha."

"So what am I suppose to do with all this pain and anger?"

Ella Mae sat up in the bed. "Listen to me, child. Forgiveness is lettin go of the pain that come wit the memories. All the pain you feelin right now is gon' pass. You'll see. Jus' relax and let go. Let go and let God."

"I'm trying."

"Try not to focus so hard, baby. Okay?"

"Yes, Mother."

"And like it or not, we gon' love ya through this." Ella Mae turned to her side, snuggled closer to Evelyn and placed her head on the pillow.

A long silence ensued.

"Mother, what's for dinner? I'm starving."

Ella Mae yielded a resounding snore.

Chapter Six

The rain brushed softly against Rowena's office window as she finalized an article before the deadline. Upon completion, she called her copy editor. "Hi Geoff, the article is done."

"Already? I didn't expect it for another couple of hours."

She giggled. "I know. But I have a few errands to run before I turn in tonight, so I started early."

"Super!"

"I'll have Morgan bring it to you right away. I'll be here another half-hour or so. Feel free to call me if you need me."

"Will do."

"Thanks." Rowena hung up the phone and did as promised. After an hour or so, she locked up and headed to the hospital to see Gail. On the way, she stopped at the mall to pick up a few outfits for her trip to South Carolina and a gift for the baby. Since the birth of Gail's baby, Rowena couldn't think of anything more than caressing her tiny hands and feet. There was no doubt that seeing the baby would trigger memories of her own loss, but she couldn't deny herself the pleasure of holding that small bundle of joy in her arms.

She strode through the sliding glass doors of the hospital and approached the service desk. The attendant directed her to the fifth floor. With her visitors pass in hand, she headed to the elevator, swinging the gift bag gleefully. When she arrived at Gail's room, a physician stood next to the bed, writing on a clipboard. Rowena hung back, until Gail spotted her standing in the doorway and motioned for her to come inside.

She entered halfway and stopped. "If you're in the middle of something I can come back."

"No," the doctor answered. "Please come in. I was just signing the discharge papers for Ms. Simms and the baby to go home," he smiled.

"Hi, Rowena!" Gail waved. "This is Dr. Memphis McDowell. Dr. McDowell, this is my good friend, Rowena Patterson."

Rowena entered and extended her hand. "Nice to meet you."

Dr. McDowell shook her hand. "The pleasure is mine, Ms. Patterson. Have we met before?"

"I don't think so," she said, her voice trailing off. Her eyes led her straight over to the see-through bassinet where the baby slept.

"Hm," the doctor said, mystified. "Oh well …. Again, it's a pleasure to meet you."

"Likewise," Rowena said, disengaged.

"Ms. Simms, is there someone coming for you and the baby?"

"Yes, Doctor. Mike is working late so my dad is coming."

"Okay then. I'll see you in a few days. You ladies have a good evening," he said, gazing at Rowena. He lingered an extra moment before finally leaving the room.

Gail blushed. "Isn't that the cutest thing you've seen in a long time?" she whispered.

Enchanted by the newborn, Rowena overlooked the doctor's exit. "She certainly is," she said, in her best baby voice.

"Of course, but I was speaking about the doctor."

Rowena looked back toward the door. "Oh, I didn't notice."

"Maybe you should have," Gail said, fixing the covers on the bed.

"How are you two doing?"

Gail shrugged her shoulders. "We're going home so…pretty good, I suppose."

"Can I hold her?"

"Sure. Go ahead."

Rowena took the tightly bound infant in her arms and held her close. "Look how tiny she is," she said softly. "What a precious gift from God!"

"Yes, she is," Gail smiled.

"She's beautiful, Gail! What's her name?"

"Eva Lynn."

Rowena's visage of impression came shining through. "Lovely choice," she smiled. "Was Eve the inspiration behind it?"

"I think you already know. Besides, we love her too, Ro."

Rowena didn't respond. She continued looking at the baby.

"We had no idea about Grady. He never once mentioned being unhappy or gay."

"To be honest, I'm not surprised."

"It really changes everything. I mean, it doesn't affect my love for him, but it definitely makes things different."

"I understand," Rowena said, stroking Eva Lynn's tiny face. "Her skin is so soft."

"Rowena Patterson, I swear if I didn't know any better, I might think you were considering motherhood."

"But you *do* know me better, Gail. Right?" she grimaced, handing Gail the baby.

"I'm only kidding, Ro. I didn't mean to scare you."

"You didn't," she said, taking a seat. "How are your parents?"

"Sad and confused. They never imagined Grady would do this to Evelyn."

"When did they find out?"

"We all found out the night Eva Lynn was born."

"Really?"

"Yeah. He told us right here in this hospital room."

"Wow!"

"Exactly."

"Well, Eve is in South Carolina with her family."

"Oh?"

"Yes. And she's getting all the love and support she is going to need, right now. In fact, I'm flying there to be with them for Thanksgiving."

Gail leaned over and placed Eva Lynn back inside the bassinet. "I owe her an apology. I'm going to call once we get settled in."

"I'm sure she would like that. Oh! I almost forgot." Rowena handed Gail the gift bag. "I brought you and the baby a gift."

"How sweet of you, Rowena! You didn't have to."

"I wanted to."

"Thanks!"

"I have to get going. Are you sure you don't need a ride?"

"Yes, I'm sure. Dad should be here any minute."

"Tell your parents I said hello and enjoy your holiday."

"I will."

Rowena planted a kiss on Gail's forehead and walked out into the hall. Dr. McDowell appeared to be waiting for someone as he stood near the nurse's station. Rowena wasn't sure if he was waiting for her but she had no intention of hanging around. She approached the elevators and mashed the down button until it lit up.

"Leaving so soon, Ms. Patterson?" he asked, approaching her.

"Yes, Dr....."

"McDowell," he finished. "You can call me Memphis."

"Only if you stop calling me Ms. Patterson. It's Rowena."

"Do you think there's a chance I'll be seeing you again, Rowena?"

"If so, I hope it's in a different setting," she smiled.

"That makes two of us," he grinned. "You have a good night, Rowena."

The elevator doors opened and Rowena entered. "Thanks! You too, Memphis," she said, without looking back. The doors closed behind her. "It would be such a waste if that fine ass man turned out to be gay," she said, pushing the lower lobby button.

*****

A day away from boarding the plane to South Carolina, Rowena couldn't shake her exhaustion. However, there was no time to rest. She had to prepare for her trip. After working a half-day, she cleared her desk, and called Morgan into the office. "Morgan, you've done such a fantastic job these past few weeks, I want to show my appreciation." Rowena handed Morgan a bottle of champagne, a silver cake-box with big red letters, and one gift certificate for a free limo ride, with Neal's Transportation Services.

Morgan's eyes lit up. "You're too generous, Ms. Patterson. Thank you so much!"

"My pleasure."

"Here's your plane ticket to South Carolina."

"Thank you!"

"Will there be anything else?"

"No. You have a wonderful four-day weekend and I'll see you on Monday."

Morgan smiled. "Enjoy your trip!"

*****

Rowena arrived home, threw her keys on the table, and checked for messages.

Beep! "Hey, Ro! I would've called the office but I didn't want to bother you at work. Girl, I can't wait to see you tomorrow. The weather here isn't bad for this time of year, as long as you don't forget to pack a few sweaters. Everyone is excited you are coming. I will meet you at the airport. Have a safe trip. Love you." *Beep!*

Beep! "Ms. Patterson, this is Morgan. Thank you, again for everything. Working with you is a pure delight. Have a safe trip. See you when you get back. God Bless." *Beep!*

Beep! "Rowena, it's Gail. I just wanted to wish you a safe trip and a happy Thanksgiving. We would really appreciate it if you would give Eve a hug and tell her we love her. By the way, Dr. McDowell asked about you during our follow-up visit. This may sound a little presumptuous, but I think he likes you, girl. *(Giggling)* Anyway, you have to call me when you get back, so I can give you the details. Talk to you later." *Beep!*

Rowena wasn't sure how to feel about the doctor's inquiries. With work and helping her best friend get her sanity back, her life was full. In fact, if Evelyn hadn't requested her presence, she'd work right through Thanksgiving into Christmas. She managed to convince herself that a few days off wouldn't hurt. Besides, she hadn't enjoyed a home-cooked meal in years and no one knew how to cook better than Ms. Ella did.

Being a frequent traveler meant having to stay organized, since packing came at a moment's notice. Certain items, like her toiletries, iPod, aspirin, and a copy of the magazine Evelyn wrote for, remained packed. Usually, Rowena packed conservatively for business but this was a different occasion. Other than the two outfits she purchased at the mall, she had no idea what to take.

She popped the sultry sounds of Jill Scott into the CD player and sorted through some clean laundry. Ten o'clock rolled around and she had not eaten all day. The rain had turned to sleet and her options were limited. McDonalds was the only place close, so it would have to suffice. She grabbed a jacket, the keys off the table and headed to Mickey Ds.

She returned with a strawberry milkshake and a large order of French fries. She sat the milkshake on the nightstand, plopped down on the edge of the bed, kicked off her shoes, and wiggled her tired feet on the soft carpet. She rumbled through the white paper bag, until she could feel the thin, hot, fries on her fingertips. She placed three of them between her teeth and savored the saltiness of the crispy potatoes as they dissolved in her mouth.

After finishing off the fries, Rowena slipped on her pajamas, switched off the lights, and turned on the TV. Falling asleep to the sound of the television was a nightly ritual and sleeping alone was starting to feel unadventurous. While flipping through channels, she wrestled with the thought of getting a pet. Lots of single women had them, she thought. And they appeared to help ward off all the disapproving stares. Something about the sophistication of a feline seemed appealing, but her schedule just wouldn't allow it.

Rowena pulled back the covers, reached for her milkshake and nestled in the center of the bed. She pulled on the straw until the sweet, cold, ice crystals danced on her tongue. "Mmmm," she moaned.

Chapter Seven

The freshly fallen snow glistened in the sunlight and 'Mr. Coffee' spit hot java into the glass carafe. On the day of her departure, Rowena woke up excited to spend the holiday in South Carolina. She peeped out of the bedroom window to survey the stillness of the neighborhood. It brought to mind, Saturday morning cereal and cartoons as a kid.

Smiling inside, she threw on her robe and followed the scent of vanilla coffee beans to the kitchen. The aroma helped to awaken her senses. She grabbed her favorite mug, filled it to the rim, and helped herself to a chocolate donut from the fridge. After enjoying a second cup, she poured the remainder of the brew into the sink. Then headed to the bathroom to shower and dress.

With a minimal amount of time to get to the airport, she called a cab and brought her things to the front door. While waiting for the taxi to arrive, she decided to call Evelyn and confirm her pickup from the airport. The call went straight to voicemail. "Eve, I hope you get this message before my flight arrives at 3 p.m. I'm on my way to the airport now and I will be looking for you when I get off the plane. I'm wearing a pink sweater and brown slacks. See you soon, sweetie. Bye."

Outside, the cab honked for her as she secured everything in the apartment. While in route to the airport, Rowena couldn't help but wonder, if her decision to skip work and hang out with Evelyn would come back to haunt her later.

*****

Mid-flight, Rowena took time to reflect. She recalled the days when she couldn't dream of anything more than poetry. The poem she found in the closet was the last one she had ever written. Two days before she penned the poem, she and her mother paid a visit to the abortion clinic. Days later, her father fell ill. A few months after, he made his transition and her mother struggled to find and keep work. Poetry gave Rowena an outlet. Unfortunately, her mother never thought much of her gift, since it couldn't put food on their table. The lack of support impeded her creativity and forced her to switch the focus to education.

"Attention passengers, we'll be arriving at the Charleston International Airport in approximately ten minutes," a soft female voice announced. Rowena gathered her things. "Thank God," she whispered, anxious to stretch her legs. She moved through the crowd and strode onto the monorail with ease. Just then, she realized she had not spoken to Evelyn. She powered up her iPhone and called again.

"Hello?"

"Eve, it's Rowena. Did you get my message?"

"I sure did. I'm outside waiting."

"Okay. I'm going to grab my luggage now. I'll be out in a few minutes."

"Okay."

Rowena approached the luggage carousel and waited. Most of the bags that spun around had little or no life left in them. The scratches and scuffmarks told of their travels. When her luggage came around, they revealed she had taken good care of them over the years. She glanced at her watch, grabbed the brown, paisley print bags, and quickly headed outside to find Evelyn. Car horns honked all around and Rowena wasn't sure which way to look. She scanned the lines of cars parked at the curbside and spotted Evelyn, several cars down, waving. "There you are," she whispered, rolling her luggage toward the SUV. Evelyn approached and they embraced for several minutes.

Rowena broke away with a smile. "I'm so happy to see you!"

"Me too! Get in," Evelyn ordered.

Rowena threw the luggage in the back seat, and climbed inside the vehicle. "Girl, what is going on with your hair?" she asked.

"I didn't feel like combing it."

Rowena laughed. "Come on, Eve. You might feel like shit, but do you have to look like it?"

Evelyn held a steady face as she stared straight ahead.

"I'm sorry. Tell me. What's going on? How are things?"

"Not so good, Ro," she said, flicking on the right blinker.

"That bad, huh?"

"Worse. My mother has told her friends all of my business and my sisters are treating me like some kind of stranger. I swear. It feels like I don't belong in this family anymore. To make matters worse, I'm sick all the time."

"Sick? What's wrong?"

"Brace yourself. This morning I went to the pharmacy and bought a pregnancy test."

"For what?"

"For one, I haven't had my period and two, my breasts are killing me. Remember, I've been through this before."

Rowena dropped her head and pretended to adjust her seatbelt as she recalled her own pregnancy. She resisted the urge to submit to the sadness associated with the thought. She shifted her body in the seat to face Evelyn. "That's right. You have."

"You'll never believe the results."

"I won't?"

"Hell, *I* certainly didn't."

"You're pregnant?" Rowena asked, trying to suppress her envy.

"Yes. I'm pregnant, Ro."

"Is that why your skin is glowing?"

"Excuse me, but I'm facing a crisis. Who cares about my skin?"

"I'm sorry, but..." Rowena paused, to allow her excitement to surface. "I never would've expected this!"

"Ro, what the hell am I going to do now?"

"Good question. What *are* you going to do?"

"I have no freaking idea and I give people advice for a living. How's that for ironic?"

"Hell, that's nothing. There are psychics everywhere who can see into other people's lives, but not their own. Trust me, you are not an original."

"Well, you're the only one who knows."

"Whoa!"

"I don't mean to hit you over the head with my shit, but girl, I'm flipping out!"

"Calm down. There is no reason you have to decide what to do right this moment, sweetie. Give yourself some time to process this."

"I'm scared to death!"

"And it's okay. Listen. You're going to be fine. Whatever you decide, I'm sure it'll work out."

"From your lips."

"Trust me. It's going to be fine."

"Having a baby is the last thing on my mind right now."

"How are you handling the sickness?"

"By staying the hell away from the kitchen. Every little smell makes me want to throw up. I've been sleeping a lot, too."

Rowena smiled again. "Good. It's not like you can't use the rest."

"I'm not even sure if rest is what I'm getting. More like agitated and annoyed at every damned thing," she sighed. "You look a little jetlagged. How was your flight?"

"Not bad. It gave me some time to think. Haven't had the pleasures of being able to do that for a while now. I've been ripping and running so much, it's beginning to take a toll on me. Truth is I'm exhausted."

"You should take a nap when we get to the house."

"Not to change the subject or anything, but I stopped by the hospital to see Gail and the baby."

"How is that not changing the subject, Ro?"

"Well ... it just came to my mind. Sorry."

"How is she?"

"She's good. She picked a name for the baby. You'll never guess what she chose."

"I'm guessing you're going to tell me, right?"

"She named the baby Eva Lynn and my heart just melted when I saw her. I couldn't take my eyes away from her precious little face the entire visit. Gail asked me to give you her love. Evelyn?"

Evelyn surfaced from a hollow daze. "Huh?"

"Are you okay? Have you heard a word I said?"

"I'm sorry, girl. As soon as you said precious little face, I started thinking about Grady. I have so much on my mind right now. I'm so glad you're here."

Rowena reached over and placed her hand on Evelyn's shoulder. "Me too."

"Are you hungry?"

"Hungry? Girl, I could eat a cow!"

"Good. Mother is cooking up a feast. The smells made me feel so nauseous that I had to leave."

"You poor thing."

Evelyn sighed. "Since I'm with child, I'm staying until the New Year."

"You should stay as long as you need to."

"I'm not staying indefinitely or anything. I do have a house and a job to attend. Besides, I think six weeks is long enough. Eventually, I'm going to have to see a doctor."

"Does this mean you're going to keep it?"

"Rowena, I don't know. Right now, I just want to focus on not throwing up."

"Okay. I won't push it."

Evelyn honked her horn as they pulled up in front of Ella Mae's house. Melvin came out to help with Rowena's luggage.

"It's only two bags," Rowena smiled.

"I got it," he smiled. "I'm Melvin."

"Nice to meet you, Melvin. I'm Rowena."

"The pleasure is mine. Come on in. Ella Mae is in the kitchen."

"Yes, Rowena. Go in and make yourself comfortable. I'll be in shortly."

"You sure, Eve?"

Evelyn looked at Rowena and forced a smile. "Absolutely! Go feed your face. I just need some fresh air. I promise I'll be in a few minutes."

"Okay. See you inside."

Rowena followed Melvin into the house. In the living room, she took a moment to marvel at all the framed photos of Ella Mae and the girls.

Ella Mae emerged from the kitchen. "Well now, look who we have here," she said, embracing Rowena. "How are ya?"

Rowena embraced her as well. "Great, now. I'm with family."

"Ya look a lil tired. Let me take ya purse. I fixed the guest room up for ya. You can go up wheneva ya get ready. I was jus' finishin up in the kitchen. You hungry?"

"Yes, but please don't go through any trouble for me."

"Child, hush! I'm gon' fix you a plate. You ain't on no special kinda diet are ya?" she asked, walking into the kitchen.

"No, Ma'am!"

"Good."

"I carried ya bags upstairs," Melvin said, returning to the living room.

"Thank you," Rowena said, following Ella Mae into the kitchen.

"Go on and sit down while I fix ya plate."

"Thank you! Ms. Ella, your house is so lovely!"

"Thank ya, child. Evelyn thinks this ole house need a makeova but I don't know. Maybe, I should call one of them television shows where they give em to ya for free," she laughed. "If only I could get them lazy girls of mine to pick up a broom," she said, without looking at Rowena.

"Speaking of the girls, where are they?" Rowena asked, scanning the room.

"I ain't sure, child. I can't keep up. One minute, they here and the next they gone."

"The last time I saw them, they were starting high school. I hear they're all grown up now."

"I wouldn't call 'em grown jus' yet, even though they'd be quick to disagree. I keep tellin 'em grown *is* as grown *does*," she said, loading up a plate for Rowena.

"I agree, Ms. Ella. Is Melvin your new friend?"

Ella Mae sat a plate of meatloaf, smothered potatoes, green beans, and two fluffy biscuits in front of her. "Yeah, child. He my *good* friend," she said, playfully nudging Rowena on the arm.

"Okay," Rowena said, laughing. "Well, congratulations to you and your *good* friend!"

"Where's Eve?"

"Oh, she said she'd be right in; something about the air. Wow, this food sure looks good!"

"Well, I guess you gon' eat it all then," she smiled.

"Oh, don't you worry."

"Jus' rememba, you family so help ya'self to whateva you want. We happy to have ya."

"I appreciate that, Ms. Ella. I'm honored to be here."

Ella Mae left Rowena to enjoy her meal. She joined Melvin in the family room, while Evelyn remained outside. Rowena grew concerned as she finished her last bite. She cleared the table and went to check on her.

Out on the front porch, Evelyn sat in a swinger, admiring the sunset. "Beautiful, isn't it?" she asked, without breaking her stare.

"It sure is," Rowena said, taking a seat next to her. "I wish we had a view like this back home."

"Yeah, it's the *one* thing I do miss about being here."

"Oh, you could probably think of a few more things you miss about this place."

"Ro, when did life become so complicated?"

"Good question, Eve. I'm afraid I don't have the answer."

"I remember long walks with my dad as a little girl. I thought I would never love a man, as much as I loved him."

"Hm. I don't think I ever have," Rowena admitted.

"Is it fair to measure a man's love with the love of your father?"

Rowena shrugged her shoulders. "What else do we have to measure it against?"

"I'm sure there's a man, somewhere out there, who disagrees," Evelyn smirked.

Rowena laughed. "You're probably right."

"Did you get something to eat?"

"Girl, yes. Your mother is such a great cook!"

Evelyn sighed. "She is. Unfortunately, I haven't been able to enjoy her cooking the way I'd like."

"Oh, no worries. I'll enjoy it for you. I wonder if her *good* friend Melvin has anything to do with how happy she looks."

"I'm sure we have no idea. In fact, I'm willing to bet he's the reason she cut her hair."

"Melvin, or no Melvin, there are some beautiful genes running through your bloodline."

"You come from a pretty decent gene pool yourself, Rowena."

"Apparently, not today. Your mother told me I look tired. She even asked if I wanted to lie down."

"You are looking a little run-down."

"Gee thanks, Eve. This is the third time I've heard that and I've only been here two hours."

"Oh come on, you know what I mean. I think you work yourself too hard, sometimes."

"That's usually what one does if one wants to pay the bills."

"Yes, and sometimes you have to take a break. You know, take some time for yourself."

"Good advice, counselor. I'll consider it whenever I get some time."

"You can be such a smart-ass."

"Only on Wednesdays."

Evelyn pursed her lips and rolled her eyes. "And every other Saturday."

"So, how come you never mentioned Melvin? He seems like a nice guy."

"I just met him myself and while I can't say much for how I've treated him, he *is* a nice guy."

"Is he the friend who knows all your business?"

"The only one that I know of."

Rowena laughed. "I don't think you have anything to worry about. He doesn't look like the gossiping kind."

"Let's hope not."

"Eve, can I be honest?"

"Please."

"I envy you right now."

"Why?"

"Doctors told me a long time ago I couldn't have any kids."

"What? How come you never said anything?"

"I got pregnant at sixteen. Mom was uncompromising when it came to feeding another mouth, so she borrowed money for my abortion. Subsequently, there were complications and now I can't have any children. I tried to pretend it didn't bother me but...."

"Girl, that's awful! And here I am bothering you with my drama."

"Eve, I'm a big girl. I can handle it. When I held Eva Lynn, the memories came flooding back like a tidal wave. Even though the abortion wasn't my choice, sometimes I feel guilty for not speaking up. There was no doubt I hated my mother back then and yet today, I still struggle not to blame her for what she thought was best."

"It had to be rough for both of you. Were you in love with the baby's father?"

"Yes. At least *I* thought we were in love. Apparently, being pregnant didn't factor into his idea of romance."

Evelyn shook her head. "As kids we think we have it all figured out."

"I know, right?"

"Seriously Ro, if I had known I would not have gone on about my problems."

"There you go beating yourself up again."

"Here I am, thinking only of what I want when people like you are out here hoping and wishing for the chance to become a mother."

"No, Eve. You have to make choices based upon what's best for you. Besides, I didn't say anything about hoping and wishing. I mean, don't get me wrong. Some day I may want to, but right now I'm absolutely positive it's not what I want or need."

"Whenever you decide, I'm sure there will be plenty of options out there for you."

"All but the natural one. What am I going to say if I meet someone and he wants children? And don't say adoption. It may work for some people, but I get the feeling all men aren't entirely satisfied with the idea."

"Yeah, I know what you mean."

"Your situation is different, Eve. All you have to do is make a choice."

"Easier said than done, Ro. I mean, with all the resentment and confusion I feel, it certainly wouldn't be fair to a child. And like I said before, I don't want to raise a baby on my own right now."

"The anger and confusion will pass, Eve. The question is why are you so convinced Grady wouldn't help take care of this baby?"

"Honestly, I don't know what he would do. Part of me knows there is nothing he wouldn't do for a child of his own. However, the other part doesn't trust him at all. This was definitely not in the cards, especially given our circumstance. It just doesn't seem ideal for a child."

"Life isn't always ideal and you have got to come to grips with that, Eve. You still love him, right?"

"What the hell does love have to do with it? What he and I shared is null and void."

"This baby deserves a chance. Life is full of mistakes, but the baby does not have to be one of them. Your pregnancy is a result of the love you and Grady once shared, nothing less."

"I don't know, Rowena. I'm still struggling with the fact that he may have only been using me to bear his children."

"If that were the case, he didn't succeed. Now, you can make a fully informed decision based on something meaningful."

"Didn't you say, ten seconds ago, that I have to decide what's best for me? Besides, I'm still very hurt and angry inside. What I really need most is time–time to sort it all out. I haven't told anyone and I'd like to keep it that way for a while."

"Okay, Eve. Your secret is safe with me. But how long do you think you will be able to keep it from your mother? She is bound to figure it out."

"Hell, she's not psychic, Rowena!"

"So you say."

"You just make sure you don't tell her. If she finds out, the whole damn world is going to know."

"Can you blame her? This will be her first grandbaby."

"Promise me, Rowena."

"I promise. Okay?"

"Fine. Let's talk about something else."

"Okay," Rowena paused. "On the plane, I thought about how much I loved to write poetry as a kid."

"Really? I never knew."

"I know. I never talked about it. The other day, I ran across a poem I wrote and it made me think about writing again. Aside from the abortion, giving up my poetry is the only thing I've ever regretted."

"Then you should write, Rowena."

"What are you passionate about?"

"The only thing I've ever been passionate about is my marriage and my job."

"Wow, are we that predictable?"

"Maybe."

"It's time to change some things."

"And how do you figure we do that, Ro?"

"By taking the time to discover what it is we like."

"Girl, I'm too old and too damn angry to find a hobby."

"I'm not talking about a hobby, Evelyn. I'm talking about something that speaks to your soul, something other than being a wife or writing advice to others. You ever feel like you're minding the gap?"

Evelyn shrugged her shoulders. "I don't know."

"I have and I don't want to anymore."

"Go ahead and do the poetry thing. Who knows, maybe you'll write an award-winning song and dedicate it to the both of us."

"Yeah, I could do that."

"I need to figure out what I'm going to do about this baby, my husband, and my future before I consider any kind of passion."

"I wish you would stop!"

"Girl, I've invested seven years of my life into my marriage and here I am damn near forty years old, starting all over again. It's pathetic."

"It's not pathetic, Eve. You are *not* the only woman in the world to start her life over at thirty-six and you certainly won't be the last. I know it isn't easy, but think of it as a chance to rediscover you. Do you know how blessed you are, to be able to start fresh and do things you never got a chance to do?"

"I hate to burst your bubble, but starting over doesn't even sound remotely fun."

"That's because you've got misery in a vice."

"Don't you mean misery has me in a vice?"

"No. I mean you have misery in a vice. You are clutching your pain so tight, I'm beginning to think you can't breathe without it. If you want to move beyond this, you have to start somewhere."

"Maybe you should write my column."

"Oh, you've got jokes."

"Once, I had a reader write me asking for advice about her teenaged daughter. She stated that when her daughter turned thirteen, it was almost impossible for them to co-exist. Everything she said or did was never right or good enough. Her daughter was extremely moody, distant and irrational. She expressed that if something didn't happen soon, she feared the relationship would end up beyond repair."

"I think I remember that story."

"After recommending a visit to their primary care physician and some family counseling, I expressed the importance of patience. Patience for her daughter and herself. There had to be forgiveness on a continual basis. And the understanding that her daughter was experiencing an added measure of insecurity. I also suggested she treat the daughter like a person rather than a child. Give her plenty of love and reassurance. As time passed, her confidence would grow and so would the relationship."

"She wrote you a few years later, thanking you for the advice, right?"

"Yeah, she did."

"I remember."

"Right now, I feel like that teenage girl. I may look normal on the outside, but inside I'm insecure, confused, and scared."

"Eve, the same little girl lives in me, as well. The difference is, she is not who we really are. She is only a reflection of how we feel."

"I have no idea who I really am."

"Maybe it's time you find out. But for starters, know that you are a spiritual being, made in the image and likeness of God, wonderful, whole and complete."

Evelyn smiled. "I like the sound of that."

"It's true. I think we both should get back in church."

"Did Mother send you out here to say that?"

"Girl, no. I'm serious."

"Speaking of Mother, we better go inside before she comes out here with a flashlight looking for us."

"You certainly know your mother, don't you? She asked about you a little while ago."

"I'm not surprised. The twins should be home shortly."

"Great! I can't wait to see them. How can you tell them apart?"

"Don't worry. You'll figure it out," Evelyn smiled.

Chapter Eight

The evening air turned chilly and the twins returned home. Ella Mae, Melvin, Rowena, and Evelyn were in the family room when they arrived.

Nyasia threw her coat across the back of the couch. "Ooooh Ma, it smells good in here," she announced, rubbing her hands together briskly. "I can't wait to taste that pecan pie. Rowena, is that you?"

"It's me," Rowena said, greeting both girls with a hug. "I don't know who's who. Both of you look exactly alike," she teased.

"One of us is prettier," Nyasia joked.

"One of us is smarter," Nyeela said, with a serious face.

"And both of you are funny!" Rowena added. "But it won't take me long to figure it out."

Nyeela poked Rowena in the side. "It's good to see you, Rowena. You're still cracking corny jokes, after all these years."

"Corny? They weren't that corny when you were younger."

Nyeela smiled. "Of course not. Those jokes came with money. I may have been young, but I wasn't a fool."

Rowena playfully grabbed Nyeela around the neck. "Ms. Ella, what are you going to do with this one?"

Ella Mae folded her arms. "Hm! I got a few ideas."

"Rowena, you haven't aged a bit. How are things?" Nyeela asked.

"Everything is everything, sweetie. I'm trying to keep up with your big sister here."

"No wonder you look so tired."

Rowena forced a smile. "Easy on the compliments, Nyasia."

"I'm just kidding, Ro." Nyasia glanced over at Evelyn. "I wish I could say the same for you, big sis. What's wrong with your hair?"

Evelyn didn't respond.

Ella Mae intervened. "Nyasia, Rowena dun told you she ain't tired, so just let her be. Where y'all been all day?" she asked, putting on her glasses.

"I would like to know *that* myself," Evelyn added, crossing her arms.

"Mama, I told you I had a few errands to run. Remember?" Nyeela asked.

Ella Mae didn't comment.

"Um... yeah," Nyasia said, sheepishly. "I was with Twin."

"How is school?" Rowena inquired.

Nyeela smiled. "Pretty good. Trying to keep my head above water."

Rowena nodded. "Okay."

"I get a little overwhelmed at times with school, work and socializing. But that's nothing new."

"You and Eve jus' like ya daddy," Ella Mae said, shaking her head. "God res' his soul. Poor man worked himself to death. I jus' don't believe you got that gene, Nyasia."

"That's not fair, Ma. I work too!" Nyasia whined.

"Not in this house! If anybody seen ya bedroom, they'd swear you was hidin a dead body in there."

"Ma, you just don't understand. By the time I get home, I'm exhausted. The only thing I want do is crawl into bed, before starting all over again."

"Welcome to my world, child. Y'all act like I'm the maid 'round here. What y'all gon' do when I ain't here no more?"

"We appreciate you, Ma. And if we didn't have you, Eve would have us."

Evelyn folded her arms. "Oh, no, I wouldn't!"

"Come on, sis. You mean to tell me we can't count on you?"

"Nyeela, you all are *not* babies anymore. You're both growing young women with your own lives, decisions and choices to make. Mother isn't going to be around forever and you need to learn how to fend for yourselves. Of course, you're always welcome to my house, but not as roommates."

"Listen to ya big sista," Ella Mae warned. "She is tellin y'all the truth."

"It's rough out there," Melvin added. "And y'all gotta be prepared. Jus' keep doin what ya doin and movin in the right direction."

"Dang! I don't feel any love in this room right now."

"Don't be such a whiner, Nyeela. It's all love."

"Whatever, Eve! Rowena, are you getting married soon?"

"Honey, no. I don't have time for a husband. My life is too hectic."

"In what way?" Evelyn smirked.

Rowena cleared her throat and forced a fake smile. "Evelyn, your cynicism is showing."

"Seriously, how is your life hectic?"

"You already know how unpredictable my work hours are and besides, I travel a lot."

Evelyn crossed her legs. "Because you don't have a man."

"Maybe, I prefer it that way, missy," Rowena said, blinking hard.

"Yeah, right. I think I just saw a tumbleweed roll by."

"So you're a comedian now, Evelyn?"

"Take it from me, child," Ella Mae added. "If you ain't careful, ya lil dry spell gon' turn into a drought. It ain't too late for you to change thangs. All work and no play make for a lonely life."

"With all due respect, Ms. Ella," Rowena prefaced. "Being alone doesn't exactly equal loneliness." She had made that statement countless times with confidence, but as soon as she uttered them to Ms. Ella, she didn't believe a word of it.

"Baby, you can color it anyway you wanna," Ella Mae said gently. "I been there and I know what it's like. Y'all worried 'bout the wrong thang. Havin a career ain't the answer to ev'rythang. Success ain't nothin, if you can't share it wit somebody."

"Mama, I keep telling you everybody doesn't want or need a man to share their successes with," Nyeela reiterated. "I think a man or woman should complement you, not complete you."

"I never said I *didn't* want a man, Nyeela. I just don't have the time right now."

"Darlin, you betta make time. It don't make no sense to live for a job, witout takin time to consida love and marriage. Trus' me. Life ain't much witout 'em. And Nyeela, what you know 'bout it? You dun spent mos' of ya life bein a tomboy."

Nyeela sucked her teeth. "Daddy never had a problem with it."

"Ya daddy was so desp'rate for a boy, I think he marked you wit them boyish ways. I'm *so* glad you grew out of it, cuz Lawd knows you wasn't gon' get no man actin like one."

Nyeela rolled her eyes. "Can we get off my case now?"

Rowena raised her hand. "Okay, I've got a confession, Ms. Ella. I've had my share of challenges with men. I'm either too much or not enough, so right now, one is the magic number for me."

"Baby, one is the lonelies' numba you gon' eva do."

Nyasia nodded. "I agree. Everybody needs somebody."

Evelyn raised a brow. "I suppose you have someone, Nyasia?"

"As a matter of fact, Eve, there *is* someone. Tomorrow, you'll get a chance to see who."

Ella Mae clasped her hands around her knee. "Good, cuz I ain't seen you wit nobody since prom. How 'bout you, Nyeela?"

Everyone's eyes slid around the room to Nyeela.

Nyeela squirmed in her seat. "What?" she asked. "Why do I have to bring my friends over for everyone's approval?"

"Well, it ain't 'bout that. But if you got somebody special, we wanna meet him. Unless you shamed of ya family."

"Mama, relax! I'm not ashamed. I just resent everybody insisting that my life has to be an open book."

"You got somethin to hide?"

Nyeela's cell phone rang. She left the room to take the call.

"Mother, you need to ease up on this relationship thing," Evelyn said, forging a frown. "I swear it's like you've become the poster girl for coupling. All of sudden, you think a woman isn't complete, unless she has a man by her side."

"I know you ain't talkin, Miss 'I gotta find Mr. Right!'"

Evelyn rolled her eyes. "Hm! Well, at least I got it honest."

Ella Mae shook her head. "I jus' don't see nothin cute 'bout you young girls bein by ya'self."

"I don't know why, since you *just* found companionship two seconds ago."

"Don't you start fussin wit me, Evelyn Simms!"

"It's Banks, Mother."

"What?"

"It's not Simms anymore, it's Banks."

"Child, please! You a Simms till them papers is signed."

"Papers or no papers, I'm still a Banks, Mother."

"Rowena, ya see how they go back and forth wit me?"

"Yes, Ms. Ella," Rowena said, her voice trailing off into a whisper. "I see where Evelyn gets it from."

Melvin cleared his throat. "What time is dinna t'morra?"

Ella Mae looked over her glasses. "Five o'clock."

"Y'all know Uncle Charles and cousin Stacey gon' be here from Nashville to eat wit us."

Ella Mae nodded and smiled. "I'm lookin forward to it."

"Nice, Melvin," Rowena said. "How old is your uncle?"

"Eighty-three and his son, Stacey, forty-two."

Rowena smiled. "It must be nice to have your youngest taking care of you at such an old age."

Nyasia walked over and sat on the arm of the sofa, next to Ella Mae. "You don't have to worry, Ma," she said, rubbing her back. "When you get that age I'll be right here to take care of you."

"That might be easy for you to say now, Nyasia," Evelyn added. "But what if you get married and your husband has other ideas? Stacey has to be good and single to take on such responsibility huh, Melvin?"

"As a matta of fact, Eve, he is. Takin care of Uncle Charles is a full-time job. He a business owna and he got good people workin for him."

"See, Nyasia, taking care of someone can require a lot of time and attention. I'm not saying you can't or won't do it, but it can be a handful," Evelyn affirmed, with raised eyebrows.

Nyasia looked intently at Evelyn. "Thanks for the advice, but this is the only mother I have. When I say she can count on *me*, I mean every single word."

"Damn! I guess I've been told," Evelyn said, scanning the room for a witness.

Rowena leaned forward and looked over everyone at Melvin. "Melvin, what kind of business does Stacey have?"

"He own a towin company and he doin pretty well for himself. Though I 'magine he do get a lil lonely sometimes."

"But if he's as busy as you say, he doesn't have much time for women anyway, which is exactly where I am." Rowena said, still trying to validate herself.

"I had a man to share my success with for seven years and where did it get me?"

Rowena sighed. "Oh, Eve."

"No," she said, holding up her hand. "I've had enough with all this talk about sharing your success with a man or woman. Trust me. At the end of the day, you can't force a person to stay or remain in love with you. Especially, if they suddenly discover that their gay."

Nyeela returned. "Someone sounds a little bitter."

Evelyn flipped her hand. "Whatever!"

Ella Mae took off her glasses. "Ev'rybody entitled to they own opinion, Eve. We got three generations in here. I'm sho we can agree to disagree. Me and Melvin a lil old skool when it come to romance, but we ain't gon' 'pologize for it."

"You should!" The twins verbalized simultaneously.

"Hey, ain't nothin wrong wit old skool," Melvin defended. "It still works."

Nyeela took a seat on the ottoman next to Rowena. "Melvin, the problem with old skool is its concepts and beliefs are somewhat outdated."

"Only cuz society always lookin for the next big thang, Nyeela. Y'all get bored too easy. Ya don't stick wit thangs the way *we* used to. Growin up, we used our 'magination and listened when our parents spoke. Wasn't no arguin and carryin on. Thangs was much simpler back then."

"But simpler isn't necessarily better, Melvin."

"I don't know. I 'preciate simple, Nyeela. Today, ev'rythang all complicated. Respec' and education is out; technology and ennatainment is in. How can ya blame these kids when society is the one raisin em?"

"Now, this is where we disagree," Nyeela said, positioning herself upright. "What you said poses a problem for me. When you all were growing up, you did what you were told, followed the rules, and never questioned whether they were right or wrong, which is why segregation and racism lasted as long as it did. Our people had no voice because of their belief system. Who says it's better? I can't speak for the children, but my generation has been taught to dig deep, find our voice, and don't take everything at face value. You know, use our minds, think for ourselves, and *not* rely on society or tradition to dictate what's acceptable and unacceptable."

"Both of you have very valid points, but who's right?" Rowena asked.

"I don't think it's a matter of who's right or wrong, Ro," Nyeela answered. "We each represent the world in its various stages of evolution. Change is inevitable and if we continue to allow ourselves to be stuck in tradition, then we miss important opportunities that only present themselves through change. Change we must and I must say I like the way we've changed."

"Give me a break, Nyeela," Evelyn said, waving her hand. "This whole new skool theory is nothing more than an excuse to do whatever you want, whenever you want."

"It may be for some, but not for me. Being able to think for myself means I get to make my own choices, Eve."

"It also means you must take responsibility for those same choices."

"Yes, Eve. I know. For *some* people, it's the very reason why new skool is a turn-off. It means you don't get to blame the other guy, when your choices don't turn out the way you expect them."

"What are you trying to say?"

"People who are stuck in traditional belief systems, like to blame the devil for everything and frankly, I don't believe *everything* is the devil's fault. For example, I don't believe it's the devil's fault when a man is attracted to another man."

Ella Mae shifted in her seat as the tension between Evelyn and Nyeela grew.

Rowena intervened. "Nyeela, I think now is a good time for you to show me where my room is. It'll only take a second."

"Good idea," Ella Mae said, putting on her glasses and scooting to the edge of the sofa cushion. "Fresh towels and blankets in the linen closet."

"Mother, have you been sharing our discussions?"

Ella Mae stood up. "Evelyn, you seem a lil cranky tonight. Ya want some hot tea?"

"I'm fine and I'd be even better if you would stop telling my business to the whole world."

Ella Mae continued toward the kitchen without commenting.

"And yes, I'll have a little tea with lemon. Please, don't put honey in it. I'm allergic."

Ella Mae turned back and looked over her glasses. "Since when?"

Evelyn didn't answer.

Nyasia snapped her finger and said, "Let's listen to some music. I feel an old skool vibe coming on. How about some Earth, Wind & Fire?"

Melvin smiled, "What you know 'bout Earth, Wind & Fire, youngsta?"

Evelyn slouched back into the sofa. "Good question, Melvin."

Nyasia inserted the CD. "Oh, I know a little something."

"Shining Star" played until everyone reconvened in the family room.

"Is that the group Earth, Wind & Fire?" Rowena asked, grooving to the music.

Nyasia nodded her head and grabbed Ella Mae by the arm. "Dance with me, Ma."

"Child, I don't hardly feel like it."

"Come on, Ma," she said, pulling Ella Mae to her feet.

Nyeela walked over and extended her hand to Evelyn. "Let's show these old folk how it's done, sis."

Evelyn paused for a brief second before reluctantly taking Nyeela's hand.

Melvin got up to join in.

The night ended on a good note. Melvin left and the ladies retired to their bedrooms. Rowena left the door ajar as she undressed into her nightclothes. Nyeela quietly approached to say goodnight. She paused to watch Rowena undress. After taking in more than an eye full, she knocked.

"One second," Rowena said, slipping on her top. She turned and pulled the door open. "Hey, Twin, I'm just getting ready for bed. What's up?"

"Not much," Nyeela said, taking a seat on the edge of the bed. "Tonight was fun, huh?"

"Yes," Rowena said, sitting next to her. "I haven't had this much fun in quite a while."

"There *are* occasions when we enjoy each other's company."

"Oh, I bet there are more than a few."

"I'm kidding. Of course there are. In spite of what it looked like, I *do* have manners."

Rowena smiled. "I know you do. Maybe you shouldn't judge yourself so much. It's okay to have an opinion."

Nyeela shrugged her shoulders. "Too bad your girl doesn't think so. One minute, she's telling me I'm a woman and the next minute, she's treating me like a little girl. I mean, I can't help it if she missed out on the big sister role. Nobody told her to run and catch the first thing smoking, looking for a man."

"Nyeela, you shouldn't be so hard on your sister. She doesn't mean any harm. She's just having a tough time."

"Yeah, well I hate it all the same. Everyone wants to dictate how we should live our lives and it infuriates me."

Rowena nodded. "I wanted to be different at your age, too."

"Precisely. Not everything has to be done the good old fashion way. Otherwise, what's the point in educating ourselves?"

"I agree. We all have to live our own truth."

"Try convincing the old skool crew. Sometimes, I just want to get the hell away from here."

"Trust me, Nyeela. It wouldn't be much different elsewhere. No matter where you are, you've got to stick to your guns and never allow anyone to keep you from pursuing whatever makes you feel free."

"I swear it's an uphill battle."

"But an uphill battle can move you upward and onward, if you do the work. Eventually, you'll get to where you want to be."

Nyeela folded her leg beneath her. "You're starting to sound like Eve."

"I know, right? Half the time, I don't know where this stuff comes from. Maybe I have been hanging with her too long," Rowena laughed.

"Are you where you want to be, Ro?"

"It's funny you ask. Eve and I were discussing that earlier. If I were to speak honestly, I'd have to say no. As a teenager, I had dreams but I allowed them to wither."

"If you don't mind me asking, what kind of dreams?"

"Dreams of being with a man whose eyes light up, whenever I walk into a room."

"Sounds eerily familiar," Nyeela grimaced.

"I also had dreams of being a poet laureate."

"Now, there's a tangible dream."

"It would've been, if I hadn't got detoured."

"Are you saying you can't re-route?"

"I don't know if I have the courage to get off of the path I'm on now."

"You put one foot in front of the other and take baby steps if you have to."

"Easy to say. Even harder to do."

"Listen. I know we've had this conversation already and I promise I'm not trying to harp on the subject. But I'm curious. Why don't you have someone special?"

"It's complicated, Nyeela," Rowena said, lowering her head.

"I mean, I understand the whole thing about not having time because of your career but look at you, you're gorgeous. You're obviously intelligent, what are you afraid of?"

"It's like I said before, someday. Not right now."

Nyeela gazed at Rowena as if she saw her for the first time. She studied the fine brown tresses nestled atop her head. Her eyes traced the contour of Rowena's pale skin and locked on her full round lips. "I guess I sound like the rest of my family, huh?"

"Honestly, this crisis Evelyn is going through makes me shudder at the thought. Besides, I've been hurt before and I don't know if I can risk it again."

Nyeela impulsively ran her finger along Rowena's back. "I really appreciate your honesty," she said. "I know exactly how rejection feels and I understand. But how do you expect to find a man who can't breathe without you, if you're shut down?"

Rowena ignored the seductive gestures. "How can you quiz me about love, when you clearly haven't signed up yourself, young lady?"

"I am seeing someone and while I'm not in love, I care for this person a great deal. I think it's better than nothing."

"That's a matter of opinion. To me, it sounds like you and your mother might share the same position after all, just expressed in different ways."

"I don't think so, Ro."

"Regardless, try not to think of it as such a bad thing, to agree with the person who taught you everything you know about love."

Evelyn walked in the room and Nyeela snatched her hand from Rowena's back. "What are you guys up to?" Evelyn asked, eyeing Nyeela suspiciously.

"We're sharing a little girl talk. Join us."

"Actually," Nyeela said, standing to her feet. "I'm going to say goodnight." She turned to Evelyn and smiled. "It's way past my bed time."

"Okay, Nyeela. Thanks for listening. Sleep well."

Nyeela winked at Rowena and left the room.

"Girl talk, huh?" Evelyn asked, with raised eyebrows.

"A little," Rowena said, ignoring her implications. What's up with you?"

"Nothing much. I couldn't go to bed without letting you know that I'm glad you're here. I'm sorry for being such a bitch this evening. I don't know if it's the divorce or the pregnancy but whatever the case, I owe you an apology."

"Listen. You don't owe me anything. This is a rough time for you and I would not be much of a friend if I couldn't understand. So, go to bed and get some rest. We've got a big day tomorrow," she said, kissing Evelyn on the cheek. "Good night."

Chapter Nine

Thanksgiving Day, Ella Mae made eggs, pancakes and sausage while everyone slept in. A friend phoned about Thanksgiving Day Service at the church. Ella Mae finished the call, helped herself to some coffee, and hurried to get dressed. On her way out, she bumped into Nyasia, who staggered half-asleep down the hall.

"Good morning, Ma," she muttered, rubbing her eyes and squinting.

"Mornin, baby."

"Where are you going this early?"

"Child, it ain't early. It's 10 a.m. and I'm on my way to church. I'm already runnin behind."

"You made pancakes?"

"Mm Hm. Go on and help ya'self. I'll be back by noon." She put her purse on her shoulder. "If Melvin calls, tell him I'll call when I get back."

"Yes, ma'am." Nyasia yawned, scratched her neck and continued to the bathroom.

Nyeela got up, put on her robe and strode down the hall, as Nyasia exited the bathroom.

"Took you long enough," Nyeela said, brushing past her sister.

"Why are you always sneaking up on folk?" Nyasia asked.

Nyeela ignored the question and slammed the door behind her.

Nyasia followed the intoxicating smell of pancakes to the kitchen.

Minutes later, the rest of the ladies filed their way into the kitchen one by one, taking a seat at the table.

"I am so excited to be here!" Rowena said. "Eve, are we going shopping tomorrow?"

"Sure, but we need to get an early start because it's going to be a mess out there."

Nyasia drowned her pancakes in warm syrup. "If anyone is interested, Twin and I know the best places to go."

"Nice!" Rowena said, reaching for the butter. "Is this a tradition for you guys?"

"Pretty much." Nyeela poured herself a glass of orange juice. "Sometimes we're able to talk Mama into going with us. She doesn't have much patience for Black Friday."

"Usually, I'm not in the mood to go either," Rowena said, taking in a forkful of sausage.

"Grady and I went every year," Evelyn announced. "I guess I get to save my money this year," she grimaced.

"Sis, look on the bright side. This will be our first Christmas together in fifteen years." Nyasia smiled. "Isn't that great?"

"I didn't realize it's been so long." Evelyn sipped her coffee. "Does Mother still have the same tree?"

Nyeela nodded. "Maybe we can pick up a new one. Lord knows it's time."

"Twin, you know how Ma is about her tree. So don't even think about bringing another one in here."

Evelyn shook her head. "It's a wonder that thing hasn't shriveled up!"

"Sis, trust me. I've tried to talk her into buying a new one, but she won't budge."

Evelyn looked up at the wall clock. "What time did she say she'd be back from church?"

"Around noon," Nyasia answered.

Nyeela rested her elbows on the table. "You know she's going to expect all of us to help her in the kitchen when she gets back. Including you, Rowena."

"I don't mind," Rowena said, licking the syrup from her fingers.

Evelyn pushed away from the table. "Well, I'm going to have to take a rain check."

"Why, sis?"

"Because I have a serious headache, Nyeela. Is that okay with you?"

"Maybe, if you tried combing your hair, your head wouldn't hurt," she smirked.

"And maybe you should mind your own damn business for a change," Evelyn said, raking her fingers through her hair. "Oh, I forgot. You don't have any."

"I have plenty of business," Nyeela argued. "But lately, we've all been preoccupied with yours."

Evelyn sucked her teeth and shot a hard look at Nyeela.

"I'm just saying. We don't usually do drama in this house," Nyeela said, sipping her juice.

"Excuse the hell out of me! I didn't know I needed permission to bring my dirty laundry home."

Nyasia put down her fork and wiped her mouth. "She doesn't speak for me, Eve."

Evelyn stood up, threw her napkin across the table, and placed her hand on her hip. "But you do agree with her, right, Nyasia?"

Nyasia ignored her twin's signal not to answer the question. "Look, Eve. I know you're devastated…."

"But you could at least make an effort to show *some* appreciation around here for your family," Nyeela interrupted. "We're only trying to support you, even though *we* had nothing to do with what happened."

Evelyn was tempted to jump across the table and strangle Nyeela. Instead, she let out a screech and stormed out of the kitchen.

Rowena looked at Nyeela with disapproval. "That was *so* not cool."

"What?" Nyeela shrugged her shoulders. "I'm tired of walking on eggshells."

"Would it kill you to think of someone besides yourself?"

"No, Rowena. What's killing me is her attitude."

"I agree with Rowena, Twin. You need to cut Evelyn some slack."

Nyeela flipped her hand. "So because she's miserable, we all have to be? I'm sick of it already."

"You are unbelievable, Nyeela!"

"Why, Rowena? Because I'm not kissing her ass all the time? Hell, as far as I'm concerned, some honesty might actually do her some good."

"For your information, no one is kissing her ass. I'm just smart enough not to take everything she says or does personally. That doesn't mean I'm incapable of telling her the truth. Evelyn is my friend and I get to show up for her in a way *you* obviously don't know how."

"Is that what you tell yourself?"

Rowena held up a firm hand. "I am not going there with you, Nyeela. I'm here for Eve and nothing else."

"I'm sorry, Ro. I didn't mean to...."

Rowena stood up and forced her chair back. "I have to go and get dressed." She placed the dishes in the sink and traipsed upstairs.

Nyasia shook her head and walked away from the table. "You never cease to amaze me, Houdini," she said, adding her plate to the sink. "I think you were born with the gift of making folk disappear."

"Oh, shut up!" Nyeela demanded. "Don't try to act all high and mighty with me," she said, getting up from the table. "You'll have plenty to worry about, when you bring your little fling in here."

Nyasia turned back and waved her index finger. "Um, excuse you. I don't have to worry about anything. But if I were *you*, I'd save some of those magic tricks for later. You're going to need all the help you can get to pull your little rabbit out of the hat." Nyasia pushed in her chair and left the room.

"Tricks are for kids!" Nyeela yelled after her. "You just watch and take notes."

Upstairs, Rowena knocked on Evelyn's door. "Eve, can I come in?"

"It's open."

"Are you okay?"

"They hate me."

"Stop it. They don't hate you. The twins don't understand what you're going through."

Tears streamed down her face. "Have I been that bad?"

"Honestly? Yes. But Eve that's allowed."

"Tell me something, Ro. Why are you being so patient with me?"

"Because I'm your friend and this is what friends do for each other. Besides, I've been hurt so I can relate. The twins haven't had their hearts broken yet."

"Nyeela makes me want to choke her sometimes."

"She's young, Eve. She has no idea the kind of woman you've become."

"What do you mean?"

"When you left here, you were a teenager. Now, you're a woman. She doesn't really know you."

"Oh, and you do?" she asked, wiping her face.

"Damn right!"

She smiled. "And just what is it that you think you know about me, Rowena Patterson?"

"I know you're much stronger than you will admit. I know there is another life, living and breathing inside of you. And he or she needs you to survive."

"Okay, Miss Rowena. We don't need to get into the whole baby situation. I get your point."

"It was just a friendly reminder. That's all."

Evelyn rubbed her stomach. "All the crazy smells floating through this house is reminder enough. Trust me."

Rowena nodded. "I understand."

"I *do* appreciate the sentiment though."

"You need all the love and patience you can get and I came here to give it to you."

Evelyn leaned her head against Rowena's shoulder. "How did I ever earn the likings of you?"

"Girl, I ask myself that question every single day," Rowena giggled. "I'm just kidding."

"You have no idea how tired I am of crying, bitching, and moaning. Twin is right. I've got to pull myself together and enjoy my family before they all turn on me."

"That's not likely, my dear. Remember, we're all on the same team —team Banks!"

"From your lips."

"Let's get you some aspirin for that headache, so we can get dressed before your mother comes home from church."

Ella Mae returned from church around noon and found the kitchen full of women. Food and dishes were everywhere and everyone worked together to help put dinner on the table.

"It's a miracle! I got one–two–three–four angels workin in my kitchen," she said. "Praise the Lawd!"

"Hey, Mama! We just wanted to lend a hand with all this food."

Ella Mae grabbed her apron and tied it around her waist. "Since y'all got thangs unda control in here, I'm gon' go and set the table. Did Melvin call?"

"Yes. He's coming early to watch the game, along with his uncle and cousin."

"Oh boy," she said, putting on her glasses. "I ain't got no beer in the fridge. Y'all know how men like to drank beer when they watchin them games."

Evelyn put one hand on her hip. "Mother, Melvin knows you don't keep beer in this house. Besides, isn't that uncle of his too old to be drinking alcohol?"

"Child, you neva know what folk be doin nowadays. And are you gon' comb ya hair at all today?"

Evelyn rolled her eyes. "Where is the bread basket? I need to unpack these dinner rolls."

"Right there ova the fridge," Ella Mae said, without looking up.

"What about the pan for the turkey, Ma?"

"Do I have to get ev'rythang 'round here? Can't you look for ya'self, child? She asked, pushing her glasses up the bridge of her nose. "I gotta set the table."

Nyasia smacked her lips. "Never mind. I'll find it. Dang!"

"Hope I fixed enough sweet corn," Ella Mae said, putting her finger on her lips. "Seem like I shudda made more."

Evelyn flashed a look at Ella Mae. "Mother, you really need to stop with all that worrying. You've got enough food here to feed a circus! Trust me. There is plenty to go around." She looked over at Nyeela. "But then again, you may be right. Nyeela can put these veggies away all by herself."

"Ha, ha, Eve. I bet you just crack yourself up. For your information, I'm not even hungry. Besides," she said, glancing at her watch. "I'm expecting a guest in a few hours."

Ella Mae spooned the corn into a deep casserole dish. "'Bout time. I can't wait to meet him. Do me a fava and brang them extra foldin chairs out the storage shed. We may need em."

"Yes, ma'am!"

"Take a rag wit ya jus' in case ya gotta wipe em down."

"I got it, Mama," Nyeela said, heading out the door. The temperature had taken a dip and it started to rain. Her guest pulled up alongside the curb and tooted the horn. Nyeela made a quick beeline to the car. "Tanvi, you're early!"

"I know," she said, climbing out of the car. "Mom and I finished earlier than expected, so I decided to come on over and help you guys. I hope it's okay."

"It's fine. I just didn't expect you this soon."

"Hello. How are you?" she said, sardonically.

"You know I'm happy to see you, babe." Nyeela said, leaning in to kiss her.

Tanvi reciprocated. "Is everything okay? Are you sure you still want to do this?"

"Mama is starting to ask a lot of questions," Nyeela said. "And it's bound to happen sooner or later, so it may as well happen now. Just so you know; my entire family is in there."

"I'm so excited!" Tanvi clapped. "I can't wait to meet them."

"Yeah well, you may want to wait until the dust settles before you get all excited. Come on around back and help me get these chairs out of the shed."

*****

Inside the kitchen, Evelyn struggled to keep her balance. She felt lightheaded but didn't want to alarm Ella Mae. "Whew! I think I'm going to go upstairs and lie down for a few minutes."

"You okay, baby?" Ella Mae took off her glasses.

"I'm a little tired. I guess the late nights are starting to catch up with me."

Ella Mae looked at her with suspecting eyes. "Well go on and lay down, then. We got it from here. Nyasia, put the Red Velvet Cake on my special cake-plate. Rowena, can you get the Banana Puddin out the icebox and slide it in the fridge?"

"Yes ma'am. I love Banana Pudding."

"The girls ain't so crazy 'bout it."

"Pecan pie is my favorite," Nyasia announced. "Ma only makes it during this time of year and I always look forward to it."

"It was ya daddy's favorite too. I used to make it more often before he passed."

"It was my mother's favorite, as well," Rowena said, sliding the dessert into the refrigerator. "She did all the cooking for both Thanksgiving and Christmas. That's the reason why the holidays are always hard for me."

"Sounds like you miss her."

"Terribly! I stay busy to keep from thinking about them. If it weren't for Eve, I'd be at home right now working my behind off. I'm so glad I came."

Ella Mae smiled. "I'm glad too, Rowena." She peeped out the window. "Who is that out there wit Nyeela?"

"Oh that's Tanvi," Nyasia said casually.

"Who? And why ain't she tell me she had more than one person comin? I swear that girl make me wanna cuss sometimes."

Nyasia shrugged. "I don't know, but my friend will be here in exactly two hours."

"It ain't more than one, is it?"

"No, Ma."

Ella Mae wiped her hands and removed her apron. "Good Lawd! What time is it?"

"It's three o'clock, Ms. Ella."

"I gotta go freshen up before Melvin gets here."

"I'm right behind you, Ma. I need to fix my hair."

Ella Mae and Nyasia went upstairs.

Nyeela and Tanvi brought in the chairs from the shed and Rowena put the stemware on the table.

"Ro, I want you to meet someone." Nyeela guided her friend over to the table. "Tanvi, this is Rowena Patterson, a dear friend of the family. Rowena, this is Tanvi."

"Nice to meet you, Rowena!"

"Likewise. Tanvi is it?"

"Yes."

"That's a lovely name."

"Thanks!"

"What does it mean?"

"It's an Indian derivative and it means delicate girl."

"Vee, I'm a little dusty," Nyeela said, wiping her hands on her jeans. "I'm going upstairs to wash my face and hands. I'll be right back."

"Okay."

"So Tanvi, are you from India?"

"Please, call me Vee."

Rowena smiled. "Okay, Vee."

"Yes. My entire family is from India. We came to America when I was three. Essentially, this is really the only home I've known."

"Do you attend the University as well?"

"Yes. This is my last year."

"Congratulations! What's your major?"

"Sociology."

"Nice! Is that where you and Nyeela met?"

"Uh...."

"I'm sorry. Am I asking too many questions?"

"No. It's fine, Rowena."

"Just trying to make small talk," Rowena smiled.

"Yes, Nyeela and I met on campus and we've been partners ever since," she said, with delight.

Rowena's eyebrows forged a slight frown. "I'm sorry, you said you've been *friends* ever since?"

"*Partners*, partners ever since."

"Partners in what?"

"She's my girlfriend," Nyeela announced, entering the room.

"You mean as in...."

"Lovers," she confirmed.

"Oh… *Oh!*"

"You said that already."

"I'm ... I ... Um, my mouth is dry. Excuse me. I need a glass of water." Rowena excused herself and walked into the kitchen. Nyeela followed. Rowena grabbed a glass and filled it with water.

"Is there something wrong?"

Rowena swallowed hard. "No. Why do you ask?"

"You left the room in a big hurry."

Rowena chugged the water and fanned her face. "I'm sorry," she said, trying to catch her breath. "I needed something to drink. I can't quench this thirst."

"You don't have to pretend, Rowena. If you have something to say, go ahead and tell me."

"First of all, I am not pretending," she said, filling the glass and turning off the tap. "Yes, you took me by surprise with your news, but I assure you, I do not have a problem with whom you date. It's your life and your choice."

"Choice… So you think it's a choice?"

"Well…." Rowena said, chugging the second glass of water.

"Apparently, I was wrong when I thought you could handle progression."

"Nyeela, you're overreacting," she said, walking away from the sink. "What does it matter anyway? It's none of my business what you do."

"You're right. It isn't your business. And I would appreciate it if you could keep it to yourself. I need to find the right time to tell Mama."

Nyasia bolted around the corner. "Tell Mama what?"

"Why are *you* so dolled up?"

Nyasia sashayed across the kitchen. "Why? Do I look fabulous?"

Nyeela grimaced. "It's Thanksgiving dinner, not a photo shoot."

Nyasia held up her hand. "Don't hate. Appreciate," she winked. "Isn't that right, Rowena?"

Before Rowena could answer, the doorbell rang. Melvin and his family arrived.

Upstairs, Ella Mae peeked in on Evelyn. "Eve, you okay in here?"

"Yes, Mother," she answered, lying across the bed. "Was that the doorbell?"

"Yeah. I gotta get back downstairs, but we'll be eatin 'bout a hour from now. You need to get up and get ya'self togetha. I want you to come down and meet ev'rybody before hand."

"Okay. I'm getting up now," she said, rolling onto her side.

"Awright." Ella Mae closed the door and returned downstairs.

Evelyn struggled to get herself together. Not only was she sick, but the emotional rollercoaster sent her crashing into an abyss of misery. She gathered some clothes and went to the bathroom to shower. Sitting on the edge of the tub, her eyes traced the lines of the subway tiles that covered the wall. Steam slowly clouded the room, but not her thoughts. Without a sound, she stripped down to her birthday suit and climbed underneath the flowing water. It temporarily dissolved the heaviness that lingered. When she finally exited the bathroom, she felt lighter and for that, she was grateful. In an effort to match how she felt on the inside, Evelyn decided to comb her hair and put on some makeup.

Downstairs, Nyeela introduced Tanvi to everyone. "Mama, this is Tanvi."

"Nice to meet ya, Tanvi!"

"You too, Ms. Banks."

"This is Melvin."

"Pleasure to meet you, Melvin."

"Good to meet ya, Tanvi."

"Please, call me Vee."

"Okay. Vee, everybody, I want y'all to meet my uncle Charles and his son, Stacey."

Tanvi waved. "Hello!"

"Stacey, can I get you or ya dad anythang?" Ella Mae offered.

"Pop, you want anythang?" Stacey repeated to his father.

Uncle Charles shook his head. "Naw."

"We fine, Ms. Ella Mae. Thanks."

"Honey, me and the fellas gon' go in the family room and watch the game till dinna get ready."

"Awright, Melvin. Y'all go right ahead. Me and Rowena gon' put the food on the table. You don't mind do ya, Rowena?"

"Of course not. I just need to run upstairs and freshen up a little bit. I promise to hurry back."

"Child, you ain't been upstairs yet? Go on then. I'm gon' get started."

"I'll be right back."

Rowena ran up the stairs and knocked on Evelyn's door.

"Come in," Evelyn said, putting the final touch on her makeup. She was fully dressed, with her hair pulled neatly into a bun.

"Whoa! Look at you," Rowena said, peeping around the door.

"The hot bath did wonders. Who knew?"

"I see," Rowena said, entering the room. "You look beautiful!"

"Thanks! Is Melvin here?"

"Yes. They are in the family room watching the game."

"How does his uncle look?" Evelyn inquired, applying a thin coat of gloss to her lips.

"Actually, he looks good to be his age. You'll see."

"I'm on my way down there now. What about his cousin?" she asked, rubbing her lips together.

"Now, *him* you'll have to see for yourself."

"Come on, Ro. Not even a hint?"

"My lips are sealed. Besides, I promised your mother I would be right back to help finish putting the food on the table."

"Stinker!"

"But *you*, my dear, are simply gorgeous!"

"Liar! Get out of here!"

Rowena rushed to freshen up. Evelyn trekked lightly downstairs to the living room. Vee and the twins were engaged in minimal conversation.

Evelyn waved. "Hey, everyone!"

Nyeela stood up. "Eve, it's nice of you to join us. Vee, this is my big sister, Eve."

"It's good to finally meet you, Eve. I'm Tanvi, but you can call me Vee."

"Nice to meet you too, Vee. Where are the others?"

"Mama's in the kitchen. Melvin, his uncle, and Stacey are in the family room."

"Oh. What are you all doing?" Evelyn asked.

"We're just chatting. Join us," Nyeela insisted.

"No. I better go introduce myself to the others and help Mother in the kitchen," Evelyn said, patting at her hair. She walked slowly into the adjoining family room and forced a smile. "Hello!"

"Evelyn, hey!" Melvin said, standing to greet her with a kiss. "You look pretty!"

"Thank you, Melvin," she smiled.

"This is Uncle Charles and my cousin Stacey. Guys, this is Ella Mae's oldes' daughter, Evelyn."

Uncle Charles nodded and waved.

Stacey stood up and extended his hand. "Nice to meet ya, Evelyn."

"Same here," she said, shaking his hand. "Call me Eve." Almost immediately, her mind went back to the night she met Grady. Her heart sank.

232 Angela Bolden-Thompson

At five-feet-six inches, Stacey bore strong shoulders and deep dimples. His clean-shaven head and butterscotch skin drew her immediately. His broad chest and washboard abs emerged through a snug fitting t-shirt. His warm and tender hands held on to her sweaty palms, as she struggled to keep her thoughts in the present. She politely eased her hand out of his and excused herself.

Evelyn walked into the kitchen.

Ella Mae smiled. "You look pretty!"

"Thanks! I feel a lot better," she said, filling a glass with tap water.

"I wish a bath could make me glow like that," Ella Mae said, admiring her complexion. "Ya hair is cute too!"

Evelyn drank the water and composed herself quickly. "How can I help you in here?"

"Ev'rythang is ready. Jus' make sho ev'rythang is in a dish, so it's easy to serve."

Evelyn put on an apron and grabbed a ceramic casserole dish. "I just met Mr. Charles and his son."

"Mr. Charles sho look good, don't he?"

"Absolutely. I suppose it runs in the family."

Ella Mae smiled. "I believe so."

"Nobody can take my daddy's place, but I'm so glad you found Melvin. He's a good man, Mother."

"I know, baby. Thank ya for sayin so."

Evelyn kissed Ella Mae on the cheek.

Rowena changed clothes, glossed her lips, and joined them in the kitchen. "What's up?" she asked, heading toward the stove.

"Mother and I were agreeing on what a good man Melvin is."

"Yes, he is," she said, removing the ham from the oven. "You can't find many like him, these days."

"Oh, I don't know, Ro. Maybe we haven't been looking in the right places."

Rowena looked at Evelyn with a blank stare. "*We?*"

"We, meaning you and I," she said, pointing her finger. "Like I said in Chicago, you and I are in the same category now."

Rowena cringed. "So what do you propose *we* do about it?" she said, winking at Ella Mae.

"I don't know what *you* plan to do, but my crying days are over!"

Rowena shifted her weight to one leg. "Really? I don't suppose a certain gentleman in the other room has anything to do with your decision."

Evelyn played coy. "Miss Patterson, I have no idea what you're talking about. Today happens to be Thanksgiving and I'm just trying to be thankful."

"I know one thang," Ella Mae interrupted. "I sho wish y'all hurry up and get this food on the table."

"Yes, ma'am!"

At five o'clock, Ella Mae summoned everyone into the dining room. She expressed that she wanted Melvin to bless the food after they all shared what they were grateful for, with each other. Ella Mae went first.

"I guess I ain't gotta tell y'all what this means to me, but I will anyhow. I'm gon' try my best not to cry. Lawd knows my soul is overjoyed right now. The birth of my three babies was the proudes' moment of my life and this one is a close second. I finally got my whole family togetha in one room. I jus' wish ya father was here to share this moment. He wudda been proud. Rowena, you cudda spent this day any way ya wanted to, but you chose to share it wit us and I'm glad ya did. It's such a blessin to have ya. Twins, I thank God for y'all ev'ryday. Y'all dun turned into some beautiful young women, but you gon' always be my babies. Ya stubborn and hardheaded too, but I'm proud jus' the same."

Nyasia folded her arms. "Ma..."

"Hush, Nyasia. I ain't finished. Evelyn Renee, I want you to hang in there, baby. I know it ain't easy facin a failed marriage but you gon' be awright. I'm jus' happy to see a smile on ya face...."

Nyeela interrupted. "That is a smile, isn't it?"

Ella Mae cut her eyes at Nyeela. "And we glad to have ya home. I love ya, suga." Ella Mae put her hand over her heart. "Melvin, you make this ole gal feel young again and that ain't a easy thang to do," she laughed.

Nyasia interrupted again. "My turn, my turn!"

"Child, if you cut me off one more time," Ella Mae threatened.

"Sorry, Ma. I'm just a little excited."

"As I was sayin, Melvin, before you came I didn't think I was gon' eva find love again. I guess God had other plans. I thank Him everyday. Mr. Charles, Stacey and ev'rybody, welcome to my home.

Ain't no strangas in this house. Eat as much as you want and enjoy ya'selves. Go on and speak, Nyasia."

"Thank you, Ma. First, I am thankful for having such a wonderful and caring Mother who is unfailing in her love and support. Ma, I don't know what I would do without you. Second, I'm thankful to have two beautiful sisters, whom I love dearly. I'm thankful for a great job and good grades. I'm also thankful for having someone in my corner that I love and trust, which you all will get to meet shortly. And last but not least, I'm thankful to Melvin for bringing some sunshine into this house. Because one thing is certain. If Ma isn't happy, nobody is," she smirked.

Nyeela smiled. "Touché!"

Ella Mae threw her hand. "Oh, hush!"

"Okay. My turrrrn," Nyeela sang. "Where do I start? I'll start with you, Twin. Even though we fight like two cats on a hot tin roof, my life is not complete without you. You are my *better* half and my best friend. No matter what challenge life has brought this family, I always knew I had you. I love you, girlie. Evelyn, I am also thankful to have you here. I know the last few days have not been our best moments together, but I love you just the same. Mama is right. You are going to get beyond this. Just believe. Oh, and the smile really does suit you.

Mama, you always say I'm a daddy's girl, but here is something you didn't know. My heart will always belong to you. I love you." She blew Ella Mae a kiss. "Melvin, I'm thankful for you, too. You make my mama happy and I hope you stay around for a long time." She smiled. "And finally, I'm thankful for friends like you, Tanvi. You already know how much you mean to me. Thank you for being in my corner." Nyeela winked at Tanvi and surrendered the floor.

Melvin cleared his throat. "It's real nice to see so much love in one room. I'm glad to be part of a wondaful and lovin bunch of people. Since Ella and me been togetha, my life been full. Ella is gentle on these ole eyes." He laughed. "But more than that, I respec' the way she love her girls. It's a good thang. And from what I can see, the apples don't fall far from the tree. I love this family and I love you, Ella.

Uncle Charles, you bein here today makes me happy. I treasure times like these, cuz we don't spend much time togetha. I'm gon' try and do betta 'bout that. Stacey, you done a wondaful job wit

Uncle Charles and I'm proud of ya. God gon' bless you in ways ya ain't gon' undastand. That's all I wanna say."

"Forgive me if I start to tear up a bit," Rowena said, swallowing a cry. "It's been a while since I've been around this much love and it's stirring me up inside. Evelyn and I have been best friends for a long time and she is just about the only family I have back home. If she had not insisted that I come here, I would be in Chicago with my head buried in paperwork. Lucky for me, I get to spend time with good-hearted people like yourselves and I am deeply grateful. Twins, you two are exceptional women. Continue to challenge yourselves and each other, so you can be shining examples for other young females. Always be true to yourselves and your heart's desires.

Ms. Ella, thank you for opening up your heart and home to me. You can't know how much this means." Her eyes welled. "And Eve, I thank God everyday for you. I love you, girl."

"I love you too," she mouthed.

"Anybody else wanna share?" Ella Mae asked.

"May I?" Stacey requested.

"You go right on."

"I know y'all don't know me very well, but I have a few thangs I'm thankful for. First, I'm thankful for Pops standin here wit a good portion of his health. I wouldn't dream of havin anotha person takin care of the man who raised me. If it wasn't for his sacrifices, I wouldn't be where I am today.

Second, I'm thankful to be in a room full of beautiful and intelligent women. Melvin told me good thangs 'bout y'all and I see for myself, he's a lucky man. Thank y'all for allowin us to be here and for lettin me share."

"I guess that means it's my turn, huh?" Eve asked. Without getting a response, she continued. "Where do I begin? Today, I am most thankful for being alive. If someone had asked me three weeks ago, I probably wouldn't have given the same answer. But today is different. I am grateful to be here. To say, I've been grouchy is the ultimate understatement. The truth is I have been angry as hell. But thank God some of it is dissipating and that's the reason I can smile," she sighed. "Starting over isn't easy. In fact, it's downright hard. It feels more like a task than anything else. I guess if I open myself to it, it could be something good. I want to thank you, Rowena for all your encouragement," she said, tipping her head. "I think Nyeela has been the most articulate in analyzing my predicament. She thinks I've gotten myself stuck in a hellhole and I'm making everyone else miserable in the process. And she's probably right. I should apologize to all of you. For that, I'm truly sorry. As of this moment, I'm going to start fresh. I'm not sure where to go from here, but I vow to move forward, one day at a time. I love you family and friends. Happy Thanksgiving. Now, can we eat?"

"Let's pray first," Melvin stated, bowing his head. "Dear Lawd, we stand here today, thankful for all ya blessed us wit, happiness, joy, strength, love, life, and each otha. Thank ya for the end of one chapta and the beginnin of a new one. Thank ya for the food and the hands that cooked it. Thank ya for the hope and friendships formed here, today. May it be eternal. In Ya Name, Father. Amen."

"Amen."

Chapter Ten

Dishes passed from hand to hand around the table. "This turkey is juicy. Who made it?" Stacey asked, chewing on a strip of turkey meat.

"Mother did," Evelyn answered.

Stacey laughed quietly. "I bet good cookin runs in the family."

Evelyn raised an eyebrow. "Are you a betting man?"

Stacey paused and scratched his neck. "Naw, not really. But if I had to put my money on somethin, that would be it."

Evelyn tore off a piece of dinner roll. "I don't know about my little sisters, but I didn't get the cooking gene. However, I can manage a few tricks from time to time," she said, pushing the bread into her mouth.

"I hate to cause dissension, but not every woman belongs in the kitchen."

"That's true, Nyeela," Stacey responded, "but it sho would be a shame if y'all grew up 'round all this good cookin and none of it rubbed off on ya."

Ella Mae picked up her glass of sweet tea. "Child, don't you pay Nyeela no mind. She got somethin to say 'bout ev'ry doggone thang."

"I agree with Nyeela," Tanvi added. "Every woman doesn't want to or *have* to know how to cook."

Ella Mae sat her drink down and squinted. "I'm sorry, baby. Now, what's ya name again?"

"Tanvi."

Ella Mae reached for her dangling glasses. "Who? Ta...."

"Tan-vi," the young lady enunciated, filling her glass with sweet tea.

Ella Mae put on her glasses and rested her elbows on the table with her fingers interlocked. "Well anyhow, it's good to have ya here. How long y'all been friends?"

Tanvi glanced over at Nyeela. "We've known each other for quite some time now."

"How come I ain't neva met you before?"

"Um...."

"Mama," Nyeela interrupted. "We've been busy and just haven't gotten around to it."

Evelyn cleared her throat, crossed her legs, and picked up her fork. "What do you do in your spare time, Stacey?"

"The shop and lookin afta Pop keep me pretty busy, Eve, so I don't get much free time. But when I do, I try to workout a lil."

"Oh." Evelyn smiled and swiped a strand of hair from her face. "Melvin mentioned that you owned a towing company. How long have you been in business?"

"'Bout twelve years," he nodded. "Thought of expandin, but I ain't had time to work on no business plan."

"Nyeela is excellent in marketing and accounting. Perhaps you two could get together and figure out your options."

"I would like that. You don't mind do ya, Nyeela?"

Nyeela put her fork down and scratched the bridge of her nose. "Um, no, I don't mind."

"Awright then, I look forward to it," he smiled. "How 'bout you, Eve?" he asked. "What you do?"

"I run an advice column for a magazine."

"Yeah, Eve gets her rocks off telling people how to handle their problems," Nyeela smirked.

"I believe he was speaking to me, Nyeela," Evelyn said, shooting her a look of contempt. "Readers of the magazine write in asking for my advice, Stacey. And I give them my opinion."

"I think it's hilarious," Nyeela said, with a wry smile.

"No one asked you." Evelyn said, putting her fork down. "Why? You don't think I'm qualified to do so?"

The doorbell rang. "Yaaaay! My friend is here," Nyasia sang. She excused herself from the table.

Ella Mae looked at her watch. "Nyeela, what time is the otha guest comin? They gon' miss all the food."

Nyeela didn't hear Ella Mae. She was completely engaged in her debate with Evelyn.

Tanvi looked up from her plate and offered Ella Mae a fake smile.

"Evelyn is actually pretty good at what she does," Rowena said. "I read her column every chance I get."

Evelyn smiled. "I love what I do. It feels good to empower other people."

"Okay, Eve," Nyeela continued. "Prove it. Let's see how good you really are."

"Nyeela, don't start," Ella Mae pleaded.

"Hypothetically speaking, let's say a woman writes to you saying she left her entire family behind, to go chasing her dream of meeting *Prince Charming*. Much to everyone's surprise, she succeeds. They buy a house, throw a big old fancy wedding and set out to live happily ever after. Seven years later, the perfect life, the perfect house, and the perfect marriage fall apart at the seams. *Prince Charming* files for divorce and announces that he's gay. What, if any, kind of advice could you give to someone in that situation … hypothetically?"

Silence permeated the room.

Ella Mae pounded the table. "Nyeela Marie Banks!"

Evelyn smiled at the audacity, shook her head, and held up a firm hand. "It's okay, Mother. I got this." She calmly placed her elbows on the table, interlocked her fingers and directed her attention over to Tanvi with a raised an eyebrow. "Vee, is it?"

"Yes."

"Tell us again. How did you and Nyeela come to know each other?"

"Why are you asking her?" Nyeela intercepted. "I told you earlier, we met on campus."

"Frankly, Nyeela, with all the talking you've done, we've yet to hear the truth."

"What truth?"

"Oh, come on now," Evelyn said, squaring her shoulders and folding her arms. "Don't be coy. You wanted to play big, bad and dirty. Let the games begin."

Ella Mae took off her glasses and waved her hand. "Wait. What games?"

Under the table, Rowena reached over and gently squeezed Evelyn's leg. "Eve, that's enough. Why don't you relax and finish your food?"

Evelyn turned a deaf ear as the tension brewed.

Ella Mae put her hands on her waist. "Somebody betta speak up and tell me what the heck is goin on."

Evelyn gazed intently into her sister's eyes. "I think Vee and Twin have a new skool secret they've been keeping from us old skool folk. Am I right, Vee?"

Nyeela's face turned rose red. "Evelyn, this is between you and me. Leave her out of it," she said, with desperate eyes.

"Please, I don't want any trouble," Tanvi said nervously.

"Too late, sweetie pie," Evelyn grimaced. "Your girlfriend should have thought twice before bringing you to the party."

Nyeela wiped her mouth, threw her napkin on the table, and stood up. "Fine. You want it? Here it is. Mama, Grady isn't the only one in this family who's gay."

"Say what, Nyeela?" Ella Mae asked.

"Who gay?" Melvin asked.

"I am."

Ella Mae's mouth flew open. "You?"

"Correct, Mama. I'm a lesbian and Tanvi is my girlfriend."

Melvin tapped Stacey on the forearm. "Time to go," he said, scooting his chair back.

"Y'all dun lost y'all eva lovin minds. This ain't the time for this here foolishness."

"This is not a joke, Mother," Evelyn said, feeling satisfied with herself. "I knew something was amiss, walking around here...."

Nyasia happily entered the room with her guest. "Everyone, this is my boyfriend, Bryson."

Uncle Charles struggled to get out of his seat.

Stacey got up to assist him back to his seat. "What's wrong, Pop? You okay?"

"What's he doin here?" he mumbled, pointing at Bryson.

"He's Nyasia's friend," Stacey said, gently grabbing the frazzled old mans arm.

"No, sir. He ain't takin me to jail," he said, snatching his napkin from around his neck.

"Hello," Bryson said nervously, scanning the faces around the table.

"Relax, Pop," Stacey said, rubbing his back. "Bryson ain't the police and he ain't come here to take you to jail."

Evelyn jiggled her glass in the air. "Somebody break out the wine. Looks like the shit has hit the fan!"

Ella Mae got up from the table. "Evelyn Renee Simms, I said y'all stop this mess!"

"Nyeela started it."

"And I'm finishin it. Now, put that doggone glass down. You don't need to be drinkin, no way."

"Why not?"

"Cuz it ain't good for that baby."

Evelyn sprung to her feet. "Who told you?"

"Neva mind! When was *you* gon' tell me?"

Evelyn looked down at Rowena. "Damn it, Rowena!"

Rowena shrugged her shoulders and shook her head. "What? I haven't said a word, Evelyn."

Nyeela folded her across her chest and shifted her weight to one leg. "And I bet you didn't tell Eve about Vee and me either, right?"

Evelyn's eyes grew. "You knew about them too, Rowena?"

Feeling completely ambushed, Rowena's mouth became arid. She stood up and surrendered her hands. "No. I swear, I just found out a few hours ago."

"I ain't likin this one bit," Ella Mae said, getting up from the table. "When y'all start keepin secrets from each otha? Neva mind. In the kitchen, right now," she ordered. "All of you!"

"Ma, what did I do?" Nyasia whined.

"Now!" Ella Mae said, pointing to the kitchen. "Rowena, you too!"

"Fellas, I think we betta leave," Melvin suggested.

"No, Melvin," Ella Mae insisted. "Y'all stay and enjoy dinna. Pour some wine. We'll be back in a minute. Bryson, take off ya jacket and stay a while."

"Yes, Ms. Banks," Bryson said, unbuttoning his coat.

Melvin introduced Bryson to the others while taking his jacket.

"You gotta excuse Pop, Bryson," Stacey explained. "He dun had a bad experience."

Bryson took a seat at the table. "It's okay," he said, with a smile.

"Have some dinna?"

"Thanks."

In the kitchen, Ella Mae demanded answers. "Somebody tell me what the heck jus' happened?"

Everyone spoke at once.

Ella Mae interrupted. "We ain't gettin nowhere wit all y'all talkin at the same time. Evelyn, why you ain't tell me you was pregnant?"

Evelyn began picking at her fingernails. "Thanks to Rowena, I didn't have a chance."

"Stop it! Rowena ain't had nothin to do wit it. Child, I ain't no fool. Have you forgot? I been pregnant twice. Anybody wit eyes can look at you and tell."

"I couldn't," Nyasia admitted.

"Walkin 'round here lookin and actin sick," Ella Mae fussed. "I don't know how you thought you was gon' keep it from me."

"I was going to tell you, Mother, after I decided what to do."

"What you mean *afta* you decide what to do?"

Evelyn drew in a heavy sigh. "You know what I mean."

"I know you had betta go and do the right thang!"

Evelyn cut her eyes at Rowena. "See what you did?"

Rowena cleared her throat. "I didn't say anything, Eve. I swear. As long as we've been friends, I have never betrayed you. You know you can't keep anything from your mother."

"Why did you betray *me*?" Nyeela demanded.

Rowena shook her head. "Nyeela, I told you earlier what you do is your business."

"You're supposed to be *my* best friend and you're keeping secrets for *Nyeela*?"

"Evelyn, stop actin like you in high school," Ella Mae insisted. "Nyeela, why did you hide this from me?"

"Hellooo!" Nyasia waved. "Can I please know why I'm in trouble?"

Evelyn jumped at the opportunity. "In case you hadn't noticed, that young man you brought in here is white?"

"Bryson? He's not white. He's just … Bryson."

"Nyeela Banks, I'm waitin for an answer," Ella Mae stated.

"Because I knew you would react this way, Mama."

"What way? Confused?"

"You are always hounding us about having a man and I knew not having an interest in one would be a problem."

"The only problem I got is all the lies. I taught y'all betta. Ova here pretendin to be somethin you ain't. You see what ya sista goin through. Ain't it taught ya nothin?"

"I'm sorry to interrupt, Ms. Ella," Rowena said, her voice cracking. "I think this is a private matter for you and your family and I really don't feel comfortable."

"You awright, Rowena? You ain't lookin so good."

"I'm a little tired."

"Go on upstairs and lie down a bit."

"Thanks, Ms. Ella. But with all due respect, I think I should leave."

"Stay. Finish dinna and sleep on it, baby."

"Yes, ma'am. I'll stay the night, but I've made my decision. I'm going to fly out in the morning."

Ella Mae put her hands on her hips. "Evelyn, what you got to say for ya'self? Ya friend say she leavin in the mornin.' Ain't you gon' 'pologize and ask her to stay?"

Evelyn folded her arms, turned her head, and shifted her weight to one leg.

"Y'all don't know how disappointed I am. Ya daddy mus' be turnin ova in his grave, right now."

"Mama..."

"Hush! I don't wanna hear anotha word, Nyeela. I jus' want y'all to go back in there and finish dinna like ya got some sense. We gon' deal wit this mess t'morra. Y'all can bet ya bottoms on it. Now, go on. We got men out there and we ain't gon' keep em waitin."

Nyeela rolled her eyes. Nyasia smiled. Evelyn sucked her teeth and Rowena struggled to keep her composure. They filed back into the dining room and took their places at the table.

"Ev'rythang awright, ladies?" Melvin asked.

"Right as rain," Ella Mae answered. "Now, pass me the ham. Bryson, baby where you from."

"I'm originally from New York, ma'am. We moved here when I was thirteen."

"You go to school wit Nyasia?"

"No, ma'am. We work together. I'm an assistant photographer."

"Aw, okay. Is ya food awright, Stacey?"

"Yes, ma'am. I ain't had a meal like this in a long time."

"I guess you gon' eat it all then," she nodded. "Mr. Charles don't say much, huh?"

"Pops ain't neva been much of a talka. He likes to sit back and watch."

"Seem like lil ole Bryson scared him," Ella Mae teased. "I thought he was gon' run on out the front door."

Laughter ensued. Everyone continued dinner as though nothing happened.

Early the next morning while Evelyn and the twins slept, Rowena packed her things and called a cab. Plagued by how quickly things turned awry, she hardly slept a wink. She never suspected Evelyn would turn on her or question her loyalty. Teary-eyed, she zipped her luggage, grabbed her purse, and quietly tiptoed down the stairs toward the front door.

Ella Mae made coffee in the kitchen. "Rowena, you gone?" she asked, peeping around the corner. "I heard ya cab outside blowin for ya."

"Yes, Ms. Ella," she said, walking over to hug her. "Thank you for making me feel at home."

Ella Mae reciprocated. "I want you to know ain't none of this ya fault," she said, cupping Rowena's face in her hand. "Give it a lil time. Thangs gon' be the same again. You'll see."

"I don't know," Rowena said, putting her purse on her shoulder. "It got pretty ugly in here yesterday."

Ella Mae grabbed her by the shoulders. "Listen. Them girls love you and so do I. Give em some time, baby," she smiled.

"Okay."

Ella Mae walked her to the door. "You come back real soon, ya hear?"

Rowena smiled. "Yes. I will."

"Have a safe trip!" Ella Mae said, waving goodbye.

*****

Exhausted beyond words, Rowena slept the entire flight back to Chicago. When she arrived home, there were two messages waiting on her machine.

Beep! "Rowena, this is Delwin. I know it's the holiday weekend but I'm having a little get together at my house tonight. If you are free, Lesa and I would love for you to attend. Of course, if you decide not to come, we'll certainly understand. Hope to see you soon. Goodbye." *Beep!*

Beep! "Miss Patterson, its Morgan. I just had to call and tell you that the gift certificate you gave me really blessed our Thanksgiving. Thank you, again. I hope you're having a wonderful time with your friends. Get some rest. You looked as if you could use it. I'll see you on Monday. Good Bye." *Beep!*

"So I've been told," she muttered. "Unfortunately, I can't say much for having a wonderful time, but at least I got some sleep." After an hour of dilly-dally, the stillness in the house grew unnerving. "Who am I kidding?" Rowena said aloud. "If I don't get dressed and go to this party, I'll be sitting here bored and depressed. Party, here I come," she said, calling to confirm her attendance.

Full of newly found energy, Rowena showered, slipped on her little black dress, and the black leather pumps Evelyn gave her last Christmas. She swept her hair up into a clean ponytail, rubbed a little gloss on her lips, and headed out the door.

Driving in silence, Rowena replayed the events that transpired on Thanksgiving Day. No matter how hard she tried, she couldn't pinpoint what went wrong. Was Nyeela right? Did Evelyn get away with more than she should have? Regardless of the details, Rowena wasn't ready to lose the only family she had left. She only wished it didn't bother her so much.

The first time Evelyn invited her over for dinner, she had changed her clothes several times before finally deciding on a denim skirt and a powder blue turtleneck. She tried to relax as she approached the door, but the excitement of gaining good friends overwhelmed her. She took a deep breath and rang the bell.

"Come on in," Evelyn said.

"Thanks," Rowena smiled. "I remembered that you like Martinis so I brought you a bottle of Grey Goose."

"Thanks," she said, taking the bottle. "Can I take your coat?"

"Sure." Rowena slipped off her coat. "You have a lovely home," she said, strolling through the living room.

"Thanks again! I told Grady you were coming and he can't wait to meet you. He should be here any minute." She hung the garment on the coat rack and took the Grey Goose to the kitchen.

"Great!" Rowena smiled.

"Come on in the kitchen," Evelyn insisted. "I'm finishing up dinner."

"Wow! Your kitchen is breathtaking," Rowena commented. "Did you do all the decorating yourself?"

"Ha! I wish. The creative genius behind this would be my husband Grady. He loves to do things like this in his spare time."

"Oh," Rowena nodded. "It must be nice."

"At times, and other times it can be a pain in the ass, if you know what I mean."

Rowena had no idea what she meant. "What's for dinner?"

"Seafood Lasagna. I hope you don't mind."

"I love seafood and lasagna!"

"Good. It happens to be one of my best dishes."

"You cook a lot?"

"Girl, no. I hate cooking. In fact, Grady calls me a restaurant fly. He says he doesn't understand why I hate cooking so much, when I come from a home with a mother who can turn a snack into a meal," she laughed.

"Really?"

Evelyn nodded. "Don't get me wrong. I've learned a few things from my mother, but I got this recipe from one of my colleagues at work. She believes a girl only needs one good recipe to impress her friends," she laughed, opening the bottle of Grey Goose. "So far it's working for me. Would you like to make the martinis?"

"Sure."

Grady returned home just as they were losing themselves in food and conversation. He didn't appear anything like she expected. Rowena imagined a tall, conservative, stately looking, man but in walked the total opposite. A man of medium build, brown skin, and mad sex appeal. Dressed in a leather black trench coat, with a grey scarf around his neck, he strode in and politely introduced himself. His charming demeanor immediately put her at ease. He

relieved himself of his outer garments, grabbed a plate, and joined them at the

table.

"Rowena, I've heard so much about you," he said. It's nice to finally meet

you."

"Same here, Grady. You've done a fabulous job decorating your home."

"You like it? I didn't think we were ever going to finish. Eve had a tough

time with all of the dust and stuff," he added. "But once the results became

apparent, she was all smiles."

"I can't deny it," she nodded. "He did do an amazing job!"

"To a job well done," he said, raising his glass. They toasted and finished

the evening with more laughter and conversation.

When Rowena left their home, she knew she had friends for life.

However, contending with Evelyn's emotional tidal wave caused

her to question the friendship. In retrospect, the events that

occurred on Thanksgiving Day, led her to face her own demons.

Without Evelyn or her job as a convenient distraction, she may

have fallen into a deep dark depression long ago. In order to take

better care of herself, a change was essential. Her desire to resume writing became an option, sooner rather than later. It would be therapeutic.

Rowena finally arrived at Delwin's house with the intention of staying for a little while. As she approached, she could feel the vibration of the music emanating from the house. She rang the bell and Delwin opened the door.

"Rowena, come in," he shouted over the music.

"Thanks. How are you?"

"Great! How about you?"

"I can't complain. It's good to see you again. Where's Lesa?"

"She's in the other room. Give me your coat and follow me."

Rowena handed him her coat, straightened her dress, and followed him through the foyer into the living room. "Wow! This looks like more than a little get together."

He shrugged his shoulders. "What can I say? These things never turn out the way you expect. Honestly, I didn't think *you* would come."

"Yeah, that makes two of us."

"How was your Thanksgiving?"

"Interesting, to say the least. Hey, Lesa!" Rowena said, waving across the room.

Lesa waved back and made her way toward them. "How are you, Rowena? I can't believe you came," she shouted, giving Rowena a hug.

"You guys were so nice to think of me. Showing up was the least I could do."

"So nice to think of you? We *are* still friends aren't we?" Delwin asked.

"Yes. You know what I meant," Rowena chuckled.

"Come on over here and let me introduce you to a few people. Greg, Lakenna, Kevin, Memphis, this is Rowena Patterson, a good friend of ours."

"Hello, everyone!"

"Hi!" They shouted in unison.

"Rowena, would you like something to drink?" Lesa offered.

"I'll have a glass of wine."

"Red or White?"

"White," she answered.

"Good choice!" a voice said over her shoulder. "Fancy meeting you here!"

Rowena turned around. "Dr. McDowell ... I mean, Memphis," she smiled.

He returned the grin. "Now, I've had the pleasure both times."

"Small world," she said, leaning in to avoid shouting.

"Yes, it is. You look amazing!"

"Thank you! How do you know Delwin and Lesa?" she inquired, pretending not to notice how good he looked.

Memphis stood five feet six inches, with fair skin and wavy brown hair. His eyes were a kiss of dark chocolate and his lips curved perfectly to produce a smile that could melt a heart of stone. "We golf together when time permits," he explained, catching her eyes.

"Oh. How nice," she said, nervously.

Lesa returned with a glass of wine. "Here's your drink, Rowena. Make yourself comfortable and help yourself to anything you see, including Memphis," she teased.

"Aren't you funny," she said, trying to deny the enchantment.

Lesa smiled and nudged her on the arm. "I'm just serious! Have a good time."

"Thanks, Lesa!"

"So ... How was your Thanksgiving?" Memphis inquired.

"Full of surprises. I spent it with Gail's sister-in-law, well former sister-in-law ... anyways. Speaking of Gail, how *is* she? And how is her little bundle of joy?"

"The last time I checked they were resting comfortably at home. I noticed how you were taken with little baby Eva. Do you have any children?"

Rowena cleared her throat and shook her head. "How does a doctor manage to get a Friday night off? Isn't there someone, somewhere in Chicago having a baby?"

"Funny you should ask. It was actually a bit slow tonight, so I took off."

"Lucky you."

"Hey, even the *best* doctors need a break, right?"

"And you're the best?"

"Can't you tell?"

"Achoo! Excuse me."

"Bless you!

"Thank you."

"Allergies?"

"Yeah. I'm allergic to bullshit."

"Oh. Okay," he laughed. "I guess I had that one coming. You're not feeling me, huh?"

"You're doing a great job feeling yourself," she said, taking a sip of wine.

He gently touched her hand. "Ah, but *you* feel much nicer. Tell me, Rowena. How can a guy like me get to spend some quality time with a beautiful lady like you?"

"Slow down, cowboy. I don't want to start sneezing again," she teased.

"Okay," he laughed. "I don't want to seem like a helicopter hovering all over you. It might make me appear suspect."

"Hm! Are you suspect?"

"Only for wanting to get to know you better"

"You're easy."

"Not easy, just taken. By you, of course."

Rowena smirked.

"What?" He smiled. "Don't tell me you feel a sneeze coming."

"I don't know," she said, putting her finger under her nose. "I think I feel a tickle in my nostrils."

"Well, I guess I better quit while I'm ahead. I wouldn't want you to break out in hives or anything. Enjoy the rest of your evening, Miss Lady," he said, raising his glass to her.

"Giving up so quickly? I didn't take you for a quitter," she taunted.

"My job is to help people get better, not make them feel worse."

"I'm only teasing. Please, I would like for you to stay."

"Good. I really didn't want to leave. I swear I've seen you somewhere before."

Rowena shrugged her shoulders. "I don't recall. But when you figure it out, let me know."

"What do you do, Rowena?"

"I write for the Tribune."

"So you work with Delwin."

"Yes."

"Nice! To be honest, I hardly ever read the papers or watch the news anymore. Too much focus on sensationalism and I get plenty of that from my line of work. Everything else is overkill."

"But there's plenty of critical information in the news. You would be surprised at how people want to stay in the know," she defended. "And with technology being the way it is, it gives us a greater platform."

"No doubt. Whether we watch it or read it, technology has given us the world at our fingertips. Maybe one day, I'll get a chance to check out your column. What's your area of expertise?"

"Current Events."

"That'll keep you busy."

"It does and I prefer it that way. I think I'm pretty fortunate to have a job where I do what I love—write."

"Oh, absolutely! What else do you write?"

"I used to write poetry in high school but...."

"But...?"

"I've been too busy to write personally. I plan to start making time for it though."

"Great! You should always make time for that which brings you joy."

"Who said anything about getting joy from it?"

"You didn't have to say it. Your eyes lit up when you mentioned it."

"You don't miss a thing, do you?"

"It's part of my training. If I tell you, you take my breath away, are you going to start sneezing again?"

Rowena laughed.

His pager went off. "So much for a slow night," he sighed.

"Hey, you said it yourself. Nobody can deliver a baby like you."

"I did say that, didn't I? I guess I better get to it then."

"I guess you better."

"Is there any chance we can finish this conversation over dinner?"

Rowena paused a moment, to give herself time to digest the obvious chemistry between them. She knew if she didn't take the time to explore it, she would have regrets. "Perhaps, you can take my card. Call me when you get some free time."

"Count on it. Enjoy the rest of your evening, Rowena."

She smiled. "Thanks!"

Memphis bid everyone goodnight and left.

Feeling bored and lonely, Rowena glanced at her watch and decided to leave. After briefly scanning the room for the hosts, she spotted Lesa and waved frantically over the music to get her attention.

"Everything okay, Rowena?"

"Yes." She smiled. "Unfortunately, I'm a little jetlagged. I think I'm going to call it a night and head on home."

"Say no more. I understand and I'm so glad you came," she said, rubbing Rowena's arm.

"Where's Delwin?"

"I don't know. He's around here somewhere, but don't worry, I'll tell him you said, goodnight."

"Thanks for everything, Lesa. I'll call you guys soon. Good night."

Rowena found her coat and walked out into the crisp night air. Under the dark blue sky, she could see her breath in front of her. She hurried to her vehicle to warm up. She switched on the radio as she drove along. "Oh, India.Arie. I love her," she said, increasing the volume. The song "Ready for Love," played to the finish. By the end of the song, Rowena was inconsolable. She pulled over to the side of the road and tried to compose herself. Her cell phone rang. She paused to catch her breath before answering.

"Hello, this is Rowena," she said, barely above a whisper.

"Hi Beautiful! It's Memphis. I hope it's not too soon to call."

"No. It's fine."

"Just checking to make sure this number was real," he laughed. *"You know how you women like to send us men off with bogus numbers,"* he teased.

"Oh," she said, trying to lighten her mood. "I guess I'm one of those women who prefer to keep it real."

"I can appreciate that. Were you busy?"

"I'm actually on my way home. I'm a little tired, so I left early."

"Well, I won't keep you. I've got a baby to deliver."

"Okay."

"Are you going to be okay?"

"Why do you ask?"

"You sound weary."

"It's been a long week."

"I'd love to hear about it over dinner."

"You don't give up, do you?"

"Afraid not. Anyway, get some rest and I'll talk to you soon."

"I will. Thanks. Goodnight."

"Goodnight."

Rowena pulled herself together and continued driving to an all night superstore where she purchased a couple of notebooks. The time had come for her to rid herself of the storm brewing inside. Once home, she undressed, slipped into her pajamas and sat in the center of the bed with her legs folded beneath her. Like an empty canvas, the blank sheets of paper invited her to purge. She wrote:

Tonight, I broke down. I couldn't keep it at bay any longer. For some reason, I feel so vulnerable and empty, like I'm missing something or someone. I've been giving to everyone except myself and here I am, all alone. Is this who I am? For the first time ever, Eve isn't speaking to me and I pray this isn't the end of our friendship. I cannot and I will not let that happen. I'm afraid to death of losing her. I wonder if she feels the same way I do. I know she loves me and she probably just needs a little space. Maybe we both do. I keep telling myself it will be okay. It has to be. Memphis,

Memphis, Memphis. Who is he? And what, in the world, does he want from me? I refuse to be hurt again. I'm so exhausted. Maybe I need to go see Dr. Kerrigo. Note to self: Make an appt. to see doc on Monday.

Rowena guzzled several glasses of water before finally going to bed.

The next morning, she experienced a prickly sensation in her legs. The tips of her toes were completely numb and she couldn't get out of bed. She lay there until 11 a.m. then forced herself into the shower, hoping to get her blood circulating. It helped, but not much. As soon as she walked out of the bathroom, the phone rang.

"Hello?"

"Hi, Rowena. It's Gail."

"Hey, Gail. How are you?"

"I can't complain. I didn't expect to catch you at home. How was your trip?"

"Interesting. How is the baby?"

"She is wonderful. I just finished feeding her and now she's sleeping. How is Evelyn?"

"Um, what can I say? She's coping."

"I don't mean to pester you about her but she has been heavy on my mind. I'm not sure when it's a good time to call her."

"Anytime, Gail. I'm sure a friendly voice would do her some good."

"Okay. I'll give her a call today. How's it going with you?"

"It's going. I haven't been feeling like myself lately. I think I need to visit to my doctor."

"What's wrong?"

"Girl, I'm exhausted."

"Been working yourself too much?"

"Yeah. I'm going to take some time this weekend and try to relax a bit."

"Speaking of doctor, I wanted to tell you what Dr. McDowell said about you."

"It's funny you mentioned him. I ran into him last night at a friend's house."

"And?"

"And what? We conversed over a glass of wine."

"Well, he wanted to know how long you and I have been friends and if you were married."

"Really?"

"Yes. I told him you were single and he couldn't believe it."

"Hm! I don't know why."

"Apparently, he thinks you're a gorgeous woman. Of course, I agreed."

"Oh, stop it."

"Really, Rowena. He's right. And girl, you deserve some love in your life."

"Thank you, Gail. That's sweet of you. Let me ask you something. How much do you know about him?"

"I know he's very professional, good at what he does, and he comes highly recommended. He is also kind, gentle, and compassionate with his patients. Between you and I, the word around the hospital is he doesn't date co-workers."

"Why is that?"

"Supposedly, he thinks it's a bad idea."

"What?"

"And he's not gay or anything, if that's what you were thinking."

"Nice, Gail. Thanks."

"So are you going to check him out?"

"Oops! Someone is at the door," she lied. "I'll have to call you back."

"Okay. I'll talk to you soon!"

The mention of Memphis not being gay both amused and relieved Rowena. She gave serious thought to having dinner with him and wondered if her life would be better with a man in it. Though she wasn't keen on dating out of desperation, Ella Mae's words kept ringing in her head. "One is the lonelies' numba you gon' eva do."

Chapter Eleven

Saturday morning brought chilly weather to South Carolina and the girls had barely spoken to each other, since Thanksgiving dinner. Ella Mae prepared breakfast and demanded that they attend. They arrived in the kitchen one by one. Ella Mae immediately ordered them to take a seat.

"Mornin," she said, putting on her glasses.

"Good Morning," they mumbled.

"Time to iron this mess out, cuz I won't have y'all in my house anotha day, ignorin each otha. Y'all already know how disappointed I am in you. Evelyn, I'm gon' start wit you, cuz you the oldes' and you know betta. I know you goin through, but darn it, you gotta get a grip! The world don't owe you nothin, cuz you dun found out ya husband is gay."

"I know, Mother."

"Well you need to act like you know."

Evelyn lowered her head and pulled on the button of her pajama top.

"You ain't neva gon' change that man. It is what it is. All you can do is thank God ya found out when ya did. That otha stuff is just a waste of energy. Let folk be who they are, so you can be who you are. It's that simple."

"It's anything but simple, Mother," she said, with a quivering lip.

"The only thang makin it hard is that attitude. Time to start lookin at life diff'rent, child. You gon' find love again, but you gotta let go of the pas.' Time to figure out what you gon' do wit ya life. You 'bout to be somebody's mama."

"I'm trying," she sniffled. "But I can't apologize any more than I already have."

"I ain't askin for no 'pologies, Evelyn. Jus' make the change. Okay?"

Evelyn nodded and wiped her tears.

"And Nyeela, you 'round here pretendin to be 'miss goody-two shoes,' when all the time you been hidin stuff."

"No I wasn't, Mama."

"Hush wit the lies! Walkin 'round here agitatin ya sistas and hidin ya lil friends," Ella Mae said, crossing her arms. "This is a lovin house and we ain't neva gave you a reason to hide who ya are."

"Yes you have, Mama."

Ella Mae looked askance at Nyeela. "When, child? I dun teased you 'bout bein a tomboy, but I always do that. God knows I ain't mean no harm. If it hurt ya feelins, you shudda said somethin. How come you ain't said nothin?"

Nyeela shrugged. "I don't know."

"I ain't neva been one to act funny wit folk. God made us all and we all his chil'ren. Whetha we like it or not, we gotta live on this earth togetha, so we may as well do it in peace. I love all my girls. Ain't nothin gon' change that."

Nyeela looked at Ella Mae and nodded.

"And Miss Nyasia, Lawd knows I dun had some uncomftable situations wit white folk in this life. But it don't mean I hate em. I judge folk by they character and not they skin color. Jus' cuz some folk is ignant don't mean we all gotta be." She drew long sigh. "I'm done now."

Nyeela cleared her throat. "I know you love me, Mama. I was scared, but that's no excuse for my behavior. Sorry for being deceitful."

Evelyn placed her hand on Nyeela's shoulder. "I love you too, baby sis. Home should be the one place you can be vulnerable and I'm sorry if I took that away from you."

"Apology accepted, Eve. And I take back all the snide remarks I made about you and Grady."

"How did you know about him?"

"I overheard you talking on the phone."

"So you were snooping?"

"Only by accident, I swear. I came to apologize about the night before and I overheard you say his name. I'm sorry."

"It's done and over with, Nyeela. Let it go."

"Ma, I wasn't trying to hide Bryson from you. I just never thought I needed to announce that I was dating a white guy. I'm sorry. I'm proud of my family."

"That ain't the point, Nyasia. You cudda brought him 'round here a lot soona."

"Yes, ma'am."

"I want y'all to promise this won't eva happen again."

"We promise."

"Awright. Now, go on eat ya breakfast. I got some errands to run. Eve, you want me to bring you anythang back?"

"Some crackers would be nice."

"Awright. I'll be back shortly." Ella Mae removed her apron and went to grab her purse. She returned with a ringing cell phone and handed it to Evelyn.

"Oh, thanks. Hello?"

"Hi, Eve! It's Gail."

"Hi, Gail. It's nice to hear from you! How are you?"

"I'm doing fine. It's nice to hear your voice, too. How's your mom?"

"Mother is fine. She is walking out the door now to run a few errands. How is everyone there?"

"They're fine. I'm expecting Mom and Dad a little later."

"Give them my love. Someone sounds a little unhappy in the background."

"Yeah, that's Eva Lynn. She just woke up. She's probably wet."

"You want me to let you go so you can change her?"

"No. I got it. Besides, I've been anxious to talk to you. How have you been?"

"I'm doing the best I can with the support of my family. Unfortunately, they're catching all the hell Grady should be catching."

"Have you spoken to him at all?"

"A couple of times, but not enough to satisfy me."

"I'm afraid we haven't seen much of him either, after he told us what happened."

"You mean, he told you the truth?"

"Yes. He did. Of course, we were shocked. Dad was a little disappointed, but you know how it goes. All in all, we still love him very much."

"The truth can be hard to handle sometimes but I guess it's better than living a lie."

"You've got a point."

"Rowena told me your inspiration for naming the baby Eva Lynn."

"It's simple. We love you, Eve."

"Thanks for saying it, Gail. The feeling is mutual."

"What happened between you and Grady changes nothing between us."

"It's nice to hear."

"Speaking of Rowena, I spoke to her this morning."

"Did you? How is she?"

"She says she hasn't been feeling well."

"Really? She did seem a little jetlagged during her visit."

"Maybe you ought to check on her."

"I will."

"Well, I won't keep you. I'll give Mom and Dad your love and I'll talk to you later."

"Okay, Gail. Talk to you soon. Goodbye."

For a moment, Evelyn considered calling Rowena, but the timing didn't feel right. She and the twins cleaned up the kitchen and went about their individual activities for the day. Ella Mae returned and took a nap. The doorbell rang. Evelyn answered the door.

"Hi, Stacey. What are you doing here?"

"I jus' wanted to stop by and thank ya mama for dinna."

"Oh, she's in her room taking a nap right now. Would you like to come in?"

"Thanks."

"Can I offer you some sweet tea or soda?"

"Tea would be nice."

"Okay. Have a seat. I'll be right back."

"Thank ya." The sole reason for Stacey's visit wasn't to thank Ella Mae for dinner, but to see Evelyn again before going back to Nashville. He didn't know how to tell her of his attraction, without coming on too strong. He wanted to remain sensitive to the challenges she faced.

Evelyn returned with two glasses of sweet tea.

"Thank ya," he said, taking a glass.

Evelyn sat on the sofa across from him. "My pleasure. How's your dad?"

"Good," he said, taking a seat. "Melvin took him fishin this mornin and now he's wiped out. We gon' be leavin t'marro."

"I see," she said, initiating a brief silence. "I should apologize for the other day. Things got a little out of hand."

"Aw, it ain't nothin. Families fight."

"Yes, but not in front of total strangers."

"We ain't strangas no more," he smiled.

Evelyn smiled. "Thank you for understanding," she said, relaxing in her seat. A few seconds passed before the inevitable crept into her mind. She swept her hair off her face and pushed the embarrassing thought into the background.

"It ain't hard to undastand somethin ya dun already been through."

"Meaning?"

"I ain't neva been married but I been in a long-term relationship before. Let's jus' say it ain't turn out the way I wanted."

"How long were you two together?" Evelyn could feel the question about his sexuality creeping up her throat.

"Three years."

She cleared her throat. "Wow! Three years is a long time to be with someone," she said, wondering if she should just go ahead and ask the question.

"Been even longa since we broke up," he continued.

"Was it a nasty breakup?"

"More hurtful than anythang."

"If you don't mind me asking, what happened?" *And are you gay*, she thought.

"I caught her and my cousin togetha."

"Ouch!"

"Yeah, I blamed myself for lettin him stay wit us while he and his wife was separated."

"Wow! How did it end?"

"He got a divorce and I was single again."

"Sounds like you were very forgiving."

"No sense in me bein miserable on account of them. I figured they was jus' desp'rate."

"I can understand him being desperate, vulnerable even, but what was her excuse?"

"I worked too much."

"Why not end the relationship then?"

"I ain't sure what was goin on in her head."

"Can I ask you a personal question?"

"Sho."

"Have you ever had any experiences with other men?"

"Experiences like what?" Stacey asked, scratching his brow.

She cleared her throat again. "Sexual experiences," she said, sipping her iced tea.

"Oh, hell no! I like to be wit women and women only."

"No offense, but I had to ask," she said, jingling the ice around in her glass.

"None taken."

"You can never be too sure these days."

"I undastand ya reason for askin.' If I was in that situation, I would ask too."

"You think you know a person after spending several years together. And then something happens and you realize you never really knew them at all."

"So true."

"Somewhere over the years, we grew apart and by the time he announced the divorce, we were already spiritually disconnected."

"Did y'all eva discuss counselin?"

"Honestly, not as much as I wanted to, but I figured I couldn't live with myself, if I didn't try everything I could to save my marriage. When he shut down, I knew we were over."

"Musta been hard."

"Sobering is more like it."

"Sometimes, we go through thangs to shake us up. I think it's a blessin really. We get so comf'table livin day to day and start takin stuff for granted. The thang is ya gotta keep movin forward and do somethin wit the lessons ya learn."

"I guess."

"Kinda hard to believe you couldn't tell somethin was up wit him."

"I had my suspicions. When he finally admitted he was gay, it made me angry as hell. I'm not homophobic or anything, but when you lose your man in such a way, the feelings are indescribable."

"I hope I ain't oversteppin too much or nothin, but why don't you try?"

"Try what?"

"Try puttin ya feelins into words."

Evelyn paused at the thought and then found the words. "Rejected, not woman enough, failure, and deceived; those are a few words that come to mind."

"See? Now you can work on fixin it."

"Somebody forgot to mention a degree in psychology."

He laughed. "Naw, I jus' know we got choices. Maybe we can't change how we got here, but we can choose how we move on."

"I guess in a sense, I already knew that but when shit happens, you tend to forget. Thanks for the reminder."

"We all need remindin ev'ry once in a while," he smiled. "Well, I should be goin. Melvin probly need a break."

"So soon? I would really like it if you could stay for dinner. I like having someone to talk to who understands. I'm sure Mother wouldn't mind."

"I don't wanna impose."

"It's no imposition, really. I want you to."

"Awright. I'm gon' call Melvin and make sho it's okay wit him."

"Great. I'll go and let Mother know you'll be staying." Evelyn trekked upstairs and Stacey phoned Melvin.

"Melvin, how's ev'rythang?"

"Fine. Uncle Charles still sleep. I guess I wore him out pretty good."

"That fresh air make him sleep like a baby, mane. I'm ova Ms. Ella's house and Evelyn want me to stay for dinna. Okay by you?"

"Go head. Ella Mae and I plan to eat dinna here tonight."

"Oh. Evelyn thought Ms. Ella was cookin dinna."

"She was before I invited her ova here. You in good hands."

"Okay," he laughed. "I'll see ya later on. Call me if you need anythang."

"I won't. You enjoy ya'self. You need it."

"Yes, sir. Goodbye!"

Evelyn returned. "Everything okay?"

"Ev'rythang is wondaful. He and Ms. Ella already made plans for dinna."

"She told me. I don't know about you, but I've had about all the Thanksgiving food I can stand. How about going out for dinner, since it's just you and I?"

"Okay."

"Knowing the girls, they'll probably grab something on the way home."

"No problem. What time we leavin?"

"It's about four o'clock now. I know a place where we can take a nice little walk, before dinner."

"Good."

"I'll just grab my jacket and we can go."

It was well after ten o'clock when Evelyn and Stacey returned from dinner. "Stacey, I've had the most wonderful evening. Thanks for helping me to get out of my head for a while."

"Naw, thank you for makin this a trip I ain't gon' forget."

"Oh, I think I had plenty of help in that area."

"That ain't what I meant, but let's keep in touch."

"I would love to. Call me anytime."

"I will and the same goes for you. Anytime you wanna talk." He kissed Evelyn on the cheek and said goodnight.

Evelyn went to her room and dressed for bed. Nyeela knocked on the door. Evelyn invited her in.

"Hey, Eve."

"Hey! I didn't hear you come in."

Nyeela sat on the bed. "You weren't here when we got home."

"Oh. What's up?"

"Nothing. Since you've been home, we haven't really been able to get reacquainted."

"I know," Evelyn said, sitting next to her.

"You look pretty tired though."

"Honestly, I'm pooped. But not too pooped for my baby sis."

"Mama told me you were out with Stacey."

"Hm! I'm not surprised."

"He seems like a cool person."

"He is. We went for a nice walk and then sat down for dinner. And you know what the best part is?"

"What?"

"He's not gay," she smiled. "No offense."

Nyeela returned the smile. "None taken."

"It seems we have a lot in common."

"Like?" Nyeela asked.

"Bad break-ups, for one."

"Who hasn't had one?"

"You haven't," Evelyn asserted.

"Never mind that. Talk to me about you."

"Me? I'm hanging in there."

"And your heart? Is it starting to heal?"

Evelyn paused to ponder the question. "Slowly," she said.

"Can I share something with you?"

"Absolutely."

"Being honest about my sexuality was just as hard as it was to hide it."

"Hm."

"I'm not trying to make excuses, I'm sharing *my* experience. If I seem angry, it's because it shouldn't be this difficult to be who you are in a world that claims we have the right to life, liberty, and the pursuit of happiness."

"Nyeela, we're all angry about something. To tell you the truth, I have never had a problem with gays and lesbians. I still don't. But I *do* have a problem with my husband coming home night after night pretending to love me, knowing all the time his heart was elsewhere. You don't know what it's like to wonder, which part of your marriage was fake and which part was real? Every woman wants to be the center of her man's world and I wasn't; not in a way that counted. Can you imagine what that feels like?"

"I imagine it must be devastating."

"When he vowed to love and cherish me, he lied."

"I don't know what Grady was thinking when he took those vows. I was in the seventh grade when I realized I liked girls."

"Really?"

"I had the biggest crush on my science teacher. I certainly couldn't tell anyone because of the obvious, but I couldn't stop thinking about her. I would make excuses to get out of my seat and go up to her desk, just to be near her. Her beauty was intoxicating."

"I wasn't around to see you and Nyasia go on any dates. Were you ever attracted to boys?"

"Not in the least. Of course, there were boys who were cute, but not in a way that attracted me. Initially, I forced myself to go out with them. I wanted to see if my feelings would change, but they didn't. Every time a boy tried to hold my hand or touch my hair, I wanted to kick his ass. It just didn't feel natural."

Evelyn laughed. "You were such a tomboy."

"I grew tired of pretending, so I stopped dating altogether. However, I quietly maintained my attraction to females."

"It's pretty noble of you to remain true to yourself. Too bad, I can't say the same for Grady. He went about this whole situation wrong."

"You have to keep in mind that there are no manuals on how to deal with these things, Eve. We're all trying to figure it out as we go along."

Evelyn nudged her in the side. "Hey, I'm supposed to be giving you advice. Not the other way around."

Nyeela giggled. "I'm just trying to help. I'm sure Grady loved you or he wouldn't have gone through the trouble."

"The jury is still out on that one, sis. Even if he did, it's still going to take some time for me to work through my resentment."

"What are you going to do about the baby?"

"I still haven't decided yet."

"Well, how much time do you have?"

"I'm not sure. If I had to guess, I'd say I'm about six weeks along."

"This means you have about six more weeks to make your decision. Not to put any pressure on you or anything, but it would be nice to have a nephew."

"Ha! No pressure there."

"Sorry," Nyeela smiled. "Your skin is glowing. Is that normal?"

"I don't know. I wish my insides were glowing."

"Hey, if I could get through Thanksgiving dinner with my integrity still intact, so can you. This too shall pass."

"From your lips. Tell me about your friend."

Nyeela smiled. "Tanvi is a gem. She's my best friend, besides Twin, of course. I feel comfortable enough to say and do anything around her. She's smart, spontaneous, and sexy as hell."

Evelyn folded her leg beneath her. "Do you love her?"

"I'm not *in* love with her."

"What the hell does that mean?"

"For me, it means our relationship isn't more important than the things I hold valuable. Personally, I think love is overrated. Two people can have great chemistry without losing themselves in love. Tanvi knows I'm not in love with her and she understands. We have a great connection but right now, my focus is on my career. I can't afford to have my nose open."

"Girl, life is too short to live just for a career. Haven't you learned anything from Mother and me?"

"Yeah and right now you sound just like her. I love Mama, but I have no intention of ending up like her, squandering eighteen years of my life mourning love. It's better to be safe than sorry."

"And you call that living?"

Nyeela shrugged her shoulders. "Works for me."

"Oh well, I guess you have to learn like the rest of us. You can't control everything."

"I'm sorry about you and Grady *and* for the way I treated Rowena. She didn't deserve it."

"You're right. She didn't. She's been great and I treated her like crap. I couldn't blame her if she never wanted to see me again."

"You haven't spoken to her?"

"No. We both need some space. I've already consumed way too much of her time with my foolishness. Truth be told, she's probably happy that she doesn't have to be bothered."

"I doubt it. Rowena loves you, unconditionally. I think she appreciates how much you make her feel needed. You know we're the only family she has. I'm going to call her and apologize first thing tomorrow."

Evelyn straightened her posture. "Answer this. Were you the least bit attracted to her?"

"Why?"

"I thought I caught you eyeing her a couple times and it struck me as odd."

"Honestly, yes. I found her quite charming, but I swear if you ever tell her, I'll kill you."

"Don't worry," she smiled. "Your secret is safe with me."

"You promise?"

"I promise, girl."

"Good."

Evelyn picked at her nails. "I think I'm going to wait until the time is right, to call her."

"Any time is the right time, when it comes to doing the right thing. But whatever!"

Evelyn glanced at her watch. "Where's your twin?"

"I think she and Bryson went to the movies or something."

"You knew all the time he was white, didn't you?"

Nyeela shrugged her shoulders. "It wasn't a big deal to me."

"Well it shocked the hell out of me."

"Why?"

"Because none of us ever dated outside of our race."

"How would you know? You weren't here."

"I just assumed…"

"The world *is* evolving, Eve. You wouldn't happen to have anything against white people, would you?"

"Don't be silly, Nyeela. I don't have anything against anyone, except Grady, of course."

"Okay. I thought I would ask because your reaction seemed a little over the top."

"Like I said, I've never considered dating outside of my race and I assumed the same about you two. That's all. I'm happy that one of you isn't afraid to open up to the experience. I wonder what his parents think."

"I don't think Nyasia or Bryson really cares what anybody thinks. I'm surprised she waited this long."

"Did you see the way she casually waltzed him in here?"

"Yeah," Nyeela laughed.

"She's so cute with her little self."

"Hey!"

"So are you," Evelyn smiled. "Looking at her is just like looking at you."

"Yeah, okay. Goodnight, Eve!"

"Goodnight, baby sis!"

Chapter Twelve

In Chicago, Rowena struggled to stay hydrated. An hour into a *Cosby Show* marathon on television, she received a text message on her cell phone:

Memphis: Hello Beautiful! This is Memphis.

Rowena: Hi!

Memphis: Had sum free time. Thought of u. Hope I'm not interrupting.

Rowena: Nope. Just bored out of my mind.

Memphis: I'm off n a few hours. Join me 4 dinner?

Rowena: Um…OK.

Memphis: How about sushi?

Rowena: Luv it!

Memphis: There's a spot in Oak Lawn. Best n town.

Rowena: A name & address would help lol!

Memphis: Chi Tung, 96th Kedzie. 7:30?

Rowena: Perfect. C U there.

Memphis: Can't wait!

Rowena had never been to Chi Tung but she had heard the food was great. Her heart palpitated as she rushed to find something comfortable to wear. After pulling her entire wardrobe from the closet, she finally decided on a pair of faded jeans and a nice crisp, white blouse. She slipped on the jeans and modeled them around in the mirror, admiring her curves. Together with the blouse, she had a perfect match. Then she realized she hadn't combed her hair all day. "Damn, I'm turning into Evelyn," she grumbled. With only an hour left to get ready, she quickly curled her hair, fastened silver hoop earrings into her ears, traced her lips with a little gloss, and dashed out the door.

During the drive, Rowena tried to rationalize why she agreed to have dinner with Memphis. It felt like centuries since her last date and anxiety was starting to mount. What if I make a complete fool of myself in front of him, she thought. Am I desperate for agreeing to dinner so soon? She pulled out a piece of gum and pushed it into her mouth. "Hell, I need to let somebody wine and dine me after the week I've had."

Memphis was waiting patiently at the entrance when Rowena arrived. She pulled up and handed the keys to the valet. Memphis took her by the hand. "Aren't you a sight for sore eyes?"

Rowena blushed. "Thanks!"

Memphis opened the door for her. "How are you?"

"Happy to get out of the house."

"That bad, huh?"

"Haven't spent that much time at home since I had the place."

"And I thought *I* was a workaholic. Table for two, please," he told the host.

"Wait a minute," she whispered, trying to catch her balance. "The room is spinning."

"Are you okay?"

"I think I need to sit down," she said, before collapsing to the floor.

Memphis shouted to the host to call an ambulance. He checked her vitals and called her name. Rowena didn't respond. The host returned with the manager, who assured him the ambulance was on the way. A small crowd gathered as Memphis took off his jacket and placed it underneath her head. He requested cold water and a wet towel from the manager. He sprinkled the water on her face and placed the towel on her forehead. Rowena opened her eyes partially, for a second or two, and then blacked out again. Memphis asked the crowd to back away and give her some air. He dabbed the towel at her cold clammy face, until the ambulance arrived.

*****

The ambulance transported Rowena to the hospital where Memphis worked. He called ahead to his colleague, Dr. Druvhi, who had a bed and an I.V. port ready when they arrived. The slight pinch of the needle in Rowena's arm woke her up. She was surprised to find Memphis at her side.

"What's going on?" she asked.

"Relax. Don't worry. You fainted at the restaurant and we rushed you to the emergency room. This is Dr. Druvhi, the attending physician and a good friend of mine."

"Miss Patterson, how are you feeling?" Dr. Druvhi asked.

"I'm not sure yet," she said. "But something cold is flowing through my veins."

"It's your I.V. drip. We implemented it to keep you hydrated. The feeling will dissipate in a moment. Do you have dizzy spells often?"

"No. This is the first time."

"Is there anything unusual you'd like to tell me?"

"I've been feeling very tired, lately."

"How long have you been feeling this way?"

"About a week now."

"Anything else?"

"Um, yes. I've been extremely thirsty."

"Okay."

"And recently I experienced a prickly sensation in my legs."

"Miss Patterson, when was your last menstrual period?"

"Oh, I'm not pregnant."

"How do you know?"

Rowena cleared her throat. "Um... I had my cycle two weeks ago."

"Okay. We're going to run a series of tests over the next twenty-four hours, which means you'll be staying the night."

"Great," she said, closing her eyes. "Just what I need. More time to watch television."

"We're going to move you to a private room, now. If you have any questions, feel free to ask myself or Dr. McDowell."

"Oh, you mean my sidekick over here?"

"We're on a date, remember?" he said, rubbing her arm.

"Well, this is one date you don't have to worry about getting the bill for," she said, rolling her eyes.

"I see your sense of humor is still intact."

"This isn't exactly how I pictured spending my night."

"Look at the positive side. At least you get to find out what's going on with you. Spinning rooms can't be fun."

"Not at my age," she paused. "And I had my mouth all set for sushi," she said, pouting.

He smiled. "No worries. I've got a rain check for that."

"Great! What's a girl have to do to keep from being stuck in this place all night? I've got people to see, things to do."

"Like what?"

"Being bored out of my mind in my *own* bed."

"You've got jokes!"

"I'm serious."

"Well if it's company you want, then company is what you're going to get."

"Don't you have a baby to deliver?"

"I'm here if they need me."

"That's right. You work here don't you? Was that on purpose?"

"No, but I couldn't be happier. Listen. I know you don't want to be here, but we have to make sure you're going to be alright."

"No. I really *don't* want to be here," she smiled. "But I like the attention."

Two male nurses came in to transport Rowena from emergency care. Memphis followed as they wheeled her to a private room.

"Is there someone you want me to call?" he asked.

Rowena drew in a sigh and lowered her head. "No. But thanks."

"You sure?"

"Yep! Can you get me some water?" she asked. "My mouth is dry."

"Sure. I'll be right back."

Rowena covered her mouth and fought back her tears. She wondered why a total stranger would go beyond the call of duty, to make sure she was okay.

Memphis returned accompanied by Dr. Druvhi and a pitcher of water. "Have you ever been tested for diabetes, Miss Patterson?"

"No. Why do you ask?"

"It appears you may be showing early signs. Tell me about your family. Any history of diabetes?"

"My father suffered from diabetes. I was young when he died, but I remember the injections he gave himself."

"Insulin injections?"

"Yes."

"I see," he said, writing on the clipboard.

"I don't mean to rude, but how long will this take?"

"Try to be a little patient — no pun intended. It shouldn't be too long now. By the way, who is your primary physician?"

"Dr. Pettis Kerrigo."

"I recommend you see him right away. In the meantime, I'll need the test results before I can make a full diagnosis, okay?"

"I understand."

"Good. Someone will be in shortly to take you down," Dr. Druvhi said, patting her on the shoulder. He smiled at Memphis and left.

Memphis gazed at Rowena with concern. "Your health is very important, you know."

She nodded in agreement. "I know. I haven't been sick in a long time, but I had planned to call him on Monday."

"I hope I'm not being pushy, but someone as beautiful as you shouldn't be lying in a hospital bed."

"Isn't so attractive, is it?"

"Lying in a hospital bed?"

"Being helpless."

"I don't want you to start sneezing or anything, but helpless hadn't even crossed my mind."

"I think I feel a slight tickle," she said, wiggling her nose.

Memphis laughed. "You're not helpless *yet*. However, if you continue to ignore your body, eventually you will be. Lucky for you, I'm here to make sure that doesn't happen."

"Lucky me. What would I do without you, Mr. Medicine Man?"

Memphis smiled and leaned in. "It's a good thing you won't have to find out," he said, lightly thumping the tip of her nose.

She blushed and bit her bottom lip.

Memphis left the room to confer with Dr. Druvhi.

Rowena's heart skipped a beat and a warm fuzzy feeling filled the pit of her stomach. The newness of it all frightened her, yet she wanted more. There were still things she didn't know about him. Why was he single? Where did he come from? And why did he care so much about her?

As promised, nurse came in to transport her to the lab. "Miss Patterson, I'm going to take you downstairs for your tests now. She pulled the curtain across the room. "First, I need you to put your garments in this bag," she said, holding up a clear plastic bag. "And then I need you to put on this hospital gown, okay?"

"Okay." Rowena did as instructed. When she was ready, the nurse drew back the curtain.

Memphis returned. "Is there anything I can get for you?"

"Some food would be nice," she answered.

"No problem. It'll be here when you get back."

Rowena smiled and sat down in the wheelchair. The nurse rolled her out of the room and down the hall. An hour later, she returned to an empty room with a tray table by the bedside. The nurse helped her into bed and pulled the tray table within reach, before leaving the room. Rowena couldn't wait to see the goodies lying beneath the cover of the plate. She was famished. She lifted the cover and found a hearty, roast beef sandwich, mashed potatoes, gravy, and a fruit cup. After eating every thing on the plate, she fell off to sleep.

The next morning Memphis returned with a bouquet of flowers and small teddy bear. Careful not to disturb her, he quietly placed the gifts on the night table and relieved himself of his coat. Slightly hovered over Rowena's body, he leaned in close to examine her peaceful demeanor. His eyes traced the contours of her face, from the top of her thin shaped eyebrows to the tip of her nose, which glistened with perspiration. A dab of pink gloss coated her full round lips. As he resisted the urge to taste them, it dawned on him why she seemed familiar to him. The memory brought a smile to his face. Lying before him was the same lady he saw in the pancake restaurant weeks earlier. The warmth of his breath on Rowena's cheeks woke her. Memphis slowly retreated.

"Did you sleep well?" he asked.

She cleared her throat and sat up in the bed. "Yes. Thank you."

"How do you feel?"

"Much better," she said, wiping the matter from her eyes. "Did I sleep all night?"

"It appears that way."

Rowena spotted the flowers and teddy bear. "Are those for me?"

"Absolutely!"

"How sweet! Honestly, I didn't know what to think when I came back and you were gone."

"Duty called. I had to go and deliver a baby."

"Oh, I forgot. Sorry."

"No need to be sorry. Did I miss anything?"

"Just a good meal."

"I'm glad you liked it," he said.

Rowena took the flowers in her hands. "These are beautiful!"

"I'm glad you like those too," he smiled.

Dr. Druvhi entered. "Miss Patterson, your test result came back positive for diabetes. Now, it doesn't mean you automatically have to have insulin shots like your father, but you will need to make some major changes and possibly take medication. A change of diet, regular exercise, and weight management should make you more comfortable."

Rowena's heart sank with the news. "Are you sure?"

"Yes. It's not as bad as it sounds. I'm going to forward all of this information to your doctor and let him make the official diagnosis. It's very important that you follow up with him as soon as possible. Okay?" he said, carefully removing the I.V. from her arm.

"Does this mean I'm free to go?" she asked, holding her arm very still.

"Yes. The nurses are preparing your discharge papers as we speak. Do you have any more questions for me?" He swiped her arm with a cotton ball and placed a band-aid over the pinhole.

"No. Thank you," she said, just above a whisper.

"Okay. You take care, Miss Patterson," he said. "Memphis, we'll talk soon." He left the room.

Memphis moved closer and took her hand. "Are you okay?"

"It's a lot to take in."

He gave her hand a gentle squeeze. "I'm right here, sweetheart."

"I'll be fine. I just need some time to process everything."

"The sooner you speak to your own physician, the better. It'll help ease any concerns you may have."

Rowena nodded.

"I'll be right back," he said.

Rowena stood to her feet and slowly walked to the bathroom to change into her clothes. She splashed a little water on her face and tried to fix her hair. Time didn't allow her to process all she had learned and she appreciated it. It would've led to a complete meltdown and that was not an option. A cry rose in her throat, but she forced it down and took a deep breath.

She exited the bathroom just as Memphis had returned with her discharge papers. She faked a smile and took a seat on the edge of the bed.

"Here you go," he said, handing her the papers. "I hope you don't mind me speeding things along."

"No. I really appreciate it."

"Will you be okay traveling by yourself?"

Rowena nodded with a frown. "Mm Hm," she said, gathering her things.

"Memphis helped her to her feet. "I got some free time, if you need me."

"You've already done enough. I don't know how I would have handled this without you. Thank you, Memphis," she said, giving him a hug.

"It was my pleasure," he said, hugging her back. His tenderness was overwhelming. She submitted to the urge to cling to him a few seconds longer — long enough to encourage her tears. Memphis sensed her despair and drew her in closer. He held her strong, giving her permission to retreat into his arms. His cologne filled her nostrils and her breathing intensified. Being in his arms caused a deep cry to surface and despite her best intention to save her meltdown for the privacy of her home, she lost herself slowly in him.

"I'm sorry," she said, avoiding his soft eyes and pulling away.

He wiped her tears. "Don't apologize."

"I'm acting like a five-year-old."

"Crying doesn't make you five, it makes you human."

"Is that what the doctors tell the screaming babies, after they've been given a shot?"

"Actually, they give them a lollipop and tell them they did great. You want a lollipop?" he teased.

Rowena smiled and looked down.

"Listen," he said, lifting her head back up. "I'll be happy to take a cab with you back to our cars and trail you home if you want me to."

Her eyes lit up. "Okay. But only to the restaurant. I'll be okay from there."

"Give me a few minutes. I'll meet you in the lobby."

Rowena nodded. The nurse brought her a wheelchair. She declined. With her flowers and teddy bear in tow, she walked to the nearest elevator. She deliberately exited in the infant ward. She strode over to the nursery where babies were crying behind the glass. Her heart melted at the sight of flailing feet and arms. She felt like a kid in a candy store. A tap on her shoulder interrupted her thoughts.

"Memphis, how did you find me?"

"This is my area, remember?" He smiled. "You okay?"

"I'm fine. You ready?"

"Your chariot is waiting."

"You called a cab already?"

"Of course!"

"You don't miss a beat, do you?"

"I aim to please when necessary."

Rowena tried to avoid being overtly casual with Memphis, but his tenderness made it hard to resist. He was reeling her in with every single smile. Inside the cab they shared, she cuddled up next to him.

"How long have you been an obstetrician?" she asked.

"About twelve years. I started immediately after my residency. Babies always fascinated me."

"Do you come from a big family?"

"No. I grew up an only child."

"Are your parents still alive?"

"My mother passed away a few years ago. I never knew my dad."

"Must've been tough growing up without a father."

"Only when I had questions about certain things. My mother did the best she could though. She was a brave woman."

"Did you grow up in Memphis?"

"No." He laughed. "But my mother did. She always said those were the best days of her life. That is until she had me, of course," he winked.

"Of course," she smiled. "Did you grow up here in Chicago?"

"Born and raised."

"Me too," she said, glancing out the window. After a short pause, she turned back to Memphis. "So if Memphis was so great, why did your mother leave?"

"She had no choice, really. The summer she graduated high school, she met my father who was a jazz musician. He played in a band down at a local nightclub in Memphis. She and her girlfriends would sneak out on Friday nights, to hear him play. One night, the two of them hooked up and she got pregnant. When my grandparents found out she was with child, they sent her here to live with my great aunt. She never saw my father again."

"That's unfortunate."

"I don't even know what he looks like. He could be the next door neighbor for all I know."

"Have you ever thought about trying to find him?"

"I don't really have a lot of information to work with and it just seems like more trouble than its worth. You know?"

"Your mother never tried?"

"She was too busy working to make sure I had everything I needed. I don't think she had the energy."

"What happened to her?"

"She passed in her sleep."

"I'm sorry."

"What about you? How come your parents didn't have more children?"

"My father started having health complications shortly after my twelfth birthday. My mother had her hands full trying to make ends meet."

"I can relate. My mother tried her best to take up the short end. Even with all her trying, I still had the *'only child'* blues."

"Same here. Losing my dad devastated my mom and me. Over the years, I tried to fill the void by keeping myself busy, trying desperately not to attach myself to anyone. I managed pretty well over the years...."

"And?"

"Then I met Evelyn."

"Evelyn?"

"My best friend. Meeting her shot a hole in my plans for solitude."

"Ah. I see."

"She's going through a rough time right now."

"Is that why she didn't meet you at the hospital?"

"It's a little complicated."

"Oh." Memphis rubbed her shoulder. "I meant what I said earlier, Rowena."

"Remind me again."

"If you need to talk or just sit in silence, I'm here for you."

Her heart melted again. "Thanks, Memphis. I'll remember that."

The cab pulled into the parking lot of Chi Tung. Memphis paid the fare and they exited the cab.

"Are you sure you're going to be okay from here?" he asked.

"Absolutely! If you keep being so kind to me, I won't be able to contain myself."

"Now, you're making *me* blush. Don't forget to follow up with your physician."

"I'll call first thing tomorrow morning."

"Great. Take care and I'll talk to you soon." He kissed her on the forehead and watched as she pulled out of the parking lot.

Despite her failed attempts to stay distracted, Rowena could no longer avoid processing all that had taken place over the past few days. She arrived home, closed the blinds, and turned off the phones. She wrapped up in a blanket, crawled to the middle of the bedroom floor, and wept like a newborn baby. She shed tears for all the pain her parents suffered, for her unborn child, for the misunderstanding with Evelyn, for her failing health and lastly, for discovering an angel like Memphis.

Chapter Thirteen

For Rowena, the morning brought a sense of relief. With her burden a little lighter, she believed she could handle the laundry list of things she had to do including making a call to the office. Without going into much detail, she told Morgan she wasn't feeling well. Morgan expressed concern, but Rowena had no time to explain and rushed off the phone. Hoping to hear from Evelyn, she checked her machine for messages.

Beep! "Hi, Rowena! This is Nyeela. I hoped to hear your voice this morning, but you're not home. I'm probably the last person you want to hear from right now. And believe me, I understand. I just want to apologize for the way I behaved Thanksgiving Day. I had no right to put you in the middle of our mess. Or treat you the way I did. I'm very sorry. You are important to this family and we love you. Call me. I'd love to hear from you. Take care." Beep!

"I love you too, Nyeela," she muttered. "Time to call my doctor." Rowena called the doctor and scheduled an appointment for eleven o'clock. She went to the bathroom, turned on the shower, and stared at her self in the mirror. The steam quickly filled the room, erasing her reflection. The idea of literally fading away frightened her. Suddenly, she realized that if she ever wanted to live a life more meaningful than the one she had, her health would have to be her first priority. With that, she undressed and entered the shower. The force of the streaming water attenuated the tension from her shoulders, while thoughts of Memphis soothed her from head to toe. After showering, she grabbed her cell phone and sent him a text message: **Going 2 C Dr. Kerrigo. Call me later?**

Memphis: Count on it☺.

*****

Rowena spent most of the afternoon giving blood samples and listening to her doctor confirm everything she learned at the hospital. Except this time, the diagnosis was Type II Diabetes. Dr. Kerrigo gave her plenty of information to go along with the medication he prescribed. Rowena never considered that her health would be a challenge. Spending the weekend with a bunch of doctors served as a rude awakening. But she took it all in stride and embraced her new lifestyle. It gave her something to do that implied she really was taking care of herself.

After leaving the doctor's office, she stopped at a little sandwich shop and ordered lunch. Now more health conscious, she ordered tuna on whole wheat and a garden salad. After lunch, she thumbed through her phone, thought of Nyeela and called.

"Hi, Nyeela!"

"Ro, is that you?"

"Yes, it's me. I got your message."

"Can you ever forgive me?"

"No worries, babe. All is forgiven."

"How are you doing? What are you doing?"

"I've been better. I'm just finishing lunch."

"Lunch ended hours ago. You working hard your first day back at work?"

"Hardly working at all. I didn't go to work today."

"Did my ears hear you right?"

Rowena laughed. "Yes, you heard right. I had a doctor's appointment."

"Doctor's appointment? Would that have anything to do with you looking so tired last week? If I'm being too nosey, just tell me to mind my business."

"Actually, I really don't want to get into it right now. But I promise I'll call you later and tell you all about it. Okay?"

"You better, Missy!"

"I promise. How is everyone?"

"By everyone, you mean Eve? She's good. She's doing a lot better than expected. But I'll leave the details for you and her to discuss. I wanted to personally apologize for my actions."

"It's all good."

"Great! I'm going to let you go and I'll be looking for your call later."

"Sure thing."

"Love you, Ro."

"Love you, too."

Rowena made a few stops before going home. One to the pharmacy to fill her prescriptions and the other to the grocery store to get healthier food. When she got home, it became painfully obvious how much junk food she actually consumed, as she cleaned out the fridge. The bottom drawer was full of sugary sodas, half-eaten snack pies and chocolaty treats. It was a wonder that she wasn't obese. One thing did bring a smile to her face. An old molded bag of salad greens in the back of the fridge made her feel like she tried.

Two weeks passed. Memphis and Rowena shared a couple of dates and spent a few afternoons cuddling in front of her fireplace. They phoned each other at every opportunity. With Christmas only a week away, Rowena rushed to give her place a holiday makeover. For the first time in years, she was going to spend Christmas with a man. It made everything that much more exciting. The shiny decorations, bright colors and tinsel made Rowena nostalgic for her mother. She had the bright idea to sit down and write a letter:

Dear Mom,

Life has been crazy. Since you've been gone, I've neglected to treat myself with love. I hid behind a wall of dysfunction pretending my job was all I needed and that I was happy. I couldn't have been more wrong. The only thing I've become good at is keeping busy while life passes me by. I really wish you could've met my friend Eve. She and her family have been so wonderful to me. I don't know where I'd be without them. Unfortunately, right now she isn't speaking to me. You know me, always trying to fix

everything; always needing to be needed. This time, I think I may have overstepped my boundaries. To make matters worse, I just found out I'm a Diabetic like Dad was and I'm frightened to death. I've since gone to the doctor and he's given me plenty of information as well as medication. This was the wake-up call I needed. Once, I heard a question asked on a talk show, "What would you do if you weren't afraid?" The truth is, if I weren't afraid, I would allow myself to love and receive love. Mom, I miss you so much! Hug Daddy for me.

Your loving daughter,

Rowena

*****

The temperature held steady in South Carolina. The Banks were busy preparing for Christmas. Ella Mae pulled out her faded white Christmas tree. It reminded her of the times when her entire family lived under one roof. Surrounded by torn boxes full of old ornaments, plenty of Nat King Cole, and more recent, bottles of red wine. A simple decorating project had the potential of turning into an all day event. Each ornament, with significant value and memory, helped fill precious hours. With Evelyn there to pitch in, the twins reluctantly assisted, whining the entire time about the way Ella Mae carried on.

"Nyasia, where them fancy decorations ya daddy bought?" Ella Mae asked, putting on her glasses.

"I think their over here, Ma."

"Well, brang em to me."

"Mama, do these lights work?" Nyeela asked, trying to untangle a string of cords.

"They was workin las' year."

"You've had these way too long. I don't think they make big bulbs like these anymore."

"Nyeela, them lights dun seen us through many a Christmas.' Quit messin 'round ova there and get them lights untangled."

"Are you sure the power won't go out if I plug these in?"

"Child, if you don't wanna help jus' get out the way. I'll do it myself."

"I'm kidding, Mama. Dang!"

"Rememba this one, Eve?"

"Mother, don't tell me you still have that thing," Evelyn said, shaking her head.

"I wish you cudda seen the look on ya face when you brung it home. I swear, I cudda lit a candle wit that smile."

"Yes, I remember. Daddy ran to get the camera so he could snap my picture."

"He made sho he got that smile, cuz you wasn't doin much of that back then."

"Adolescence does that to you, Mother."

Ella Mae held up a reindeer ornament. "Nyeela made this one in the fourth grade. You rememba, child?"

Nyeela rolled her eyes. "How could I forget, Mama? You remind me every year."

Ella Mae smiled with pride. "You was upset, cuz the paint got smeared."

"No. I was embarrassed because you kept putting it on top where everybody could see it."

"I can't believe you still have this angel after all these years," Evelyn marveled.

"It belonged to ya grandmotha. It was the las' thang she gave ya father before she passed. And Herman put it in a safe place ev'ry year till Christmas came 'round."

"Once, I found it and used it to bless all my dolls. Daddy found out and whipped my butt," Nyasia recalled. "Then after he calmed down, he explained to me why he did it. I never touched that thing again. Not even to put it on the tree."

"Twin, you were always playing with stuff that wasn't yours. Do you remember the time I caught you playing with my softball trophy? You told me you needed it for the Statue of Liberty. Because your dolls were touring New York City."

"That's right! Whoever heard of New York City without Lady Liberty?"

"Nut!"

"Well, it's true." Nyasia insisted.

"Grady and I used to put up our tree on Christmas Eve. Christmas was his favorite holiday."

"Have y'all talked?" Ella Mae asked, finishing off her wine.

"No. I've been thinking about calling him though."

"You oughta."

"Maybe I will, Mother."

"This wine is gettin mighty low."

"Sounds like that be a mighty good thing."

"Mind ya business, Nyeela. And brang me anotha bottle out the fridge."

"Why me?"

"Cuz I said so! You ain't too old to get knocked out," Ella Mae threatened.

"You better do what she says, Twin," Nyasia warned. "Things could get pretty ugly in here."

"Will y'all look at this tree? Ain't it somethin?"

"Yes it is, Mother."

"And it didn't take all day like it usually does," Nyasia added.

"Now I can finish wrapping gifts," Evelyn stated.

"Speakin of gifts, Nyeela and Nyasia, I need y'all to help me wit somethin later."

"How much later, Ma?"

"Why? What you gotta do, child?" Ella Mae asked, with her hands on her hips.

"Since we finished kind of early, I thought maybe Bryson and I could go out tonight," Nyasia said, with a twinkle in her eyes.

"Lawd! Y'all can't be still for two minutes," Ella Mae fussed. "Can't you go out wit Bryson some otha time?"

"I guess," Nyasia huffed.

Evelyn's cell phone rang. "Hello? Hi, Stacey," she smiled, leaving the room.

"Stacey?" Nyeela asked. "Hm," she smirked.

Evelyn continued out of the room. "How are you?" she asked.

"Pretty good," he answered, hearing the smile in her voice. *"How 'bout ya'self?"*

"Oh, I can't complain. We're just finishing the Christmas decorations."

"I went and bought us a real tree yestaday. Pops like the way they smell. I ain't no good at decoratin though."

"Don't feel bad. It's a group effort over here. How is your dad?"

"Not bad. He takin a nap as we speak. I been thinkin 'bout ya a lot lately and I was wonderin if it was okay to come visit for Christmas."

"Really?"

"Only if it's okay."

"Of course. I would love you to come for Christmas. What about your dad?"

"*Well, the travel may do him good. He don't get out much and Cousin Melvin wanna see him again.*"

"Then it's a date."

"*Awesome. So how you been, lately?*"

"Each day seems better and better. Being here with my family has been a tremendous help. To be honest, I miss him, Stacey."

"*Y'all dun shared the last seven years togetha and gettin through this ain't no overnight thang.*"

"At least the tears aren't flowing as much."

"*That's good to hear. I can't wait to see ya again.*"

"That's sweet!"

"*Okay, see you in a few days.*"

"Good deal. Bye."

"*Bye.*"

*****

It was the last day of work before Christmas Eve, in Chicago. Rowena prepared for the office Christmas party. Fresh out of the shower, she sat on the edge of the bed, massaging lotion into her legs and wondering what it would feel like to have Memphis' strong, gentle, hands on her thighs. If things kept going the way they were, it wouldn't be long before she would find out. Until then, she planned to savor every moment of their foreplay. She snapped out of her daze and took a moment to journal.

Dear Mom,

Today is a good day. You'd be happy to know that I'm putting myself first, and it feels good. The medicine I'm taking is helping so I'm not as tired these days. I'm also back at work, but not all day like before. See, I really am taking care of myself. I met someone and he is a doctor. His name is Memphis and lately it seems we've been growing close. I find myself incredibly attracted to him. I feel comfortable talking to him and we talk about everything. He makes me laugh. He's witty and charming. He loves art and music as much as I do. I believe I just might be ready for love. We have plans to spend Christmas together. I feel so honored to know him. He takes his time with me and he's very gentle. He reminds me so much of Dad. I struggled not to fall in love with him, but I believe I'm losing that battle. Love you.

Rowena.

*****

Although it had been a trying year for her, Rowena's work never suffered. She never dreamed of receiving an award for it, but the Universe had other plans. She arrived at the office early to make a few phone calls. Morgan walked in with coffee and pastries.

"Good Morning, Miss Patterson," she greeted.

"Good Morning, Morgan. Thanks for the coffee."

"You're welcome. I know you can't eat these things, so I grabbed you a whole wheat bagel."

"How thoughtful of you. Thanks!"

"No problem. I also have your gift. Would you like it now? Or do you want to wait until the party?"

"Speaking of gifts, I have one for you as well. Everyone else will have to wait until the party. I want you to have yours now."

"Wait a minute. Let me go and get yours." Morgan hurried to her desk, grabbed the gift, and hurried back to Rowena's office. "You go first," she said, handing her the gift.

Rowena carefully peeled away the wrapping to find a Saul Williams CD entitled, "Amethyst Rock Star." She was delighted. "Oh, wow! How did you know?" she smiled.

"It's my job to know," Morgan blushed.

"He is my favorite poet! Thank you, so much," she said, giving Morgan a bear hug. "Okay. Now it's your turn." Rowena handed her the gift bag.

"No. You didn't," she said, covering her mouth.

"Yes. I did!" Rowena smiled.

"Pink UGGS!"

"Size seven, right?"

"Yes. How did you know?"

"It's my job to know," she winked.

"Miss Patterson, thank you so much!"

"You're welcome. Now skee-daddle. I need to finish these calls before noon. Merry Christmas!"

"Merry Christmas!" Morgan exited the office.

Rowena stuck the CD in her bag and resumed work. Later, during the party, she received an award for outstanding work. Recognition from her colleagues ended the day on a high note.

Dear Mom,

You wouldn't believe what happened at work today. I got an award for all my hard work at The Tribune. I've never received an award for anything in my entire life. It seemed weird, yet validating. There's no question in my mind that I can do anything. I have someone I can share my hopes and dreams with, now. I'm so grateful. I haven't felt this way in a long time and it's scary. I'm willing to give it a shot, even though I don't know how things will turn out. Sometimes, when I'm alone, I can feel you and Dad watching over me. I hope I make you proud. I'm learning that I can't control everything that happens in life, but I can make better choices and hope for the best. I love and miss you, deeply!

Rowena.

*****

After a long and eventful day, Rowena welcomed the silence that flowed in her house. She relaxed for a few moments, before calling Memphis.

"Hi," she greeted.

"Hey, you!"

"Are you busy?"

"Not at all. I'm getting ready to do my rounds. How is everything?"

"Wonderful! You won't believe what happened to me today."

"You realize you're madly in love and want to spend the rest of your life with me."

"Can you be serious for one second?"

"Baby, I am serious."

"I received an award today at work."

"Congratulations! That's great!"

"Thanks!" Rowena smiled.

"I guess that's cause for celebration."

"What did you have in mind?"

"A lot!"

Rowena laughed. "What time do you get off?"

"Damn! I forgot I'm working late."

"We can save it for tomorrow. I'm pretty partied out myself."

"You sure, Princess?"

"Yes. I get to have you for the whole day, right?"

"Wrong. I get to have YOU for the whole day."

Rowena bit her lip. "What time will the party begin?"

"What time do you wake up?"

Rowena laughed. "You're a party animal!"

"Well?"

"9 a.m. and bring breakfast with you."

"Done. See you in the A.M."

"Bye."

She lay across her bed amazed at the fact that initially, she hadn't paid Memphis much attention. Now, she couldn't get him out of her head. He wasn't shy about telling her how much he adored her, something Rowena could never grow tired of hearing. Every morning, before she opened her eyes, thoughts of him flooded her mind. At night, when she closed them to sleep, he occupied her dreams. The world felt like a smaller place when they were together. She rolled over and realized she hadn't cleaned up, nor had she wrapped Memphis' gift. Intoxicating thoughts of him, furnished her with plenty of energy to get things done.

Christmas Eve, Rowena rose early to shower and dress. When the doorbell rang, she was more than ready. "Good morning," she smiled, opening the door.

Memphis saluted her with a soft kiss. "Good morning, beautiful!"

"Mmmm," she said. "You taste like cinnamon."

"And you smell good enough to eat!"

"Careful now, Doc. You could get a cavity fooling around with me."

"You promise?"

She blushed. "What's in the bags?"

"Fuel." He handed her two brown shopping bags. "We might need it for later on."

"Are you getting fresh with me?" she asked, leading him to the kitchen.

"This *is* a party, right? I'm just saying."

"Hm."

"And we got the whole day, remember?"

She turned back and flashed a smile. "I didn't forget."

"What's a party without your favorite?"

"Sushi?"

"That's right! We never got a chance to enjoy it on the first date, so I thought we'd give it another shot."

"Ah, a thinking man. I like that!"

He stopped as they passed through the family room. "Nice tree!"

"Thanks! It's my first real tree."

"Really? I can never find the time to go pick out one."

"Yes. Time is something you definitely need. Especially, to find a good one."

"That's why I don't have one. It's pathetic, I know."

"They *do* have artificial trees, you know. And some of them come decorated already."

He lowered his head and surrendered both hands. "I digress."

"Smart man," she smiled, continuing toward the kitchen.

"Hey, I make love not war."

"Then we're going to get along just fine," she said, placing the bags on the counter.

"My mother raised me right."

She hopped up on the counter. "What's in the other bag?" she asked, peeking inside the sack.

"Just what the doctor ordered. Breakfast."

She grabbed a plate and passed it to him. "Good. I'm starving."

"Let's get this party started," he said, preparing her a plate.

"These look delicious," she said, taking the plate of strawberry waffles.

"There is plenty where that came from so dig in."

She placed a forkful in her mouth. "Mmm. Where did you get these?"

He filled his plate and walked over to the table. "I got them from our favorite pancake house."

Rowena swallowed hard and tilted her head sideways. "How do you know where my favorite pancake house is?"

"I saw you there about a month ago," he said calmly.

Rowena hopped down from the counter with her plate and joined him at the table. "Say what?"

He placed a strawberry in his mouth. "Remember, I kept saying you look familiar?"

Rowena nodded. "I remember."

"Well, when you were in the hospital, it came back to me."

Rowena wiped her mouth. "This is awkward. And a little confusing."

"Okay, hear me out." He paused and swallowed. "When you walked in the door that day, I was completely mesmerized," he said, reaching for his latte.

Suddenly, Rowena remembered. "*You* were the one staring a hole in me that day!"

"A hole?" He laughed. "Really?" He took a sip from his latte.

"Are you kidding me? I was so annoyed and pissed! I must've been red as a tomato."

"I'm sorry. I couldn't take my eyes off you or that pink jogging suit you were wearing."

"Hell, I thought you were some kind of pervert. I haven't been back there since."

"I couldn't help myself." He laughed. "But I didn't mean to frighten you."

"I'm afraid you failed in that department. Why *were* you staring so hard?"

"It's too embarrassing to say," he said, looking down at his plate.

Rowena let out a hiss. "Hell, I'm the one who's embarrassed!"

"You really want to know?"

She nestled down in her seat and folded her arms. "I'm listening."

"Okay. I was standing over by the periodicals, minding my own business, waiting for my order and all of a sudden, you, a beautiful, lively young thing, walked in the door. You were so fine! The way your hair fell against your face, carried me back to my childhood when I was a young boy, sitting next to my mother, sucking my thumb and stroking her hair." He winced and shook his head. "I can't believe I just told you I used to suck my thumb."

"Your secret is safe with me," she sneered. "Now, finish the story."

"You walked in there like you were on a mission. The drive and focus in your face, impressed me," he said, squinting his eyes.

She covered her face. "Oh God!"

"Don't hide now. You wanted to hear the details, right?"

She removed her hands. "I'm so glad I didn't look crazy, like the night I had before that.

"Crazy night?"

"Yeah. But that's another story. Let's get back to the point."

"The point is I couldn't take my eyes off you."

"You have no idea how embarrassed I am right now," she smiled. "Go on."

"Then I noticed your shoes."

"My shoes?"

"Yeah. Did you know that a woman's shoes can tell you a lot about her?"

She frowned. "What?"

"If a woman's shoes are nice and clean, then she works smart and not hard. But," he said, holding up his index finger. "If they're dirty and beat up, then she might be a little heavy footed." He laughed.

She threw her napkin at him. "Get out of here!"

"A little something to put you at ease."

Rowena shook her head. "What in the world am I going to do with you?"

"I can think of a few things."

"Finish the story, please!"

"Shoes or not, I had an instinct about you."

"Hm," she said, rubbing her chin. "Anything else?"

"Not that I was looking or anything, but I couldn't help noticing how well-defined your legs were."

"So you *are* a pervert," she smirked.

"Not at all. But they did turn me on."

"Okay. That's it."

"Wait. I'm just getting started."

"I'm covering my ears."

"You'll be happy to know I skipped over your hind parts."

"Yeah, right," she said, raising her brow.

"I did. But very slowly," he laughed.

She shook her head. "You're crazy."

"Seriously. When you glanced around the room, I couldn't speak or move. I never did get my food that day. Once I found my legs, I had to get out of there."

She wiggled her nose. "Uh oh! I feel a sneeze coming on."

He laughed. "Go ahead and sneeze. It's the truth, so help me, God," he said, holding up his right hand.

She got up and poured herself a glass of juice. "Do you believe in fate?"

"I suppose."

She took a sip. "Hm."

The phone rang and startled them both. "I'm sorry. I'll go and turn off the ringer," she said. "It's Christmas Eve. There will be no business today."

Chapter Fourteen

In South Carolina, Evelyn finally decided to call Rowena, but the call went straight to voicemail. Instead of leaving a message, she joined her family in the kitchen for breakfast.

"Good morning, everyone," she greeted, with a smile.

"Mornin, baby! That sho was a lotta tossin and turnin you did las' night," Ella Mae acknowledged, sipping her coffee.

"How did you know I tossed and turned all night?"

"Jus' rememba, ev'ry closed eye ain't sleep," she winked. "Mama knows ev'rythang."

"Do you know the winning lottery number for today? I could use a couple million," Nyeela sneered.

Ella Mae answered with a serious face. "I know that mouth is gon' get you in serious trouble one day, missy."

Nyeela smacked her lips. "I'm just kidding, Mama. Dang!"

"Twin, please stop agitating Mother," Evelyn pleaded. "It's Christmas Eve."

Nyasia tore off a piece of toast and placed it in her mouth. "Evelyn, you look pretty for someone who hardly got any sleep. Is it the pregnancy?"

Evelyn pointed her finger at them. "Do you all practice this stuff overnight? I swear, Nyeela asked me the same exact question, hours ago."

Nyasia shook her head. "I'm just saying. Look at you! You're cheeks are full of color. Obviously, you didn't look this way when you first got here."

"Maybe it does have something to do with the pregnancy, Nyasia. I don't know. One thing I *can* say is I look way better than I feel. My breasts are sore and I can barely keep anything on my stomach. So before you go getting any ideas, it isn't all it's cracked up to be."

"Don't worry. I have no desire to bear any children, right now. I want to be married *before* I have kids," she said, munching on some bacon. "Anyways, Bryson already has a son."

Evelyn's eyes grew. "Does he?"

"Mm Hm," Nyasia said, picking up her fork.

"How old?"

"Three."

"Did you know that when you met him?"

"Yeah. He told me right away."

Evelyn poured herself a glass of orange juice. "How do you feel about that?"

"It's okay," she said, shrugging her shoulders. "I mean, that's part of life, right?"

"What the baby's mama got to say 'bout you and Bryson?" Ella Mae inquired, taking off her glasses.

"She passed away two years ago. Killed by a drunk driver."

Evelyn covered her mouth. "That's terrible! How is he handling it?"

Nyasia placed a forkful of rice in her mouth. "Bryson or the baby?"

"Both," Ella Mae and Evelyn said in unison.

"Bryson has his moments," she said, pausing to swallow her food. "I wish I could say the baby was too young to remember, but you never know. He appears to be doing fine though. Bryson shares custody with her parents."

Evelyn shook her head. "That's heavy."

"Is he comin by this evenin?"

"I'm not sure, Ma. His family expects him to be home."

"I undastand. His family, what kinda people are they?"

"We haven't exactly had a chance to get to know each other, yet."

"But you have met them, right?" Evelyn asked, sipping her juice.

"Briefly. They seem like nice people. So don't worry, Ma. I see that look on your face."

"Who worried? Child, I ain't worried." Ella Mae waved a dismissive hand. "I was jus' bein nosey, that's all."

Nyasia got up to empty her plate. "Yeah. Okay, Ma."

"Evelyn, why don't ya have a glass of milk? It's fresh."

"Ugh! No, Mother. I hate milk!"

"You hate milk?" Ella Mae raised a brow. "Well, you betta figure out a way to like it."

"Why?"

"Child, cuz you gotta drank it while you carryin that baby."

"Says who?"

Ella Mae put on her glasses. "Says ev'ry doctor in the world. That's who."

"Isn't there some kind of pill I can take instead?"

"I don't know nothin 'bout no pill."

"I'm sure with all the technology out here today, there's bound to be a pill I can take, instead of drinking that awful milk."

"Listen. This ain't 'bout you no more. That baby gotta get vitamins and stuff."

"I know, Mother. But it's so disgusting. The thought of it makes me want to gag right now."

Nyeela pushed away from the table. "Can you spare us the agonizing pain of watching you spill your guts all over this table, please?"

"No problem, sis. If I feel the urge coming, I'll just push the pause button until I make it to the bathroom."

"I'm just saying. *I* don't want to see it."

"Okay, enuff! Nyeela, clear the table. I gotta go make some phone calls this mornin."

"No church service today, Mama?"

The twins giggled.

"Not till t'morra. Why? Y'all wanna go?"

"No!" They answered.

"I'll go with you, Mother."

"Wondaful!" Ella Mae stood up. "I'll be in my room," she said, leaving the kitchen.

Evelyn folded her arms and looked at the twins. "What's the problem? How come you all don't want to go to church with her?"

"Girl, it'll be hours before you get out of there."

"Oh, it can't be *that* bad."

Nyasia raised her eyebrows. "Okay, sis. Don't say we didn't warn you," she said, leaving the room.

Nyeela put her hand on Evelyn's shoulder. "Trust me. When you finally get out of there, you are going to be hot, bothered, and hungry."

"Oh, stop it."

"Go ahead. See for yourself."

"Where are you going? I thought Mother asked you to clear the table."

"Could you do it for me, please? I have to make a quick run before everything closes. I promise I'll be back in an hour."

"You two are pathetic, I swear! I don't know how Mother puts up with it."

"Thanks, Eve." Nyeela blessed her with a kiss. "I love you!"

"Hm!" Evelyn rolled her eyes and cleared the table. She wondered what time Stacey and Mr. Charles were going to arrive. She ran upstairs to shower and dress.

An hour later, Stacey had arrived. Evelyn opened the door and displayed her pearly whites. "Stacey, Merry Christmas!"

"Merry Christmas!"

Ella Mae trotted down the stairs to see who rang the doorbell. "Hey there, Stacey!"

"Ms. Ella, Merry Christmas!"

"Where Melvin at?"

"Oh, he at the house wit Pop. He told me to tell ya he'll be here this evenin."

"Awright. Can I get ya somethin?"

"Naw. But thank ya."

"Well, come on in. Eve, take his coat."

"Yes, Mother." Evelyn reached for his coat.

"Child, ain't you tired from all that drivin?"

"No, ma'am."

"Lawd, I don't know how y'all young folk do it."

He smiled. "I'm good, Ms. Ella."

"Ya hungry?"

"No, ma'am."

"You sho? We got plenty to eat in the kitchen."

"Yes, ma'am."

"Well, I'm goin back to my room then."

"Good to see ya, Ms. Ella."

"You too, baby." Ella Mae returned upstairs.

Stacey turned to Evelyn and smiled. "How are you today?"

Evelyn led him over to the couch. "Pretty good."

"Ya look good!"

"Thank you, Stacey!" Evelyn said, taking a seat. "You're just full of compliments."

He sat down next to her. "You do!"

"I believe the pregnancy has something to do with it."

"It's workin for ya, huh?"

"So they say."

"What's been goin on? Have ya spoke to ya friend yet?"

"I tried calling her this morning but the voicemail picked up. It didn't seem right to leave a message, so I didn't. I'll try again later."

"I been meanin to ask how you feel 'bout bein back home. I reckon it was a lil tough in the beginnin."

"It's been ok, I guess. Yes, there was a lot of tension at first, but I'm... *We're* adjusting."

"That's good to hear."

"I plan to go home after the New Year."

"Oh yeah?"

"Yes, I think it's time. Have you ever been to Chicago?"

"Naw, but I wouldn't mind visitin one day."

"You should."

"How long have you been there?"

"Since I was eighteen."

"That long, huh?"

"Yeah. Come visit. You'll have a great time. There's so much to see and do and I would love to show you around."

"I jus' might do that."

"Bring your Dad. My place is big enough and he could get plenty of rest."

"You don't think ya ex gon' have a problem wit that?"

"Please. He's living his life. Doing his own thing."

"I jus' don't wanna be caught in the middle of no drama."

"I understand. You can stay in a hotel, if it will make you feel more comfortable."

"We'll see. How does next year sound?"

"It's funny to hear you say next year, when it's only a few days away. This year flew right past me. I'm still trying to catch my breath."

"Yeah. These years jus' fly right on pass."

"I remember Valentine's Day as if it were yesterday. Grady brought home some beautiful red roses and chocolate covered strawberries for me. Then he whisked me away to see *The Color Purple*. When we got home, the lights were low, soft music played in the background, and the smell of burning incense filled the room. He poured some wine and we sipped on that until we both fell asleep. He was so romantic."

Stacey remained silent.

"And then all of a sudden, he wasn't."

"No explanation or nothin?"

"Nope, just a cold shoulder."

"That's too bad."

"Indeed. At least I can talk about it now."

"Did ya forgive him?"

"Not quite, but I'm working on it."

"Take ya time."

"Oh, I couldn't speed it up if I wanted to."

"Forgiveness is a tricky thang."

"Mother says forgiveness is letting go of the negative emotions that come with the memories."

"It's true."

"Who knows? I just might come out on the other side of this."

"I rememba when I didn't think I would eva see the otha side again."

"Now look at you," Evelyn smiled.

"It was by the grace of God."

"Hm."

"Have y'all talked yet?"

"Me and Grady? We have. But there is still so much that needs to be said."

He nodded. "I see."

Nyeela returned with Tanvi. "Hi, everybody. Remember Tanvi?"

"How could we forget?" Evelyn mumbled.

"Merry Christmas!" Tanvi greeted.

"Merry Christmas, Vee," Stacey and Evelyn responded.

"Come on in, Vee," Nyeela directed. "Make yourself at home. I'll be right back."

"Sure!" Tanvi took a seat on the couch. "How's everyone?"

"We're good," Evelyn said. "How about you?"

"Good. Excited about the holidays," she smiled.

"Oh yeah? Any particular reason?"

"Something about this time of year brings out the good in people."

"I agree." Evelyn smiled. "What are you guys planning to do this evening?"

"Nyeela wants to spend Christmas Eve here with you guys."

"Oh. Isn't that cute. Where do you live?" she asked.

"I live close to the school campus," Tanvi stated.

"I see. If you don't mind me asking, what do your parents do for a living?" Evelyn inquired.

Tanvi clasped her hands around her knee. "They run a small printing company, just outside of town."

"Really? Will you be working the business someday?"

"According to them I will, but I have my own plans."

"And what are your plans?"

Her eyes lit up. "Well, I'd like to open up a social center for lesbian teens, that don't really have a place to go otherwise."

"Nice!" Evelyn said. "I think it's great to reach out and help others. I believe in that, wholeheartedly."

"Nyeela told me. She also told me that you're good at what you do."

Evelyn laughed and waved a dismissive hand. "Girl, you don't have to lie for Nyeela."

"No. Its true, Evelyn."

"*Nyeela* told you that?"

"Yeah. She's really proud of you."

"If she heard you telling me this, you'd be yesterday's news!"

"I know. Please don't tell her I said anything."

"My lips are sealed," Evelyn pledged.

"Don't look at me," Stacey said, raising both his hands. "My name is Benn-it and I ain't in it."

Evelyn laughed.

Nyeela returned to the living room. "What did I miss?"

"Did you forget you had company?" Evelyn questioned. "Where were you?"

"Mama asked me to help her with something."

"Help her with what?"

"Eve, why are you all up in my kool-aid?"

"Because you shouldn't be so rude."

Nyeela nudged Tanvi. "You didn't mind, did you, babe?"

"Not at all," she smiled. "Who decorated the tree? It's beautiful!"

"We...."

"Mother did," Evelyn interrupted. "We helped."

"Great job!"

"Nyeela, where is your twin?"

"I don't know. I haven't seen her since this morning."

"Hmm. I don't remember her saying anything about having other plans," Evelyn said, chewing at her lip.

"Me either," Nyeela replied. "I assumed she was spending the evening with us. Maybe Mama knows."

"Knows what?" Ella Mae asked, walking down the stairs.

"Of Nyasia's whereabouts."

"She jus' called and said she was on her way. Bryson comin ova here, tonight. Melvin on his way, too," she announced.

"I guess we better get dinner started then, huh?" Evelyn asked.

"Naw, child. I ain't gotta worry 'bout cookin. Melvin brangin dinna wit him," Ella Mae said, with pride.

"He cooks too?"

"Hush, Nyeela!" Ella Mae demanded.

"I'm saying… If Melvin can cook, you may have found yourself a keeper, Mama."

"Go away from me, child," she said, waving her hand.

"Now I see why he was tryin to get rid of me."

"Stacey, you ain't know ya uncle could cook?" Ella Mae asked.

"I did. But I ain't neva seen it."

"Can *you* cook?" Evelyn asked.

"A little. I had to learn so Pops could get a decent meal."

"Y'all put on some music. Where my Nat King Cole CD?" Ella Mae asked, reaching for her glasses.

"Mama, can we please listen to something else this time?" Nyeela whined.

"How 'bout a lil Motown Christmas?" Stacey suggested. "I can grab the CD outta my car."

"Yeah. Go get it. Child, y'all don't know nothin 'bout that."

Nyeela rolled her eyes up into the air. "Here we go again with the old skool stuff."

Tanvi shimmied her hips. "What's wrong with old skool? I happen to like it."

"You never told me you like it."

"Because I know you don't care for it, Nyeela."

"Just because I don't care for it, doesn't mean you can't share it with me."

"Duly noted."

Stacey returned followed by Nyasia and Bryson.

"Here we go," Stacey announced, pulling the CD out of the case.

"Go on and put it in." Ella Mae directed.

Stacey complied.

Nyasia took of her coat. "Remember Bryson, everybody?"

Ella Mae waved. "Merry Christmas, Bryson! Come on in."

"Merry Christmas!" Bryson handed Ella Mae a bottle of champagne with a ribbon tied around it.

"Thank ya, suga. Go on and make ya'self at home." Music emanated from the speakers. "Now, this is the Christmas I been waitin for," Ella Mae said proudly.

*****

The sun had already set in Chicago. Memphis and Rowena sat in front of the fireplace with half a bottle of wine.

"How's the writing coming along?" he asked.

"Good. I find it to be therapeutic especially during this time of year."

"Yeah, this time of year can be hard for a lot of people."

"Lately, I've been listening to a CD my assistant gave me and it inspired me a lot. I've been writing almost every day."

"Anything you want to share?"

"I do have a little poem that I wrote."

"Good," he said, rubbing his hands together briskly. "Let's hear it!"

"You're making me nervous."

"Don't be nervous. It's just you and me, baby. It's a gift to be able to put your thoughts and feelings into words."

"You promise not to laugh?"

"Cross my heart," he said, drawing an *x* across his chest.

"Okay. I wrote this one a few days ago. I call it, A Sundae Kind of Love."

"I like it already," he smiled.

"Seems as if I've found myself a Sundae kind of Love - one that has ignited my Saturday night. It's a sinful dose of my favorite ice cream. Two heaping scoops of Butter Pecan, nestled inside a long, slim, banana, drenched in a silky caramel sauce. Sprinkles of sexy almonds collaborate on top with the enticing cherry. They please and tease my eyes with inch upon inch of scintillating temptation. Visually, I devour it completely. Still, I want to consummate our relationship. I grab the spoon and courageously step out of my comfort zone. Ready to dip and slip it right between my lips, I hear a voice in my ear. "Take your time. Enjoy your dessert, baby girl." I pull back, inhale deeply and slow down a bit—allowing myself a sample. The cream on my tongue is smooth like jazz, the caramel hot like summer on a wet, July day. Each portion I push inside me is richer and much sweeter than the last. Over doing it causes indigestion--the kind that makes the heart hurt. So again, I pull back and re-pace myself. I play around the outside and work my way in--trying to make this Sundae kind of love, last past Saturday night."

Memphis clapped. "Damn! That was hot!"

"Don't lie," she said, covering her face.

"Look at me," he said, pulling her hands away from her face. "It was beautiful!" He pulled her close and gave her a deep passionate kiss. "And so are you."

"Memphis," she whispered.

"What?" he asked, tracing her face with kisses.

"I told my heart not to do this," she muttered, closing her eyes and enjoying his kisses.

"Your heart can't hear, baby. It was made to feel," he said, finding his way back to her lips.

"Well, I'm feeling like I love you," she said, breathing heavily and looking up at him.

His heart swelled. He stopped and looked into her eyes, "I've been waiting to hear you say those words." He planted a wet kiss on her lips.

Rowena's insides stirred. She wanted him as much as he wanted her. He took his hands, slid them down the small of her back and gently massaged her. She moved her neck slightly to the side as he trailed it with warm kisses, tasting every inch of her skin. The heat between them intensified. He returned to her lips. She could taste her own perfume on his tongue. It added to the sweetness of his lips. He gently nibbled at her earlobe then slipped his tongue in her ear. Rowena could hardly take anymore. She pulled away and looked at him with intimate eyes. He laid her down in front of the fireplace. "Can I make love to you?" he asked.

She closed her eyes. "Please."

He showered her with more kisses as he slowly undressed her. Rowena's body lit up like a fire as she lay there thirsting for him.

He slowly removed his shirt, never taking his eyes from hers. She admired the strength in his arms as they supported his weight above her. She leaned forward and kissed his broad, naked chest. Memphis closed his eyes and took pleasure in the feeling of her mouth on his skin. Rowena panted and her sensuality heightened. He reached for a condom and methodically placed it on himself. He returned to her, showering her with more kisses. Rowena lifted her pelvis so he could easily find his way inside. He gently entered and let out a hiss. "Mmmm," he moaned. Rowena's insides throbbed as he filled her up. Her misconceptions about love melted and she lost herself in his rapture. Her body tingled with every thrust. In and out, up and down, their bodies intertwined, moving in a rhythmic motion. "Damn, I love you, girl," he whispered before letting out a small whimper. They became one, reaching their climax together. He held her tight and she relaxed in his arms. The fireplace crackled next to their perspiring bodies. They nestled close under the orange glow and soon, were off to sleep.

Rowena woke up an hour later resting in his arms, vulnerable, yet safe. She lay there taking it all in and owning the moment. To be in love with someone who loved her back, opened her up in a way she never thought possible.

Memphis woke up and kissed her on the forehead. "Feliz Navidad," he whispered.

"Mmm," she moaned. "Right back at you, Santa." She walked her fingers along his bare chest.

"I gave my elves the day off. But first, I instructed them to prepare your gift," he announced, sitting up.

"You didn't."

"Of course, I did." He smiled. "There's more to this sack of bones than you think." He stood up and walked over to where his coat lay.

Rowena held her face. "Memphis! What is it?"

He reached into a bag hidden under his coat and pulled out a big black book. "I had this made special for you," he said, walking back over and handing her the leather bound book.

"Oh, my goodness!" Her eyes lit up. "What is it?"

"Open it," he directed.

Rowena sat up and nervously pulled the blanket up around her chest. She took the book in both hands and slowly ran her fingers along the shiny gold letters engraved on the cover, *Memphis Blessings.* She flipped open the cover to the first page and read the dedication:

I'm a bit of a romantic. Ever since the age of seventeen, I dreamt of meeting my soul mate. I started writing her love letters twenty years ago. Once a year, every New Year's Eve, I described how I pictured her in my mind, how I would love her and take care of her, forever. When I saw her in that restaurant for the first time, I *knew* she had walked right out of my dreams. I left there confident she'd be mine, so I published these letters just for her. Rowena Patterson, *you* are my blessing!

Rowena's heart melted and tears streamed down her face. "Memphis, I don't know what to say."

"You don't have to say anything. Just let me show you how much I appreciate the blessing." He leaned in and kissed her.

Several moments passed before she spoke. "I have something for you, too." She wiped her tears.

"Oh boy!"

"I haven't bought a gift for a man in years. I hope you like it." Rowena stood up, with the blanket wrapped around her body, and walked to her bedroom. A moment later, she emerged with a long box covered in Christmas wrapping. "Merry Christmas!"

He peeled away the wrapping, removed the cover and inside he found a *state of the art* golf driver with his initials engraved. "Baby, this is the shit right here!"

"I guess that means you like it?"

"You better believe I like it. I love it! I can't wait to use this bad boy!" He kissed her. "Thanks, baby!"

"You're welcome. Are you hungry?"

"Like you wouldn't believe. What time is it?"

"It's about four in the morning."

"What can we eat at this time of morning?"

"We still have the sushi you brought before we got into something else?"

"You mean *sex* wasn't on the menu?"

"Um, I don't think so."

"Well to hell with the menu, tell me how to get more of what I had earlier."

"Don't worry, there's plenty where that came from, right now we need to eat some real food."

Chapter Fifteen

Christmas Day in South Carolina brought beautiful sunny weather. Ella Mae and Evelyn returned from church and despite the twins forewarning, Evelyn enjoyed herself. However, she did feel a little famished. "Mother, I'm going to grab me a snack, change my clothes, and then I'll help you prepare for company."

"Go on and feed ya'self, child. I'm goin to change my clothes."

Evelyn made herself a sandwich and took it upstairs to eat while she changed. A half-hour later, they both convened in the kitchen.

"I really enjoyed church service this morning," she said

"I been tryin to get them twins to go, but I jus' can't get them to do nothin these days," Ella Mae complained, putting on her glasses.

"They're practically grown, Mother."

"They ain't too grown to go to church, Eve!"

"Yes, but you raised them to be God-fearing women. Trust that and let it go."

"I'm gon' have to pray 'bout that," she said, turning on the tap. "They might be grown, but they still live unda my roof and ev'ry time they walk out them doors, I worry."

"I understand. Do you want me to talk to them?"

"I sho would 'preciate it, baby," she said, taking the milk and chopped onions out the fridge.

"Okay. Don't you ever get tired of cooking?"

"If I didn't cook, child, y'all wouldn't eat," she said, pulling a skillet from the cabinet.

"Well, it may not seem like it, but I do know how to find my way around the kitchen. Though I'd much rather have someone else cook for me."

"It's a good thing ya husband didn't mind all that restaurant food. But it sho ain't healthy."

"I guess. But you're right. There is nothing like a home-cooked meal."

Ella Mae walked over to the fridge and took out the butter. "Eve, I got somethin I wanna say to you. I know you thought ya daddy and me had a perfec' marriage but child, ain't no marriage perfec.' We jus' didn't like makin a fuss."

"Is that why I've never seen you two argue?"

"That's right," she said, spooning the butter into the skillet. "Sho, we disagreed from time to time, but we picked our battles."

"Hmm."

"Yeah, he got on my nerves 'bout as much as you and the twins did. I'm sho I got on his jus' the same, but we was real good friends. Good friends don't let the sun go down wit bad stuff between 'em. We didn't hold no grudges or go to bed mad."

"How come you didn't share this with me before now?"

"Cuz you was always mad 'bout somethin," she said, adding flour to the melted butter. "You ain't neva want me tellin ya nothin."

Evelyn lowered her head. "It wouldn't have made a difference, anyway."

"Maybe not wit Grady. But ain't Rowena ya good friend?"

"Yes and I'm going to fix everything with Rowena. I promise."

Ella Mae nodded and stirred. "That situation wit Grady sho is a shame. But it ain't the end of the world. Life is full of chances to make a brand new start."

"Something the minister said struck a chord with me. When he said, unto us a child is born, I knew the message was for me. I wanted to turn a deaf ear, but when he said, a gift to all humanity and what we choose to do with the gift is entirely up to us, I just couldn't ignore it. Especially the part about being accountable."

"It's the truth, ain't it?"

"It is. So I've decided to keep the baby, Mother."

"Praise the Lawd!" Ella Mae smiled. "My prayers dun been answered," she said, hugging her. "I'm so happy!"

Evelyn's eyes filled with tears. "Yes, Mother."

"This gon' be the best Christmas eva," she said, taking off her glasses and turning off the stove. "I'm gon' be a granny."

"Yes, you are."

"Have ya told Grady yet?"

"I'm going to tell him when I get home. We have a lot to talk about."

Ella Mae leaned against the sink. "What's goin on wit you and Stacey? Y'all spendin a lotta time togetha."

"Nothing. We're just friends. He's been a nice shoulder to lean on, that's all."

"Well, jus' rememba you still fragile," she said, folding her arms. "Whateva feelins you got for him could be misleadin. Careful not to break his heart."

"I won't, Mother," she pledged. "Trust me. I'm not even *halfway* thinking about a man right now. I like Stacey and I value his friendship. I wouldn't dream of hurting him."

"Awright then, let's get this food goin," she said, putting her glasses back on. "Folk gon' be here soon enuff. I would ask ya where them twins at, but it ain't gon' do me no good."

"Why?"

"Cuz I need 'em and they ain't here."

"Don't worry. They'll be here, Mother. Meanwhile, I can help you. I'm not handicapped."

"Well, let's get to it, child." Ella Mae dished out her requests back to back. By the time she finished, Evelyn had grown tired and had no desire for company.

When the twins finally returned, Evelyn lit into them. "Where the hell have you two been? I've been working like a hog around here! And you two are off gallivanting, God knows where."

"Eve, calm down," Nyasia insisted.

"What is your problem? And who are you yelling at?" Nyeela asked.

Evelyn folded her arms and looked at Nyeela angrily. "Mother has been looking for you two all afternoon. *That's* my problem, Nyeela!"

"We figured you guys would be in church all day, so...." Nyeela explained.

"So what!"

"Melvin asked us to drop by for a minute," Nyasia stated. "And we ended up staying longer than we intended."

"Melvin? What's he got to do with this?" Evelyn asked.

Ella Mae entered the living room. "Where y'all been? Y'all shudda been here hours ago and what's this 'bout Melvin?"

"Nothing. He'll be over within the hour and we're sorry for being late. Dang!"

"What can we do?" Nyasia asked.

"Nyasia, take out the trash and Nyeela, go make some sweet tea," Ella Mae directed. I'm goin to lie down for a minute. Wake me when Melvin gets here," she said, going up the stairs.

"Okay, Ma," Nyasia responded.

Evelyn followed the twins into the kitchen. "You two need to be a little bit more considerate of Mother."

Nyeela drew in a deep sigh. "Eve, what are you talking about?"

"I'm talking about coming home at a decent hour, Nyeela. I'm talking about doing more around this house, besides treating Mother like a maid."

"What? How dare you accuse us of treating Mama like a maid."

"She was talking to you, Nyeela. Not me," Nyasia announced, grabbing the trash out of the can.

"I'm talking to the both of you!" Evelyn rectified.

"Girl, you have no idea what you're talking about," Nyeela said, dismissively as she reached into the cabinet for the tea bags.

"I know she doesn't feel appreciated. Every time she asks either of you to do something for her, you always have something else to do," Evelyn fussed.

"And how would you know?" she asked, tossing the tea bags into the pot. "You've only been here a hot second, your *damn* self! And already, you think you know everything. That's what rattles my nerves about you, Eve. You've got advice for everybody else and your own life is screwed up!"

"My life may be screwed up, Nyeela, but what does that have to do with your lack of support around this house?"

"I do a lot to support Mama. At least *I'm* here. You live on the other side of the planet and barely come home to visit. How can you fix your mouth to say anything about what we do?"

"Because I can."

"You don't give a damn about this family, Eve. The only reason you're here is because your shit is all over the place. You're not fooling anybody."

"Nyeela, I think you better close your mouth."

"No, Eve. I'm sick of you acting as if you're here to set things straight. You might be some kind of savior to your readers, but here, you're nothing more than a damsel in distress. As far as I'm concerned, if you don't like what's going on in this house, you can high-tail your ass right on back to where you came from!"

378 Angela Bolden-Thompson

Evelyn slapped Nyeela across the face.

Nyeela grabbed her face and stared at Evelyn with hurt and disbelief. "You better be glad that baby is in your stomach or…"

"Or what?" Evelyn asked.

"Or I would kick your ass!"

Evelyn squared her shoulders and leaned in close to Nyeela's face. "You go right ahead and try. And I swear to you, you are going to wish you hadn't!"

"Go to hell, Eve!" Nyeela ran upstairs to her bedroom and slammed the door.

Evelyn turned to Nyasia. "She had that one coming."

Nyasia shook her head and slammed the bag back down in the can. "I am so sick of all this fighting between you and Nyeela."

"I will not allow her to disrespect me."

"Evelyn, I love you. But if this is going to continue, I'm not sure you being here is a good idea," Nyasia huffed.

"Well, everything doesn't revolve around the two of you, Nyasia. You all are way too selfish. Mother is getting older and she can't continue to worry about you two."

"No one is trying to make her worry, Eve."

"Well, she does. You all don't help around this house the way you should. You don't come in at a decent hour. And she can't keep standing over that hot stove everyday, cooking food that you all hardly take the time to eat."

Nyasia raised her eyebrows and shifted her weight to one leg.

"It's not fair, Nyasia."

"I know," she admitted.

"Things have got to change around here."

"I was going to wait until the New Year to say this, but Bryson and I are thinking about moving in together," Nyasia announced.

"Why do you have to move in with Bryson? Why can't you get a place by yourself?"

"I can. I'm just not ready to live by myself."

"What about Twin? Have you asked her?"

"Yeah, but she hasn't shown much interest."

"Maybe she doesn't think you're serious. Both of you have good jobs, it's time for you to be independent and move out. Give Mother a break. Let her enjoy life with her new boyfriend."

"I'll talk to Nyeela again."

"Good. Now listen. I'm sorry about what just happened, but your sister crossed the line. You know I love you guys and I only want what's best for you, right?"

"Yeah, but you and Nyeela need to find a way to get along. All this drama is working my nerves."

"That girl needs to bridle her tongue!"

"Hm! I wonder where she gets it from," Nyasia said, pursing her lips.

"Evelyn rolled her eyes. "I'll give her some time to calm down before I go talk to her. Meanwhile, somebody has to make the sweet tea."

"Don't look at me," Nyasia shrugged.

"Mother, isn't going to like this, but what the hell," she said, shaking her head. "Damn! I wanted to take a nap, too."

"Is there any more trash to go out?" Nyasia asked.

"I'm not sure. Check the bathroom."

Nyasia went on to empty the trash and Evelyn put forth her best effort to make the tea. Afterwards, she went upstairs to talk to Nyeela. She knocked gently on the door.

"Go away, Eve!"

"Nyeela, we need to talk," she said, entering the room.

"Get the hell out of here!"

"I will not," she said, taking a seat on the bed. "You and I are going to finish this, so we can have a merry Christmas."

Nyeela turned on her side with her back to Evelyn. "I don't have anything to say to you."

"Fine. Don't talk. Just listen. I'm sorry about what happened downstairs. I had no business putting my hands on you, but sometimes you go way too far."

She turned to face Evelyn. "Who are you to tell me what I can or cannot say? You don't have the right!"

"I'm your big sister. I changed your pissy pampers and wiped your snotty nose. So you owe me a modicum of respect."

Nyeela sat up. "Respect is earned, Eve. And in case you haven't noticed, I'm not wearing pissy pampers or sporting a snotty nose. You've been acting as if this family owes you something, because your husband deceived you. You were the one who chose him, Eve, not us. Maybe you need to stop pointing fingers and take responsibility for your actions."

"I'm trying, Nyeela."

"Try harder! We haven't seen you in years and all of a sudden, you show up acting all concerned trying to tell us how to do things. I don't think so!"

"Oh, so because you're all grown up now, nobody can tell you anything?"

"No, Eve. *You* can't tell me anything."

"What is your problem? Why are you so angry with me?"

"You tell me, since you know everything."

"No, I don't, Nyeela. Enlighten me."

"Because you left," she said, with a broken voice. "You left us here all alone after Daddy died."

Evelyn reached over to console her.

Nyeela flinched. "Don't touch me!"

Evelyn retracted her hand. "I'm sorry."

"How could you? You knew Mama needed you," she sobbed. "We needed you. But I guess chasing a man was more important."

"That's not fair, Nyeela. Daddy's death hurt me too."

"But it wasn't just about you. Burying him devastated Mama and you knew she was in no shape to raise us alone. Anybody with eyes could see she needed you." She wiped her tears. "Everybody else knew it too. Everybody except you."

"Nyeela, I never meant to hurt her or you."

"Well, guess what, Eve? You did. I suppose congratulation is in order! You got your man."

"Listen. Leaving here wasn't easy for me. When Daddy left me … us, I didn't know how we were going to make it. I couldn't handle Mother's grief and mine at the same time. I didn't know what else to do. I had to get out this house. Once I got myself situated, I offered to have one of you come live with me, but Mother refused."

"Can you blame her? We were all she had left. How could you even suggest such a thing?"

"What do you want me to say, Nyeela? I only did the best I knew how to do. I was young at the time and yes, it may have been selfish. I won't deny it. But we all make mistakes…." Her voice trailed off, as she realized the significance of her words. Her eyes slowly welled.

"Say it again, Eve."

"We all make mistakes," she repeated, lowering her head. "You're right. I'm sorry."

Nyeela wiped her nose. "And we've forgiven you. Now it's time for you forgive too."

"How come no one said anything?" she asked, wiping her tears.

"Mama never wanted to burden you. We didn't have a right to make a fuss, if she didn't."

"Did she ever express any anger toward me?"

"Never. All she ever wished for you was happiness. No matter how much she struggled. But you never came back to make sure we were okay."

"Yes, I did. But it was still too fresh. All the memories here with Dad, still haunted me."

"You only came back once and your visit was so short, I can barely remember it. I grew tired of waiting for you to walk through those doors."

Evelyn listened intently as her sister voiced her pain.

"I felt like we weren't good enough to be a part of your life," Nyeela continued. "And I resented you every single day because of it. Mama always encouraged us to call you whenever we needed you, but that was useless. Nothing you could say would ever fill that void. It just fueled my determination to prove my worthiness."

"How so, Nyeela?"

"By working overtime to be the best."

"Being the best doesn't make you worthy, sis. You were born worthy. You mattered to me and you still do. I thought of you guys all the time. And if I could do it all over again, I swear I would do things differently. I love you, baby girl, with all my heart. And I never meant to hurt you. I just wanted to be a good example."

"We didn't need a good example, Eve. We had Mama for that. What we needed was a big sister."

"I can't change the past, Nyeela. But I can be here for you now. I promise I'll make every effort to visit more often. After all, you're going to be an aunt."

"What?" her voice softened. "You're keeping the baby?"

"Yes." Evelyn smiled and wiped Nyeela's face.

She hugged Evelyn. "Are you serious?"

"I am."

"Yay!" She sniffed. "I'm so happy for you, Eve!"

Evelyn moved a strand of hair from Nyeela's face. "We're going to be a family again, baby girl. I promise!"

"I'm sorry for being so harsh with you, Eve."

"The truth can be harsh and it's okay. I promise I'll never put my hands on you again."

"You better not. Next time, I might have to hurt you."

Evelyn laughed. "Remember who taught you how to fight in the first place."

The doorbell rang. Evelyn wiped her face and rushed downstairs to get the door. Nyeela followed and Nyasia woke Ella Mae.

"Merry Christmas," she greeted, inviting Stacey, Melvin and Uncle Charles inside. Nyeela and Evelyn relieved everyone of their coats. "You all are just in time, dinner is about to be served," Evelyn announced.

"Not before we open them gifts," Ella Mae said, trekking down the stairs.

"Oh. Okay, Mother."

"I wanna go first," Ella Mae stated. "Stacey, do me a favor, baby."

"Anythang, Ms. Ella."

"Go upstairs, down the hall to the las' room on the right and brang me that big ole box."

"Awright."

"Mother, how on earth did you get a big box up those stairs?"

"I paid a few extra dollas," she said, reaching for her glasses.

"Baby, I wudda helped you," Melvin said.

"Ain't no sense in both of us gettin bent out of shape."

"You right 'bout that. I need my back for otha thangs."

"Ewe!"

Melvin laughed. "What?"

"Don't be nasty," Nyeela said, turning up her lips.

Stacey returned with the box. "Here you go. Where you want it?"

"Set it right there next to Eve," Ella Mae directed. "It's for her."

Evelyn pointed to herself. "Me? What is it?"

"Open it and see."

She ripped off the wrapping paper. It was a brand new, classic, convertible, baby crib. "Mother, this is so nice!"

"Me and the twins was hopin you could use it. We glad to know you will."

Nyasia's eyes grew. "She will?"

"Yes, I will."

"Yay!"

"Mane, I'm gon' be a step granddad!

"I reckon so, Melvin. Nyasia, you next. It's the one wit the blue wrappin."

Nyasia searched frantically through the gifts for blue wrapping paper. She found it and smiled sheepishly at Ella Mae. "No noise," she said, shaking the box.

"Child, jus' open it."

"Okay, okay!" With everyone watching, she carefully opened the neatly wrapped package and pulled out a huge, white, laminated, book full of family recipes. "A cookbook!"

"Yes. It's time y'all learn how to cook for ya'selves. Since you was the firs' to show int'rest, I thought you should be the one to have it."

"Thanks, Ma!"

"It ain't jus' any ole cookbook. It's been in this family for years. I added a few pages and I had it restored jus' for you."

"Aw! Thanks!" She planted a kiss on Ella Mae's cheek.

"Merry Christmas! Your turn, Nyeela."

"What color should I look for?"

"Same color, diff'rent name," Ella Mae, clarified.

Nyeela's gift sat on top of the others. She reached over, picked it up, and shook it. "It's not a rock is it?"

"Naw, it's a brick." Ella Mae laughed. "Go on and open it, girl," she insisted.

"Ha ha ha!" Nyeela opened the gift and found a heart shaped pendant with a picture of her and Ella Mae inside. On the back it read, "Mama's Finest Work." Nyeela covered her mouth. "It's beautiful, Mama! Thank you." She bent over and hugged Ella Mae's neck.

"From my heart, baby."

"Yes, Mama."

Melvin held up his finger. "Ella, I think you oughta go next."

Ella Mae pushed her glasses up on the bridge of her nose. "Awright," she smiled.

Melvin pulled a small gift box out of his pocket and handed it to Ella Mae.

The room grew silent.

"Ella Mae, we been seein each otha for two years now," Melvin stated. "And if you would have me, I want us to spend the res' of our days togetha. I dun seen how you operate 'round here and I like it." He knelt down on one knee and took her hand in his. "Ella Mae, will you be my wife?" He opened the little black box and revealed a 1-karat, solitaire-diamond ring.

Ella Mae straightened her posture and took off her glasses. Her hands trembled and her eyes welled.

Everyone waited silently for her answer.

She looked at Melvin and nodded her head.

"I can't hear ya," he said.

"Yes, Melvin. I will," she said, sticking out her ring finger.

Melvin slid the ring on her finger and everyone clapped.

"Lawd, have mercy! I can't believe it," she said, admiring the ring. "Ain't it pretty?"

Evelyn smiled. "It's beautiful, Mother!" She turned to Melvin and hugged him. "Welcome to the family!"

"Is this what y'all was doin earlier, when I couldn't find ya?" Ella Mae asked, putting her glasses back on.

"Melvin wanted our blessing and we gave it to him. Ma, you deserve to be happy again."

"Aww! Thank ya, Nyasia."

"I wasn't gon' do it witout y'all's blessin. I love ya mama, but I know y'all love her more. I promise to take good care of her."

"You've done a fantastic job so far," Evelyn said, rubbing his back.

After all the gifts were open, everyone sat down for dinner.

"Who dun made the sweet tea? Cuz Nyeela sho didn't."

"I tried, Mother. But nobody can make it the way you and Nyeela can."

"I thought I told Nyeela to do it."

"I started to, Mama, but Eve...."

"I told her to let me do it," Evelyn interrupted, forcing a smile.

"Well, you gon' have to learn the proppa way to make it, cuz this here is jus' plain awful."

"Ma, Twin and I have something to tell you."

"What is it, Nyasia?"

"Since you and Melvin are getting married, we've decided to go ahead and get our own place together," Nyasia announced, looking at her twin with hopeful eyes.

Ella Mae wiped her mouth with a red linen napkin. "What? When did y'all decide this?"

"Yeah. When did we make that decision?" Nyeela asked, looking confused.

Nyasia kicked her under the table. "Earlier today. Remember?"

Evelyn nodded in approval.

"Oh, yeah," Nyeela smiled. "I remember."

"We figured since you and Melvin were getting married, you'd probably want your own space," Nyasia continued.

Ella Mae shook her head. "I don't know."

"Maybe you can let the girls have the house, Ella," Melvin suggested. "You can come live wit me, if you wanna."

"Makes complete sense to me, Mother," Evelyn added. "You can check on the girls whenever you want and the house can stay right here in the family."

Ella Mae sat back in her chair. "I don't know, y'all. I been in this house ova forty years."

"Oh, come on now, Mother. This house isn't going anywhere. Besides, you've been to Melvin's house a hundred times. It's practically your second home. I think the girls are responsible enough to take care of things. You've raised them to be strong, smart, and independent. Now, you need to trust them."

"Honestly, Ma, we'd rather live here than somewhere else," Nyasia added.

"Melvin, you sho you want me livin wit you?"

"We gettin married, ain't we?"

"Yeah."

"There ya go!" Melvin smiled.

Chapter Sixteen

A few days later, Evelyn sat contemplating whether she should return home for New Year's Eve. Even though things were just starting to improve with the twins, she needed to get home. Starting the New Year on bad terms with anyone, including Grady didn't feel right and she couldn't allow anger any more room to grow. Plus, she missed Rowena terribly. She made a decision to go home and put things in order.

It was late into the evening when she headed to the kitchen to talk with Ella Mae.

"Are you okay, Mother?"

"Yeah, baby. I'm jus' sittin here enjoyin a cup of tea and thankin God for bein so wondaful. How you feelin?"

"I'm good," she said, taking a seat. "I've been doing a little reflecting myself and I think it's time for me to return home. I have some things I need to take care of before the New Year."

"You sho?"

"Yes."

"Okay, baby."

"I'm really glad I got a chance to spend time with you and the twins. I don't know what I would have done without you."

"You wudda figured it out, same way ya always have."

"Oh, I don't know about that, Mother."

"Well, you can't give us all the credit. Some of it belongs to God, Stacey and Rowena."

"That's true and I'll thank them in my own way. But first, I want to apologize to you."

"For what?"

"For leaving you and the twins here alone after Daddy died. It was wrong and I'm really sorry."

"Hush, child. You ain't gotta be sorry for goin to find ya own path."

"No, Mother. I never should have left you and I'm so sorry. If I could do it all over again, I would stay here with my family."

Ella Mae took her hand. "Evelyn, you jus' gotta let that go. I have. Sometimes, we can't help the thangs we face or the mistakes we make. So go on and let ya'self off the hook."

"I didn't realize how much you all needed me."

"I neva wanted my life to be a burden to my girls."

"Mother, you can never be a burden to me. If it weren't for you, I wouldn't be here. I need you and I had forgotten just how much."

"Aw, baby. I neva stop prayin for y'all."

"I appreciate that and I love you more than you'll ever know."

Ella Mae cupped Evelyn's chin in her hand. "I love you too, baby."

"And please stop worrying so much. You've raised us to be who we are. Let us make you proud."

"Child, I am proud of y'all. But I ain't gon' eva stop worryin or prayin. You jus' wait. You gon' see what I'm talkin 'bout soon enuff."

"Well, I thought the point was to pray and not worry. Or if you're going to worry, don't pray."

"Child, please. You gon' see."

"Okay, Mother."

"Do me a favor."

"What's that?"

"Learn how to let folk help ya out from time to time."

Evelyn chuckled. "Yes, Mother. I know I need to surrender my ego. I'm working on it."

"Child, you gon' be awright," Ella Mae said, patting her on the hand.

Evelyn pulled off Ella Mae's old wedding ring and placed it in her hand. "Remember this? You gave it to me when Grady and I got married."

She smiled. "I rememba."

"I don't need it anymore. One of the twins should have it now."

"You sho?"

"Positive."

"Okay," she sighed. "I guess Nyasia gon' be the one to get it, cuz it sho ain't Nyeela." She shook her head. "But you neva know. She might change her mind."

"Mother! Have you been paying attention? Being gay is not a phase. I had to learn that the hard way. Whatever you do, please don't say that to Nyeela."

"Child, please. I ain't scared of Nyeela," Ella Mae said, looking over her glasses."

Evelyn leaned over and kissed her on the forehead. "I love you. Thanks for allowing me to be me. I won't let this family down again."

"You jus' focus on takin care of my precious grandbaby."

"I'm going to miss you so much!"

"I ain't goin no where. Go on home and get ya life in orda. And let Grady know 'bout that baby."

"Well, it wouldn't do me any good to try and hide it now. I'll be showing soon enough and someone is bound to see me."

"I'm gon' be prayin for ya, honey. If ya need me, call!"

She smiled. "Yes, Mother."

"Next time you visit, you gon' be givin me away," Ella Mae chuckled.

"I can't wait! Any ideas about a wedding theme?"

Ella Mae waved a dismissive hand. "Child, I ain't thinkin 'bout no weddin theme."

Evelyn shook her head. "Whatever, Mother! It's your wedding."

"Its gon' be strange leavin the girls in this big ole house by they self."

"The *girls* are growing young ladies. They'll be fine in this house."

"Awright."

"Besides, you and Melvin can look in on them whenever you want."

"You right. I forgot."

"That's why I'm here. To remind you," she smiled. "I'm going to say goodnight now, Mother," she said, rising from the table. "The twins can take me to the airport in the morning." Evelyn pushed her chair in.

Ella Mae stood up. "Okay. Night, baby," she said, giving her a hug.

Back in her room, Evelyn was content with her decision to return home. She grabbed her cell phone and noticed she missed a call from Stacey. Before returning his call, she phoned Nyeela to confirm her ride to the airport.

After three rings, Nyeela answered. *"Hello!"*

"Nyeela?"

"Yes."

"It's Eve. I tried to wait around for you guys to get home, but it's getting late. Where are you?"

"I'm saying goodnight to Tanvi. What's up?"

"I've decided to return home sooner than expected and I need you to take me to the airport in the morning."

"So you're leaving us again, huh?"

"Please, don't make this any harder than it has to be."

"I'm just kidding. Dang!"

"I have some business to take care of back home and there's no sense in putting it off, you know?"

"I understand, sis. I'd be happy to take you to the airport."

"Really?"

"Yeah."

"I'll look forward to it, then."

"See you in a little bit."

"Thanks, baby girl."

Evelyn sat on the bed thinking about Ella Mae's advice regarding Stacey. Although, she found Stacey very attractive, she knew it was too soon to trust him or her feelings. He made it easy for her to believe life could be full again and she wanted to remain open to the possibilities. She decided to return his call.

"Hi, Stacey! How are you?" She could hear the smile in his voice, as he returned the greeting.

"Good! How 'bout you?"

"I can't complain. I've been doing some thinking and I've decided to return home tomorrow."

"Really?"

"Yeah. It's time."

"Jus' rememba to be gentle wit ya'self."

She nodded. "I hear you. I'd like to start the New Year with a clean slate, you know?"

"Ev'rythang gon' work out fine. You'll see. I'm gon' miss ya."

"Oh, we'll talk often. But if you want to visit, you'll have to fly to Chicago. Think you can handle that?"

"Blindfolded wit one hand tied behind my back."

"I'm going to hold you to it. How is your dad?"

"Pops is good. I think travelin back to back like that wore him out."

"Bless his heart!"

"How's Ms. Ella? She ready to move?"

"I think so. Once she makes the transition, she'll be okay. She's having a tough time wrapping her head around leaving the girls."

"I undastand."

"But she certainly loves Melvin enough to try."

"Melvin is pretty excited too."

"I'm so happy for both of them."

"What time is ya flight?"

"8 a.m."

"Okay. Promise me you gon' take care of ya'self."

"I promise."

"Good. Get some sleep. Call me when ya get home, no matta what time."

"I will. And Stacey?"

"Yes?"

"Thank you for everything. I'm glad we met."

"I'm the lucky one! Good night, Eve."

"Good night."

The next morning, Evelyn and the twins headed to the airport. She couldn't leave, without giving them a few friendly reminders.

"Girls, it wouldn't hurt you to attend church with Mother sometimes. Even if it's only once a month. You both know how much it means to her."

"We know."

"Remember, our parents worked hard to pay for that house and Mother is entrusting the two of you with it. I'm sure you'll do your best not to let her down, right?"

"Sis, you can spare us the long speech about not wrecking the house. Nyasia and I have already discussed how we're going to honor our parents' legacy. You can relax. We'll work hard to maintain the integrity of the house. We're not total idiots."

"Just checking. Honestly, I know you'll make her proud."

"Can you make sure you send my niece or nephew down to visit over the summers?"

"Um, Nyasia, speak for yourself. I have no desire to baby-sit for an entire summer."

"What you say, Nyeela? No babies for you, huh?"

"Not if I can help it."

"Thanks, guys, but my little angel won't be going anywhere, until he or she can talk. I need my child to be able to tell me what goes on."

"I know that's right," Nyasia remarked. "Bryson is the same way with his son."

"Well, here we are, ladies," Nyeela said, pulling up to curbside check-in. "I love you, Eve and hope to see you soon."

"Nyeela, you're welcome to visit anytime you want. Both of you."

"You *are* coming back for our graduation, right?"

"I wouldn't miss it for the world! Nyasia, can I call you when I need a recipe?"

"Of course!"

"And don't be in such a big hurry to play house. Take it from me. You have plenty of time for that. Live your life and enjoy your family. Okay?"

"Yes, Eve."

"Both of you keep in touch with me."

"We will. You better go before you end up staying," Nyeela teased.

Evelyn exited the vehicle. "Love you both! See you later," she said, blowing the twins a kiss and entering the sliding doors to the airport.

*****

In Chicago, the flutter of butterflies in her stomach, made it difficult for Rowena to concentrate, as she sat behind her desk. She wasn't able to eat or sleep much and lived for moments when she could hear Memphis' voice.

Morgan entered, interrupting her thoughts. "I'm sorry, did I startle you?"

"A little," Rowena smiled. "But it's okay. What's up?"

"I'm taking orders for lunch. What would you like?"

"Actually, I'm not hungry."

"But you have to eat something, don't you? My aunt is a diabetic. When she doesn't eat properly or if she skips a meal, her blood sugar drops tremendously."

"You're right, Morgan. Thanks for the reminder. Let's see. What do I want from Potbellys? I think I'll have a turkey sandwich on whole wheat, with everything except mayonnaise. Okay?"

"Um, did I say I was ordering from Potbellys?" she asked, confused.

"Didn't you?" Rowena asked, even more confused.

"I don't think so, but I am headed that way," Morgan smiled.

"I could've sworn I heard ... Oh well, lucky guess, I suppose," she said, shrugging her shoulders.

"Are you okay?"

A huge grin surfaced. "I'm great, Morgan," she answered.

"Okay. I'll get these orders in."

"Thanks." Her phone rang. "This is Rowena."

"Ooohhh! I love hearing your name. But you know what I love even more than that?" Memphis asked, in a sultry voice.

"No. Tell me." She bit her bottom lip.

"I love me some you."

"You love you some me?"

"With my whole heart."

"Well, guess what?"

"What?"

"I love me some you, too!"

"How's it going?"

"I can't get any work done. I keep spacing out, thinking about you. My assistant just asked if I was okay," she giggled.

"Check this out. I've been getting on the elevator, going from floor to floor trying to find a little privacy to call you. I've been caught randomly smiling when nothing is funny."

Rowena laughed. "Oh my God! Me too. It's so embarrassing."

"I know. I just shrug it off as an inside joke."

"I can't even think that fast."

"Baby, we got it bad and that ain't good."

"Says you. This is *excellent* for me!"

"I haven't been lovesick in a long time. I don't know what to do with myself."

"I know what you mean. It hurts so badly, yet it feels so damn good!"

"Damn, I love you, girl!"

"I love you back," she whispered, twirling the cord around her finger.

"I better get back to work now."

"Call me later?"

"Count on it. Bye."

"Bye."

Rowena took a deep breath. "I need to go for a walk or something." She wrote a note to Morgan: **I'm going out for a bit. I'll be back. You can reach me on my cell.**

She placed the note on Morgan's desk, grabbed her coat and walked to the elevators. Her mind flashed back to her recent conversation with Memphis. She smiled hard. When the elevator doors opened in front of her, there was an awkward silence. Rowena straightened her face, cleared her throat and entered the elevator with her head down. She wanted to go straight to the top floor and scream to the world that she was in love. But who would care? Instead, she exited in the lower lobby area, unsure where to go next. Feeling light and jovial, she hugged herself in the chilly air and walked across the street to buy gum from the newspaper stand. Her mouth felt dry and she figured the gum would help. After making her purchase, she returned to the building where she ran into Grady.

"Grady! What are you doing here?"

"Hi, Rowena! Um, I just finished a meeting with my attorney."

"Oh. Well, happy holidays to you," she said, forcing a fake grin.

"Thanks! How have you been?" he asked, trying to pursue a conversation.

"I've been great! I can't complain at all. You look well!"

"Thanks. I had a wonderful Christmas with my family and I feel pretty good."

"How is your precious niece?"

"Spoiled."

"Already?"

"You know how it goes with the first grandbaby/niece/child. She goes from arm to arm."

"Well, she certainly is beautiful!"

"Yeah. How is Eve?"

"I don't know."

"Come on, Rowena. I'm not trying to be nosey. I really want to know how she's doing."

"I get it and I'm not trying to be rude. But you'll have to call her to find out, because I haven't spoken to Eve since Thanksgiving."

"Why?"

"Look, I don't want to get into it, right now. But you should call her. I'm pretty sure there are things you two need to discuss."

"I don't know. The last time we spoke left much to be desired."

"This is a difficult process for both of you."

"I never wanted to hurt Eve. I just didn't know what else to do, Rowena."

"I'm the last person who needs an explanation. You should be talking to her."

"I'm just saying."

"Grady, do yourself a favor and call her. I have to get back to work."

"There is nothing I can say that will make this easy for either of us."

"I understand," she said, with a heavy sigh. "It's a hard pillow."

"Very emotional."

"Imagine how she must feel."

"That's why I haven't called. I figured she needed some space."

"I see."

"I can't believe you two aren't speaking."

"Grady, I never said we weren't speaking. Besides, you need to worry less about us and focus on how the two of you are going to work through this."

"I guess I've been told!"

"Hey, this is a little uncomfortable for me as well."

"I'm sorry. I didn't realize."

"Hopefully, things will be back to normal soon and you guys can put all of this behind you."

"I'm praying for us," he said.

"Well, I have to get back to work. It was nice seeing you, Grady. Happy holidays!"

"Thanks! Same to you, Eve."

Rowena hurried back into the building and boarded the elevator. Talks of Evelyn and Grady ruined her euphoria. When she returned to her desk, there was a message from Nyeela: **Ro, Eve is on a plane heading home. You two should talk. Love you, Nyeela.**

Rowena smiled at the note. Obviously, one of them would have to put their pride aside and make amends. Rowena prepared to assume the role.

Chapter Seventeen

Evelyn's flight landed at Chicago's Midway Airport just as evening began to fall. She wanted nothing more than to relax in the comforts of her own home. Prior to her flight, she arranged for Gail to pick her up from the airport.

"Thanks for picking me up, Gail," she said, getting into the car. "I know you have a busy schedule with the baby. I just didn't know who else to call."

"I'm happy to do it, Eve."

"How's the baby?"

"She's wonderful. She still doesn't know the difference between night and day, but we are working through it."

"Where is she?"

"She's with Mom. They really enjoy spending time with her."

"I bet!"

"We practically moved in with them during the holidays. But Mike and I plan to spend New Year's alone."

"Oh, okay."

"How was your visit with the family?"

"Good. I feel rested, relaxed, and much stronger."

"I can tell. Your skin is glowing and everything. You look great! Seems like you got what you needed and that's what everyone wants for you, Eve."

"Everyone?"

"Mike, Mom, Dad, and I. We're praying for you to get through this."

"You've all been so supportive. Thank you. God is good."

"Yes, He is! Grady spent Christmas with us, you know."

"How would I know?"

"You two haven't spoken?"

"Briefly, but nothing to shift the momentum. So ... how is he?"

"He seems okay. I mean, I guess he is. I don't know. We love you both."

"Gail, relax. I'm not asking you to choose sides. Grady is your brother and your loyalty should be to him. I'll be fine."

"I want you to be happy. Just promise me you won't shut us out. I want very much for Eva Lynn to know her aunt."

"Hey, no need to worry. I love you guys just as much and I promise not to shut you out. Grady and I will have our opportunity to talk before the year ends. There are a lot of things to say."

"Okay. I guess Rowena couldn't get away from work, huh?"

Evelyn raised a brow. "Girl, you know Rowena. Everything is work, work, and work."

"I know. Speaking of her, my doctor has been asking about her. Did she tell you?"

"No. She didn't."

"His name is Memphis and he is one fine piece of chocolate. You know how Rowena tries to act all nonchalant when it comes to men. I guess it shouldn't surprise me that she didn't mention him to you."

"Gail, can you pull over into this parking lot. I need to run inside of Walgreens and grab some milk, right quick. I'm almost sure I don't have any at home."

"Oh. No problem."

"Thanks."

"Do you need to stop at the grocery store before you get home?"

"No. I'll just grab some milk. I won't be long."

"Okay, hun."

Gail had a tendency to be quite nosey and a motor mouth at times. Evelyn found it very annoying. She exited the car and quickly entered the pharmacy. Just as she was about to pay for the milk, Gail strode through the sliding doors.

"I forgot, Eva Lynn needs baby wipes," she called out to Evelyn. "I left the car doors unlocked for you."

"Great!" Evelyn said, heading out towards the car. "I hope she doesn't take all damn day," she grumbled, throwing herself inside the car. "I'm ready to get home and get the hell out of these clothes." She sat there and wondered if it would be a huge mistake to tell Gail that she was going to be an aunt. If she ran to Grady with the news, it would only complicate things even further. Besides, Evelyn wanted to be the one to tell him.

She still couldn't believe she would be a mother in less than nine months. Some little person would soon look to her for answers and while she was poised to give advice, this would be something entirely different. There were times when she thought she had all the answers. Now, there was only uncertainty. She even felt uncertain about her ability to continue the advice column. It didn't seem to suit her anymore. Was it responsible to consider a career move at this stage in her life? Sure, she had a degree which gave her options, but circumstance dictated that she re-evaluate her life and everything in it. Fortunately, she had plenty of money saved up to cushion things, until she made a decision.

"Oh, good. Here she comes," she mumbled.

"I hope I wasn't too long," Gail said, getting into the driver's seat. "I had a hard time trying to find the brand we use. Her skin is so sensitive and I have to make sure I'm consistent with the products."

"I see. How do you know which products to buy?"

"I don't. I just go with what works and when it doesn't, I go with something else. Sometimes, the doctor will recommend a certain brand but generally, it's up to the parent."

"Hm. Tell me something. How does it feel to be responsible for someone other than yourself?"

"Honestly, it's an adjustment. But I'm not complaining."

"An adjustment, huh?"

"Yeah. Why do you ask?"

"For what it's worth, it seems like you're adjusting pretty good for a first time mom."

"Ha! That's only because I have plenty of help. Mike and my parents make a huge difference. I couldn't imagine being a single mom. I'd probably be overwhelmed."

"Oh, I don't know, Gail. There are single mothers out there who have that very same support."

"If they're lucky. But let's face it, most single mothers don't have a fraction of the support I have."

"True. Thank God, you or I don't have to worry."

"Right. Are you thinking about motherhood?"

"Why do you ask?"

"Because you said you or I. No offense, I'm just asking."

"None taken. You just caught me off guard with the question. What time is it?"

"It's a little after seven."

"Where did the time go?" Evelyn asked.

"The days always seem to go faster during the winter, don't they?"

"Yeah. I guess because it's getting dark much quicker."

"I suppose," Gail said, pulling into the driveway.

"Thanks so much for coming to pick me up, Gail. I can't tell you how much I appreciate it."

"No problem, Eve. Can I help you with your bags?"

"No, I can make it. Thanks. Give my love to Mike and your parents and happy New Year."

"Thank you! Same to you. Say hello to Rowena for me."

"Good night." Evelyn grabbed the milk, climbed out of the car. She unloaded her luggage onto the driveway and gently closed the trunk. She turned toward the house and approached the front door at a snail's pace. The closer she got, the more her heart started to pound. Placing the key in the door was like standing on an emotional land mine. Any sudden moves could cause an explosion. Memories flooded her mind like a tsunami.

"I can do this," she said, coaching herself into turning the key. She gave the door a hard push and squared her shoulders. Taking deep breaths, she stepped inside and slowly closed the door behind her. She briefly surveyed the living room before moving slowly into the kitchen. She placed the milk in the fridge and grabbed a bottle of water. After taking a few moments to gather herself, she rolled in the luggage from the driveway.

Emotions began to stir again as Evelyn approached her bedroom. She paused in the doorway waiting for them to pass. Much calmer, she checked the closet to see if Grady had been there to get his things. He hadn't. She sat down on the bed and recalled her brokenness. The memories produced a deep sigh from her chest. And although she felt much stronger, the thought of it all still saddened her. She marveled at how thirsty she had been for a man. Who or what had she been running from? Before she could complete that thought, the phone rang. She hesitated before answering.

"Hello?" she said wearily.

"Hi, Evelyn!"

"Rowena!" She smiled.

"I heard you were back and I was in the neighborhood," Rowena said, her voice shaking.

"Well, are you coming by or what?"

"I'm in your driveway," she answered, returning the smile with her voice.

"Ok. I'm coming to the door now," she said, hurrying down the hall to the front door. She opened the door holding the cordless receiver to her ear. Rowena got out of the truck and approached with her phone to her ear. The two women stood face to face teary-eyed. Rowena hung up the phone and slowly approached her best friend.

"Rowena, I'm sorry," Evelyn said humbly.

"Me too."

Moments passed, as they embraced.

"Come inside," Evelyn insisted, breaking away.

"I didn't mean to pop up like this, but I had to come," Rowena said, holding her hand.

"I'm glad you're here. I missed you so much." Evelyn hugged her again. "You look great!"

"Thanks and so do you." Rowena acknowledged. "I've never seen you more radiant. How are you?"

"I'm good," she smiled. "Coming back to this house hurt at first, but I'm okay." She offered Rowena a seat on the sofa.

"How long have you been home?"

"Ten ... fifteen minutes, tops," she said, sitting next to her.

"Did you take a cab from the airport?"

"No. Gail picked me up."

"Oh boy! How did *that* go?"

"It wasn't so bad. I had a tough time keeping the pregnancy from her."

"Hmm. How's that coming along?"

"Actually, the morning sickness has subsided considerably. And as you can see, I've gained a few pounds. Otherwise it's a lot better than expected," she said, placing her hand on her stomach.

"How is the family?"

"Everyone is wonderful! Melvin asked Mother to marry him."

Rowena's eyes grew and a smile emanated. "What? Get out of here!"

"He proposed on Christmas Day and she said yes."

"How sweet!"

"And once they're married, Mother will move in with him and leave the house with the twins."

"Awesome! The twins could use their own place, not that it's any of my business."

"Stop it. We are *still* family and the girls love you."

"That's what I like to hear." Rowena smiled.

"How have you been?"

"I've never been better. Unfortunately, when I got back from South Carolina, I received some shocking news regarding my health."

"Shocking?"

"Yes. I found out I'm a Diabetic."

"My goodness, Rowena!" Evelyn placed her hand over her heart. "I'm so sorry. Is there anything I can do?"

"Continue being my friend," Rowena said, with soft eyes. "Other than that, it's all on me. I need to watch my diet, take my medicine and exercise regularly."

"Wow! That news hurt my feelings."

"Mine too. I literally felt like someone yanked the rug from beneath me."

"How are you dealing with it?"

"Well, my last visit to the doctor went very well. My sugar levels are under control and I'm taking better care of myself. All in all, I'm doing great!"

"That's a relief." She rubbed Rowena's arm. "I'm sorry for not being here for you."

"Girl, you have your own problems to deal with. Besides I wasn't completely alone," she said, blushing.

"Oh? Gail didn't say anything about you being sick."

"Are you serious? I wouldn't let Gail help me with a sore throat, let alone something that life changing. Don't get me wrong. She's a sweet person but come on now. You know better." She frowned.

"You're right. My bad. Forgive me. Who nursed you back to life?"

"His name is Memphis," she said softly.

"The doctor?"

"How did you know he was a doctor?"

"Gail."

They laughed.

Rowena shook her head. "See what I mean? I should've known she couldn't keep it to herself."

"She mentioned his interest in you, but she said you didn't reciprocate."

"Well, not at first. To me, he was just another white coat. I had no interest in having a relationship, nor did I think I would ever see him again. But we ran into each other after Thanksgiving and something about him drew me in," she said, playing with her keys. "His persistence ushered in a new reality."

"What do you mean? Are you dating him?"

"Eve, I'm in love with him."

"Rowena!" Evelyn stood to her feet, "You *are* kidding, right?" she asked, walking into the kitchen.

"No, Evelyn. I'm not," Rowena said, following her. "Look at me. I feel like I'm in the spring of my life."

Evelyn looked at her. "Girl, you sound like a crazy woman."

"Oh, this is not the ranting of a crazy woman. I'm in love, Eve."

"Sounds a bit dramatic to me."

"Listen. Before Memphis, I was running around here working myself half to death. Pretending as though I didn't know how empty my life had become. Since he came along, I realized I was working my way to a slow death. I don't want to do that anymore."

"Wow!" Evelyn grabbed a glass from the cabinet. "You should see how your face lights up when you talk about him. If I didn't know any better, I'd swear you found your soul mate." She poured herself a glass of milk.

Rowena smiled. "It doesn't matter how you spin it. I'm in love, Eve."

Evelyn looked at the glass with her nose turned up and sat it down on the counter. "I don't know if I should be jealous or happy for you."

Rowena's smile faded. "Why?"

"I mean, I know we haven't spoken in a while, but how could this be? Do you even know him enough, to classify this as love?"

"Trust me. I know the difference. I fought myself on every level not to feel this way. When it came down to it, I couldn't cheat myself anymore. I've been available to everyone else and emotionally checked out when it came to my own life. It's not fair to keep mistreating *me*."

"Ok. I get it. You need to do *you*. So where does this leave me?"

"Why would this affect *our* friendship?"

"I'm just saying. If this Memphis person is suddenly the missing piece to your puzzle, where do I fit in?"

"You know what, Eve? You never give me credit for doing the right thing by you. In all the years we've known each other, I've never done one thing to hurt you, not one."

Evelyn sighed. "Rowena…."

"No. Let me finish. Throughout our entire friendship, I've never been jealous of Grady or put you in a position to choose between him and me. You're my best friend and I love you, but you've got some serious trust issues."

"I know and I'm sorry. You're all I have this side of my family and I don't want to lose you."

"If you learn to trust me, you won't."

"I do trust you. I'm just foolish at times. Forgive me?"

Rowena walked over to Evelyn and placed her hand on her shoulder. "Of course, I do. Nothing is worth holding a grudge. Especially, when two people truly love each other."

"I can attest to that! I definitely learned a huge lesson on forgiveness. Sorry for being paranoid."

"There is enough room in my life for the both of you."

"So … when do I get to meet him?"

"How about New Year's Day?"

"Deal."

"I can't wait!"

"My best friend is in loooove," she sang, hugging Rowena. "Congratulations! I remember what love used to feel like."

"You *can* have it again, you know."

Evelyn shook her head. "Not until my heart has had time to heal. You remember Melvin's cousin, Stacey?"

"The cutie who kept giving you the eye over the turkey?"

"Was he? I didn't notice," she blushed, looking down at her hands. "Anyway, he and I got to know each other pretty well in the last few weeks. I can honestly say, because of people like him, you, and my family, I'm a lot stronger today."

Rowena nodded and a smile emerged. "I'm so proud of you, Evelyn Renee!"

"And me, you. I want you to be the baby's godmother."

"Girl, I would be honored! When did you decide?"

"A few days ago. I thought about how selfish I had been, living only for myself. Don't get me wrong, I still don't think there's anything wrong with pursuing your dreams and goals, but I'm knocking on forty years. It's time for my life to be about something or someone other than myself. You asked me back home what I was passionate about and the truth is I've never even taken the time to find out. I always thought I had everything, but in retrospect they were just distractions."

"How so?"

"Just things to keep me from taking a good, hard look at myself."

"Exactly!"

"You too, huh?"

Rowena nodded. "I hid my unresolved issues in my work and our relationship, not realizing that we can't be in the driver's seat all the time. Sometimes we have to be willing to take a ride."

Evelyn laughed. "Yeah. And enjoy the mistakes and goof-ups along the way."

"Right!"

"You know what I see right now?"

"What?"

"I see two young girls finally growing up."

Rowena nodded.

"When my daddy died, I never allowed myself to grieve. Instead of staying with my family and going through the process together, I abandoned them when they needed me most and I will always be sorry for that. I've been given another chance to make things right and I'm going to do it."

"Sounds like you've had time to work it out."

"Oh yeah," she laughed. "I've had *plenty* of time."

"Who knew a vacation could do this much good."

"Thank you for pushing me to go. And for being by my side."

"I'll always be here for you, Evelyn. But I should've given you more space to grieve. I can be overbearing, sometimes. Even though I mean well, I tend to overstep my boundaries a bit."

"No, Rowena. You didn't overstep any boundaries. Listen, I don't want to harp on the subject. Let's move on, please."

"Moving on. Oh! Before I forget, I ran into Grady today."

"How did that happen?"

"I was returning from a break at work and he was visiting with his attorney."

"Really?"

"Yes. He mentioned he hadn't spoken to you and asked how you were. I told him to call and find out."

"He knows how to get in touch with me if he really wants to."

"He told me he was going to give you a call."

"I don't know what he's waiting for; he still hasn't gotten any of his things."

"Give it some time, Eve. Maybe he wants to take it slow. You have to consider that this is rough for him, too."

"I just know I'll feel much better when he comes to get his stuff. Then we can *both* move on."

"Are you planning to tell him about the baby?"

"I haven't decided yet. I'm figuring it out as I go along."

"I understand. You know, I did some serious soul searching and asked myself what I would do if I weren't afraid."

"Good question."

"I'm not telling you what to do, Eve. But you should take some time to consider the answer for yourself."

"Thanks. I will," she smiled. "Well, I have to change my clothes and do some grocery shopping. There isn't a thing to eat in this house."

Rowena laughed. "Yeah, I know. I'll get out of your way. I'm glad you're home. Call me later?"

"Absolutely!"

Rowena gave her a hug and left. Evelyn changed her clothes and prepared to go to the grocery store, when she heard keys jingling in the door.

Chapter Eighteen

Grady returned home for the first time to retrieve his things. "Oh! I'm sorry, Eve. I didn't realize you were going to be home. I thought you were coming after the New Year."

"Well, I changed my mind," she said, trying to maintain her composure. "And you really should have called first."

"I said I was sorry. I didn't know you were going to be here."

Evelyn stood there with her arms folded, in silence.

"You want me to come back later?"

"No, it's fine. We need to talk."

"Happy holidays to you! You look nice," he said, reaching out to touch her.

Evelyn retracted herself from his reach. "I feel good. No thanks to you."

He graciously accepted the rejection. "How is your family?"

"They're great! Spending time with them has done wonders for me."

"I can see that," he acknowledged.

"How is your family?" she asked.

"Good," he nodded. "But, enough about them. Let's talk about us."

"Fine." She squared her shoulders and sat down on the sofa.

"I know the pain is still raw and I don't want to patronize you."

"Don't. Let's cut past the bullshit and get to the facts."

"Eve, I don't want to fight either."

"Neither do I."

"I saw my lawyer today."

"Anything I should know?"

"It's pretty simple. You'll keep the house and I'll pay alimony."

"I wish it was that simple, Grady, but things are a little more complicated."

"Why?"

She wanted to tell him about the pregnancy, but couldn't form the words. "Because you married me knowing you were attracted to men!"

His posture sank and he lowered his head. "You are never going to forgive me for this are you?"

"Damn it, Grady! Would you forgive me, if the shoe was on the other foot?"

"What do you want me to say, Eve? I was wrong for deceiving you, I know. I'm a complete idiot. It's true."

His honesty prompted some relief. She sat back and crossed her arms. "So far, we're off to a good start."

"Okay," he said, turning to face her. "You were right and I was wrong."

"This is the part where you get to tell me why, Grady."

"I didn't have the courage to be true to myself. I hated growing up different, listening to my peers make fun of people like me. I wanted to shrivel up and die. Consequently, I decided to fashion another image of myself. An image that people everywhere, even you, could love."

"That's where you went wrong."

"What's wrong is not being free to be myself."

"So because you lack the courage to stand up for yourself, you punish others with deceit?"

"I wasn't looking at it that way."

"Grady, vowing to spend the rest of your life with someone who expected you to be something you wasn't, is insane!"

"I know. At the time it was the only card I had."

"Not good enough."

"It's true."

"Well, that doesn't cut it for me, Grady."

"I know I've ruined everything and I couldn't feel any smaller if I tried."

"I hope you don't expect any sympathy from me. Your wounds are self-inflicted. You chose to be deceitful."

"Maybe I expected marriage to cure me."

"Are you trying to be funny, Grady Simms?"

"I'm trying to find an answer that will satisfy you."

"Well, dig deeper. Because what you're telling me is bullshit and you know it."

"Okay, Eve. I was afraid, very afraid."

"Of?"

"Of what my parents would think? My friends, hell, even you."

"Selfish…." she said calmly.

"Excuse me?"

"Yes, Grady! You were selfish as hell and hurtful," she said, shaking her head. "But, I can't put all the blame on you."

"What do you mean?"

"Part of the responsibility is mine for marrying you."

"It is?"

"Yeah. If I hadn't been in such a damn hurry, maybe someone your age, without a woman or a child would've posed as a red flag for me."

"There are plenty of men out there who don't have a woman or a child. It doesn't mean they're gay, Eve."

"From now on, it will raise all kinds of questions for me."

Grady shrugged his shoulders. "Well..."

"I won't leave anything to chance."

"Can you at least accept that the love was real?"

"Do you really expect me to? After all of this?"

"I don't expect anything, anymore. But I did and I still do."

"I won't lie. I still love you very much, Grady, but I wish to God I didn't."

"I don't want anything from you, Eve. I came here with the best intentions. I know I've been an ass to you and destroyed your trust in me. I'm not going to sit here and pretend otherwise. But all my cards are on the table and whatever you choose to do from this point on is completely up to you."

"I really want to hate you, Grady."

"I deserve that."

"But I know it won't do me any good."

"For a long time, I...."

"Did you cheat on me?" she asked, cutting him off mid-sentence.

"I was never unfaithful."

Evelyn didn't know why she asked. She didn't believe him. "At what point in our relationship, did you decide you wanted out?"

"When I realized we couldn't progress as a couple. I got real honest with myself and I just couldn't do it anymore."

"I found a calendar of naked men in your office. How can you expect me to believe you were attracted to me?"

"Because I was. That was…"

"Was the sex between us real?" she asked, interrupting again.

"As real as it gets."

"Why me?"

"Why not you? I considered myself very lucky to have you. Any man would be."

Evelyn lowered her head. "I remember you telling me, that I would always find my reflection in your eyes. I thought you were being romantic at the time but now, I don't know what the hell you meant."

"At the time…."

"My parents really loved each other. And I promised myself that someday, I would have what they had. After Dad died, Mother struggled to raise the twins. I never wanted that to be me. So I resisted the idea of family and I never told you because I was afraid of losing you."

"I knew you were avoiding it, but I didn't know why. Part of me assumed that you didn't think I was man enough to be a father. The other part of me thought it had something to do with your ambition. I let it go for a while, but when Gail shared the news of her pregnancy, it stirred up those feelings all over again. By then, I had hoped you would change your mind."

"I wasn't ready and I was afraid you were going to hate me for it."

"I hated not being able to maintain what I started."

"That's what happens when you bite off more than you can chew."

"Would it have been fair for me to continue lying for the rest of my life?"

"Hey, you did this to yourself, Grady! If you had chosen honesty in the *first* place, then we wouldn't be in this predicament."

"That's a dead issue, Evelyn. What you see, standing before you is the real deal. Hate me or love me, I'm gay."

Evelyn gazed at him, with soft eyes. She waited for the man she fell in love with, to walk over, gently shake her, and tell her to wake up. It's only a bad dream. But that man was dead. The man standing in front of her looked and sounded like him, but he was only an imposter.

"You know what? I think we both need to consider this a lesson learned," she advised. "I will always love the good times we shared,

Grady. You were a very sweet and romantic husband. I would like to remain friends."

"I'm glad to hear you say that. Me too!"

"It's going to take a lot of patience and willingness on both our parts. We have to remain civil to each other, no matter what."

"I agree."

"Have you drawn up the divorce papers?" she asked, rising to her feet.

"We're halfway there, why? Are you in a hurry?"

"I just need to know because . . . well . . ."

"What is it, Eve?"

"Would you like something to drink?" she asked, heading to the kitchen.

Grady followed. "No. Is everything okay?"

Evelyn stopped and faced him. "This has been a tough decision for me to make. I've wrestled with it for weeks and well ... I'm about nine weeks pregnant."

"Huh?" he said, with a blank stare.

"Yes."

"Are you serious?"

"The last time sealed the deal."

A huge grin emerged. "Oh, man! I'm going to be a dad. Wow!"

"You know this changes things dramatically, right? I mean, in addition to alimony, there will be child support payments, and visitation rights to consider."

"Oh, Eve. This is the best news I've heard in a long time," he said, teary-eyed. "Thank you!"

"I didn't do it for you."

"I know," he said, taking a deep breath. "Whatever you need, you got it. This baby won't want for anything. I promise."

"I'm not worried at all. You should know the baby and I are going to be tested for HIV."

"Whatever makes you comfortable. Do you want me to get tested too?"

"Yes. That would make me very comfortable. To be honest, I wasn't even sure I wanted to keep it."

"Ouch!"

"Well, it's true."

Grady remained silent.

"I guess forgiveness played a huge role in my decision. Truth *is* I needed forgiveness too. At the end of the day, we all have our own issues to work on. Besides, I'm thinking of someone other than myself for a change."

"Thank you. I know this couldn't have been easy."

"No. It wasn't easy, Grady."

"I don't know what to say. I'm a bag of mixed emotions right now."

"*You?* I've been a sack of anger, hatred, bitterness, resentment, and rage. Oh, did I mention anger?" Evelyn shook her head. "You have no idea the amount of shit I had to wade through, just to be able to scratch the surface of forgiveness. So I could care less about what you are feeling, right now."

"I guess I've been told!"

"I guess you have," she said, rolling her eyes.

"When do you want to schedule this testing?"

"Right after the New Year," she said.

"Okay. Is there anything else you need from me?"

"I suppose the answer is no for now. Should anything change, you'll be the first to know."

"What about maternity clothes?" he asked.

"It's on my list of things to do."

"Can I go with you? I mean, do you mind?"

"Please, Grady. Don't push it. I don't know if I can handle you, right now."

"Shopping used to be our favorite thing to do together."

"Key word. *Used to be*. Things change."

"Fine. I'll just get my things and be on my way."

Evelyn grabbed his arm. "Listen, Grady. I know you want to be involved with the baby, and I'm all for it. However, you and I are a different matter. Yes, I want to be friends, but I need time. There are still so many things I need to work through."

"I understand, Eve."

"I also plan to live my life."

"Which translates to dating, right?"

"Not especially. But I do reserve the right to see whomever I please, whenever I please, without interference from you."

"Hey, I have no intention to keep you from living your life. I'm sure whomever you choose, will be someone of which I would approve."

"Don't be arrogant. This is not a request for your approval. You don't get to have a say about whom I can or cannot have in my life."

"Why are you so defensive? Do you have someone already?"

"None of your damn business!"

Grady surrendered both hands. "Fine!"

"Now, promise me we will always put our child first."

"You have my word, Eve."

"Good." Evelyn grabbed her keys and headed to the grocery store.

*****

As she strode around the aisles of the grocery store, Evelyn replayed the previous conversation with Grady in her head. She wondered if he was capable of being a good father. She also wondered if she would be okay with him having a gay partner. A frown emanated as she continued to mull over the complexities she faced. She fulfilled her shopping and proceeded to the checkout line. After paying for the groceries, she treaded out to the parking lot, cart in tow, and scanned the rows of cars to remind herself where she parked. "There it is," she whispered, heading toward the vehicle. Completely aware of her surroundings, she noticed someone following close behind. She unlocked the trunk and loaded everything inside, while keeping one eye on the person behind her. A heavy, middle-aged, man casually sauntered past her and quietly got into his vehicle, a few cars down. Evelyn placed the basket in the cart-stall and returned to her car.

The man pulled up alongside her and rolled down his window. "Aren't you 'Ask Eve'?" he inquired.

Evelyn nodded. "I was. Yes."

"Was?" he asked, looking confused.

"Please! Don't ask," she insisted, shaking her head.

The man shrugged his shoulders, rolled up his window and drove away.

Evelyn could hear Rowena's voice, in her head asking, "What would you do if you weren't afraid?" Her frown slowly gave way to a smile.

THE END

About the Author

Angela Bolden-Thompson resides in South-Suburban Illinois, with her family. Mrs. Bolden-Thompson believes in the power of both the written and spoken word. She uses them as a source of inspiration for herself and others. Particular to those who struggle with self-esteem issues, it is her intention to empower such individuals to celebrate who they are.

Mrs. Bolden-Thompson writes part-time. This is her second novel. She is currently working on a third. Find her on Facebook at www.facebook.com/1NovelistABT.

For more information, or to request her presence at your event/place of business, send an email to iwritebookz@gmail.com. Your feedback is important. Post your review at www.amazon.com.